HF497724

Amadis of Gaul

Vol. 2

Vasco Lobeira

Originally Published by
Printed by N. Biggs, for T. N. Longman and O. Rees
1803

Contents

AMADIS of GAUL. Book the First.

CHAPTER 36.

Amadis and Galaor were within two leagues of London when they saw Ardian the Dwarf coming towards them as fast as horse could gallop. Never trust me, quoth Amadis, if he comes not with the news of some great mishap to seek us. Presently the Dwarf came up and related all his tidings, and how Oriana was carried away. Holy Mary, help me! cried Amadis: which way did they take her?—By the city is the nearest road. Amadis immediately spurred his horse, and gallopped amain towards London, so confounded with the terror of this news that he never spoke word to Galaor, who followed him full speed. They passed close by the town without stopping a minute, only Amadis enquired of all he saw which way the Princess had been taken; but as Gandalin passed under the windows where the Queen and her Ladies were, the Queen called him, and threw the King's sword to him, which was the best sword that ever Knight girded on; take it to your Master, quoth she, and God speed him with it! and tell Galaor that the King went from hence with a Damsel this morning, and is not yet returned, and we know not where she has led him. Gandalin took the sword and rode as fast as he could after Amadis, who coming to a brook missed the bridge in his hurry, and forcing the horse to leap the tired animal fell short into the mud; then Gandalin came up to him and gave him the sword, and the horse which he himself rode. Presently they turned aside from the road to follow the track of horsemen, and there they saw some woodmen, who asked them if they came from London, for if a Knight and a Damsel be missing there, said they, we have seen an adventure; and then they told them what they had beheld. Who is it that has taken them? quoth Amadis; for he knew it was Lisuarte by the description. They answered, the Damsel who led the Knight here called loudly for Arcalaus. Lord God! quoth Amadis: let me but find that traitor!—The woodmen then told them how the party had separated, and said that one of the five Knights who went with the Damsel was the biggest Knight they had ever seen. Amadis knew that that was Arcalaus; and bidding Galaor follow where the King went, he spurred on after Oriana. By sunset the horse could carry him no farther, and he being greatly distressed, saw a little to the right of the road a Knight lying dead, and a Squire by him holding his horse. Who slew that Knight? cried Amadis. A traitor that passed by, carrying the fairest Damsel in the world by force, and he slew my master only for asking who they were, and here is no one to help me to remove the body.—My Squire shall help you: give me your master's horse: I promise to give you two better in return. He told Gandalin to follow him after the body was disposed of, and gallopped on. Towards day-break he came to a hermitage in a valley, and asked the Hermit if he had seen five Knights pass carrying with them two Damsels? Do you see yonder castle? he replied: my nephew tells me that Arcalaus the Enchanter is lodged there, and with him two fair Damsels whom he hath taken by violence. By God the very villain whom I seek!—He hath done much evil in this land, replied the Hermit. God remove him, or mend him!—Then Amadis asked him if he had any barley for his horse; and, while the horse was feeding, enquired who was the Lord of the castle. Grumen, said the good man, cousin to Dardan who was slain in Lisuarte's court, and therefore the King's enemies put up there. Now God be with you, father! quoth Amadis; I beseech you remember me in your prayers! which way to the castle?—Amadis followed the path which the good man had pointed out, and came up to it, and saw that the wall was high and the towers strong. He listened and could hear no sound within, and that pleased him, for he knew that Arcalaus was not gone forth; and he rode round, and saw that it had only one issue. Then he retired among some crags, and, dismounting, stood holding the bridle, and with his eyes fixed upon the gate, like one who had no will to sleep. By this the morning broke, and he removed farther across a valley to a hill that was well wooded, for he feared that if those of the castle saw him they would suspect there were others at hand, and therefore not come out. Presently the gate opened, and a Knight came out, and went to a high eminence and looked all round; then returned into the castle. It was not long before he saw Arcalaus and his four companions come out, all well armed, and among them Oriana. Ah, God! quoth he, now and for ever help me in her defence! They drew near him, and he heard Oriana say, Dear friend, I shall never see thee more, for I go to my death. The tears came into his eyes; he descended the hill as fast as he could, and came after them into a great plain, and then cried, Arcalaus! traitor! it becomes not one like thee to carry away so excellent a Lady! Oriana knew the voice, and shook all over; but Arcalaus and the others ran at him. He took his aim at Arcalaus, and bore him right over the crupper; then turned his horse and smote at Grumen, so that the point and part of the stave of the spear came out at his back, and he fell down dead, and the spear broke in him. Then he drew the King's sword, and laid about with such rage and violence, and felt such strength in himself, that he thought if the whole plain were full of Knights they could not stand before him. We are succoured! quoth the Damsel of Denmark: it is the fortunate Knight! look at the wonders he performeth! Ah God protect thee, dear friend! cried Oriana: none other in the world can save us. The Squire who had her in his keeping seeing what had passed, cried out, Certes I shall not wait till those blows come upon my head which shields and helmets cannot resist! and he put the princess down, and rode off full speed. By this Amadis had cut thro' the arm of another, and sent him away howling with the agony of death; and he cleft a third down to the neck. The fourth began to fly, and Amadis was after him, when he heard his Lady cry; and looking round, saw that Arcalaus had mounted again, and was dragging her up by the arm. Amadis soon came up to them, and lifting up his sword dared not put forth his strength lest he should slay both, but with a half-blow he smote him on the shoulder, and cut away part of the cuirass and the skin; then Arcalaus let Oriana fall, that he might escape the better. Turn, Arcalaus, cried Amadis, and see if I be dead as thou hast reported! but he in fear of death spurred on, and threw his shield from off his neck for speed. The blow made at him just reached his loins with the sword-end, and fell upon the horse's flank and wounded it, so that the beast rode away more furiously. Amadis, albeit he so hated the Enchanter, did not pursue him further, lest he should lose his mistress, he turned towards her, and alighted and knelt before her, and kissed her hand, saying, now let God do with me what he will! I never thought to see you again. She being among the dead was in great terror, and could not speak, but she embraced him. The Damsel of Denmark going to hold his horse saw the sword of Arcalaus on the ground, and admiring its beauty gave it to Amadis; but he seeing it was right glad thereof, for it was King Perion's sword which had been placed in his cradle, and which Arcalaus had taken when he enchanted him. Presently Gandalin came up, who had travelled all night long: a joyful man was he seeing how the quest had ended.

Amadis then placed Oriana upon the Damsels palfrey, while Gandalin caught one of the loose horses for the Damsel, and taking her bridle they left the place of battle. But Amadis as they went along reminded Oriana how she had promised to be his; hitherto, said he, I have known that it was not in your power to show me more favour than you did; but now that you are at full liberty, how should I support disappointments without the worst despair that ever destroyed man! Dear friend, quoth she, never for my sake shall you suffer, for I am at your will: though it be an error and a sin now, let it not be so before God.—When they had proceeded about three leagues they entered a thick wood, and about a league farther there was a town. Oriana, who had not slept a wink since she left her father's house, complained of fatigue: let us rest in that valley, said Amadis. There was a brook there and soft herbage; there Amadis took her from her palfrey: the noon, said he, is coming on very hot, let us sleep here till it be cooler, and meantime Gandalin shall go bring us food from the town. He may go, replied Oriana, but who will give him food?—They will give it him for his horse, which he may leave in pledge, and return on foot. No: said Oriana, let him take my ring, which was never before so useful: and she gave it to Gandalin, who, as he went by Amadis, said to him, he who loses a good opportunity, Sir, must wait long before he find another. Oriana laid herself down upon the Damsel's cloak, while Amadis disarmed, of which he had great need, and the Damsel retired farther among the trees to sleep. Then was his Lady in his power, nothing loth; and the fairest Damsel in the world became a Woman. Yet was their love encreased thereby, as pure and true love alway is.

When Galaor returned, the Damsel prepared the food; and, though they had neither many serving-men, nor vessels of gold and silver, yet was that a sweet meal upon the green grass in the forest.

CHAPTER 37.

Galaor rode on after the King so fast as his horse could carry him; still following the track of the horsemen. About vespers he met a Knight who cried out to him, whither so fast? stop and tell me! I have no time, quoth he.—By St. Mary, you pass not so! tell me, or fight me! But Galaor still rode on.—Certes, Knight, cried the stranger, you have committed some villainy that you fly so fast: defend yourself! Galaor turned as if to meet him in his career, but dexterously moved aside, so that the Knight's horse in his speed carried him a good way on. Ah, coward! cried the Knight, when at last he turned, thou shalt answer me or die! and he ran at him again full tilt. Again Galaor avoided the encounter, and rode on as fast as he could. When the Knight saw him far before, he said, as God shall help me, he shall not escape so! and knowing the country well, he struck across by a nearer way, and took possession of a pass. Faint-hearted coward! quoth he, chuse now of three things: fight, or turn back, or answer me! I like neither, replied Galaor, and you are discourteous: if you want to know why I go so fast, follow me and see; I should lose time in telling you, and you would not believe me, it is for so great an evil. The Knight answered, In God's name then go on, and I will follow thee though for these three days.

In about half a league's time they saw one Knight running after his horse, and another gallopping away from him. He who was with Galaor knew him on foot, for he was his cousin, and he caught the horse for him, and asked him, how is this? He replied, I was riding along thinking upon you know what, when that Knight yonder gave me such a thrust on my shield that the horse fell upon his knees and threw me. I drew my sword, and called to him to do battle; but he only cried out, remember to answer another time when you are spoken to! and so he rode away. By my faith in God, let us follow him, and see you how I will avenge myself. I cannot, said his cousin, now, for I must keep this Knight company for three days; and then he related what had befallen him with Galaor. Quoth the other, certes either he is the greatest coward in the world, or he goes upon some great adventure: I will forego my own vengeance to see the end of this. By this Galaor was far before them, for he did not tarry a whit, and they rode after him. It was now drawing towards night. Galaor entered a forest, and soon lost the track, for it was dark, so that he knew not which way to take. Then he began to pray to God to guide him that he might be the first to succour the King; and thinking that those horsemen might have led the King apart from the road to rest themselves, he went along the bottoms listening every where if he might hear them. The Knights thinking he had kept the road, rode straight forward about a league till they came through the forest, and not seeing him there they imagined he had hidden himself, and they turned aside to lodge in the house of a Dame hard by.

When Galaor had searched the forest throughout, and found nothing, he resolved to proceed, and ascend some eminence the next day to look about. So recovering the road, he went on till he came into the open country, and there he saw before him in a valley a little fire. Thither he went; it was some forgemen, and they seeing him come among them in arms, took up lances and hatchets to defend themselves; but he bidding them not fear, besought them to give him some barley for his horse. The which they did, and he gave the beast his supper. They would have given him also to eat, but he would not; only he lay down to sleep, requesting them to wake him before day-break. The night was two parts gone, and Galaor lay down by the fire, completely armed. At dawn he rose, for he had not slept much for pure vexation, and, commending them to God, he took his leave. His Squire had not been able to keep pace with him, and thenceforth he vowed if God prospered him, to give his Squire the better horse. So he rode to a high hill, and from thence began to look all round him.

The two cousins had now left the Lady's house, and it being now day they saw Galaor on the eminence, and knowing him by his shield rode towards him. As they drew nigh they saw him descend the hill as fast as horse could carry him. Certes, quoth the one, he is flying and concealing himself for some mischief: if I come up with him, God never help me if I do not learn from him what he hath deserved. But Galaor, thinking nothing of them, had just seen ten Knights passing a strait at the entrance of the forest, of whom five rode first and five behind, and some unarmed men went in the middle. These he thought to be the villains with the King, and went towards them like a man who has devoted his own life to save another. Coming near, he saw Lisuarte with the chain about his neck; and then, with grief and rage that defied danger, he ran at the first five, exclaiming, Ah, traitors! to your own misfortune have you laid hands upon the best man in the world! The five at once ran at him; he smote the first so sternly, that the wood of his lance appeared through his back, and he fell dead; the others smote him with such force that his horse fell upon his knees, and one of them drove his spear between Galaor's shield and breast-plate. Galaor forced it from him, and striking at another with it, nailed his leg to the horse, and left the broken lance in them; then putting hand to sword, the others all came at him, and he defended himself so bravely that every one wondered how he could bear up against such blows. But being in this great press of danger, it pleased

God to succour him with the two cousins who were in his pursuit, who seeing his great chivalry, exclaimed, Of a truth we wrongly called him coward: let us go help the best Knight in the world! With that they ran full tilt to his assistance, like men who knew their business, for they had each been Errant Knights for ten years, and the one was called Ladasin, the sword-player, and the other Don Guilan the pensive, the good Knight. At this time Galaor had great need of their aid, for his helmet was hacked and battered, his harness open in many places, and his horse tottering with loss of blood; yet he felt assured that, if his horse did not fail him, he should bring it to a good end. But when the two cousins came to his help, then he bestirred himself more hopefully, for he marvelled at their prowess. The load of blows was lightened, and he had room for action. When the Cousin of Arcalaus saw how things were going, for his Knights were falling on all sides, he ran to Lisuarte to slay him. Those who were with the King had fled, and he got from off the palfrey with the chain about his neck, and caught up a shield and sword from the ground, and received upon the shield the blow that was meant for his death. The sword passed a palm's length through the rim of the shield, and with its point reaching the head made a slant wound to the skull; but the King smote at his enemy's horse in the face, so that the traitor could not repeat the blow, and the horse reared and fell back upon the rider. Galaor now on foot, for his horse could not move, ran to him to smite off his head; but the King called out not to slay him. By this the two cousins had made an end of their last enemy, and then turning round they knew the King, to their great wonder, for they knew nothing of what had happened; and they took off their helmets, and knelt before him. He raised them up, saying, By my God, friends, you have succoured me in time! great wrong, Don Guilan, hath your mistress done me in withdrawing you from my company, and for your sake I lose Ladasin also. Guilan was ashamed at these words, and his cheeks crimsoned, for he loved the Dutchess of Bristol and she loved him, and the Duke always suspected it was he who had entered his castle when Galaor was there.

Galaor had now taken the chain from Lisuarte, and fastened it round the cousin of Arcalaus; they took the horses of the dead, one for the King, and one for Galaor, and rode towards London. They halted at the dwelling of Ladasin, and there found Galaor's Squire and Ardian the Dwarf, who thought his master had taken that way. A Squire was sent forthwith to inform the Queen of Lisuarte's safety. They rested that night; and, as they set forth on the morning, their prisoners confessed how all that had passed had been concerted with Barsinan, that he might make himself King of Great Britain; which, when Lisuarte heard, he spurred on in greater haste.

CHAPTER 38.

The woodmen had carried the news of Lisuarte's imprisonment to London; immediately there was a great stir in the city: the Knights all ran to horse, and gallopped to his rescue, so that the whole plain seemed full of them. King Arban of North Wales was talking with the Queen, when his Squires brought him horse and arms, and a Page said to him, arm yourself, Sir! what are you doing? there is not a Knight of all the King's company, except yourself, who is not gone full speed to the forest. And why? quoth Arban.—Because they say ten Knights are carrying away the King prisoner. Holy Mary! exclaimed the Queen; I always feared this! and she fell down in a swoon. Arban left her to the care of her Ladies, all making loud lamentation, and armed himself. As he was mounting, he heard a great cry that the Tower was taken. Holy Mary! quoth he, we are all betrayed! and then he knew he must not leave the Queen. By this time there was such an uproar in the town, as if all the people of the world were there. Arban drew up his two hundred Knights before the Queen's palace, and sent two of them to discover the cause of the tumult. They went to the Tower, and saw that Barsinan had got possession of it, and was killing some and throwing others from the walls, for he had six hundred Knights with him, besides footmen, and the King's Knights suspecting nothing had all gone to their master's rescue. The townsmen hearing this, ran all armed as they could in haste to the Queen's palace, and there also Barsinan went that he might take her, and get possession of the crown and throne. When he arrived he found Arban ready for defence. Arban, quoth he, you have hitherto been the wisest Knight of a young man that has been known: see now that you lose not your wisdom. Why do you say this? cried Arban.—Because before five days end Lisuarte's head will be sent me, and there is no other in this land who can and ought to be King except myself, and King I will be! I give you the kingdom of North Wales which you now hold, because you are a good Knight and wise: so retire now, and let me take the crown and throne, for whosoever opposes me shall lose his head. Villain and Traitor! quoth Arban; and then began a sharp conflict, wherein many were slain, which lasted till night, for the streets being narrow Barsinan could not avail himself of his numbers, and King Arban so behaved himself that he that day saved the Queen.

At night both parties retired: the Queen then sent for Arban; he went to her armed as he was, and wounded in many places, and, when he came before her, took off his battered helmet. There were five wounds in his face and neck, and his countenance was all bloody; but it seemed a beautiful face to those who, under God, thought him their protector. But the Queen seeing him, wept aloud with great pity: Ah, good nephew, God defend thee! what will become of the King? and what will become of us? Of him, quoth Arban, we shall have good news; for ourselves, fear nothing from these traitors: your vassals who are with me can defend themselves in their great loyalty.—But, Nephew, you are not in a state to bear arms, and what can the others do without you?—Fear not, Lady, so long as life is in me I shall not forsake my arms.

Barsinan, who found his people had need of rest, took twenty Knights with him in the morning, and went to a post which Arban's High Steward kept. They at the barrier took their arms to defend themselves, but Barsinan cried out that he came to speak with them, and make a truce till noon; to which Arban, being advised thereof, assented willingly, for the most part of his company had been so hardly handled that they could not bear arms. Barsinan then went to Arban, and said he would make a truce for five days. Agreed, said Arban, but provided that you shall not attempt to take any thing in the town; and that if the King comes, we immediately act as he may order us. I grant all this, said Barsinan, that there may be no more battling, for I value my own Knights, and I value you who will be mine sooner than you think. I will tell you how: the King is dead, and I have his daughter and will make her my wife. God forsake me then, quoth Arban, if ever thou shalt have truce with me, since thou art a partaker in the treason against my liege Lord! go and do thy worst! And before night Barsinan made three attacks upon him, and was repulsed.

CHAPTER 39.

Meantime Amadis asked Oriana what Arcalaus had said to her. He told me not to grieve, said she, for within fifteen days he would make me Queen of London, and give me Barsinan for my husband, to whom he was to give me and my father's head, and be made his High Steward in return. Holy Mary! quoth Amadis: Barsinan, who seemed such a friend! I fear lest he do injury to the Queen. Dear friend, cried Oriana, hasten on! I must to my sorrow, replied Amadis, for else I should have delighted to pass four days here in the forest with you, if it had pleased you. Oriana answered, God knows how willingly! but great evil might happen thereby to this land, which if God pleases will one day be yours and mine. As soon as it was morning Amadis armed himself, and leading his Lady's bridle, rode on as fast as they could towards London; and every where they met the Knights, five by five, and ten by ten, as they were seeking the King; more than a thousand they met, and told them which way the King was gone, and how Galaor was in quest of him. When they came within five leagues of London they met Grumedan, the good old Knight who had fostered the Queen; twenty of his lineage were with him, and they had been all night long scouring the forest. He seeing Oriana went towards her weeping: Oh God, Lady, what a good day with your coming! but what tidings of the King? They told him what they knew, and Amadis said to him, Take you charge of Oriana, and bid all the Knights that you shall meet turn back, for if numbers can succour him, there are already more than enough gone: I must go with all speed to protect the Queen. With that he gallopped away: at the entrance of the city he found the Squire whom Lisuarte had sent with the news of his deliverance, and learnt also the state of the city. So entering as privately as he could he went to Arban, who embraced him right joyfully, and asked, what news? As good as heart could wish! quoth Amadis: let us go to the Queen. He took with him Ladasin's messenger, and kneeling before Brisena, said, Lady, this Squire has left Lisuarte safe and well, and I have left Oriana with your fosterer Grumedan; they will soon be here, but I must go look after Barsinan. He then changed his shield and helmet that he might not be known, and bade Arban throw down the barriers, that the traitors might come freely on, for by God's help they shall pay dearly for their treason! The barriers were thrown down, and Barsinan prest on at the head

of his people, thinking that all would now be his, for his own men were many
and his enemies few, and he was eager to seize the Queen. The King's party
gave back being overpowered, then Amadis went forth; he had on a rusty
helmet, and a plain shield hanging from his neck; but he was soon judged to
be a good one, and he went on making his way through the press; and having
the good sword of Lisuarte by his side. He forced his way to Barsinan and
encountered him; drove his lance through shield and corselet, and left the
broken spear in him half way of its iron; then drew he his sword, and smote
off the crest and top of his helmet, and the scalp of his head, for the sword
cut so finely that Amadis could scarce feel the blow he gave; with another
stroke he sheared thro' gauntlet and hand, and the sword passing through the
bone of the wrist, fell on the leg and entered in half through. Then Barsinan
fell, and Amadis turned upon the throng, and King Arban so prest them that
they who could escape slaughter ran to the Tower, and made fast the gates.
Amadis finding he could not force entrance readily, went back to Barsinan,
and finding him still alive, ordered that he should be carried to the palace
and kept till the King's return. Then the strife being over, he looked at the
bloody sword which he held in his hand. Sword! quoth he, in a happy day
was the Knight born who shall wield you! and certes you are well employed,
for being the best in the world, you belong to the noblest King! He then
disarmed himself, and went to the Queen; and Arban was laid in his bed, as
there was great need, for he was sorely wounded.

At this time King Lisuarte was hastening to London. Of the Knights
whom he met, some he made turn back, others he sent through the vallies
and by all roads to recal their comrades from their search. The first whom he
met were Agrayes and Galvanes, and Solinan and Galdan, and Dinadaus and
Bervas, all six together making great moan; who when they saw him would
have kissed his hand, but he joyfully embraced them. Sir, said Dinadaus, the
whole city are in quest of you like mad men. Nephew, replied the King, take
some of these Knights with you, and carry my shield that you may be the
sooner obeyed, and turn back all whom you meet. This Dinadaus was one
of the best Knights of the King's lineage, and well esteemed among all good
Knights, as well for courteous bearing as for his good chivalry and prowess.
When they came into the high road to London they fell in with Grumedan,
the King's so dear friend, who was conducting Oriana home; and I tell you
their pleasure was exceeding great, and the old man told him how Amadis
was gone to the Queen's succour. Presently they heard news what Barsinan
had done, and how King Arban had defended the city, and how by the coming
of Amadis all had been ended and the traitor taken. By the time the King
reached London, there were in his company more than two thousand Knights.
When he came to the palace, who can tell the joy that was made? Immediately
he had the Tower surrounded, and having made Barsinan and the Cousin of
Arcalaus confess the whole manner of their treason, they were both burnt
in sight of their own people, who having no provisions, neither any remedy,

in five days came to the King's mercy, and he executed justice upon some
and pardoned others. Thus ended this treason, but it was the cause of much
enmity between the countries of Great Britain and Sansuena, for a son of
Barsinan, who was a good Knight, came afterwards against Lisuarte with a
great power.

These dangers over the court proceeded as before, making great pastimes
and festivals as well by night in the town, as by day in the fields. On one of
those days the Lady and her sons arrived, before whom Amadis and Galaor
had made their covenant with Madasima. They seeing her went honourably
to bid her welcome. Friends, said she, you know wherefore I am come: what
will you do in this case? will you not keep your promise, for to-day is the
time? In God's name, replied Galaor, let us go before the King. Let us go,
quoth she. Then coming into the presence, the Lady made her obeisance and
said, Sir, I come here to see these Knights perform a covenant which they
have made; and then she repeated what they had promised to Madasima, the
Lady of Gantasi. Ah Galaor, cried the King, you have undone me! Galaor
answered, better this than to die: if we had been known, all the world could
not have saved our lives; and now the remedy is easier than you imagine.
Brother, remember you have promised to follow my example! Then Galaor
related before the King, and all the Knights present, by what treachery they
had been taken. Sir King, said he, I now forsake you and your company for
the sake of Madasima, the Lady of Castle Gantasi; for it is her will to do you
this displeasure, and whatever others she can, for the hatred she bears you.
Amadis affirmed what his brother had said. Have we performed our covenant?
then said Galaor to the three witnesses; they answered, yes, truly, you have
acquitted your promise. In God's name! quoth Galaor, and now you may
return when you please, and tell Madasima that she hath not made her terms
so cunningly as she thought, as you may see. Sir, we have kept our covenant
with Madasima, and forsaken your service; but it was not stipulated how long
we were to be out of your service, therefore we are free to use our own will, and
freely again enter your service as before. At this Lisuarte was greatly pleased,
and said to the Lady, Certes these Knights have fairly acquitted themselves
of a promise so treacherously obtained, and just it is that they who deceive
should be themselves deceived. Tell Madasima, that, if she hates me, she
had it in her power to do me the greatest ill that could happen; but God,
who has preserved them from other perils, would not suffer them to perish
by such hands. If it please you, Sir, said the Lady, tell me who these Knights
are?—Amadis and Don Galaor his brother. What! was Amadis in her power?
cried she: now God be praised that they are safe, for certes it had been great
misadventure if two such good men had so perished? She will be ready for
pure vexation to inflict the death upon herself which she designed for them.
Truly, quoth the King, that would be more justly done. So the Lady went
her way.

CHAPTER 40.

Twelve days together did King Lisuarte continue his court, and, when it broke up, though many Knights departed to their own lands, it was a wonder how many remained, and in like manner many Dames and Damsels continued to abide with the Queen. Among those whom the King received into his company were the cousins Ladasin and Guilan the pensive, both good Knights, but Guilan was the better of the twain, for in the whole kingdom of London there was none who surpassed him in worth; but so absent was he, that none could enjoy his conversation or company, and of this love was the cause, and that to a Lady who neither loved him nor any thing else to such an excess: her name was Brandalisa, sister to the Queen of Sobradisa, and married to the Duke of Bristol.

The day came whereon that Duke was summoned to appear and answer the appeal of Olivas. The Duke arrived, and was courteously by the King received. Sir, quoth he, you have summoned me to answer an accusation: he who made it lies, and I am ready to acquit myself as you shall judge right. Then uprose Olivas, and with him all the Errant Knights present. Lisuarte asked why they all arose. Grumedan answered, because the Duke threatens all Knights Errant, and therefore we are all concerned. Certes, quoth the King, a mad war hath he undertaken! there is not in the world a King so mighty, or so wise, that he could bring a war like that to good issue! but retire you at present, and seek not now to avenge yourselves: he shall have full justice. All then withdrew, but Olivas, who said, the Duke who standeth before you, Sir, hath slain my Cousin-german, who never by word or deed gave him occasion of offence: I therefore accuse him as a traitor for this, and will either make him confess it, or kill him, or force him out of the lists. The Duke told him he lied, and that he was ready to acquit himself. The combat was fixed for the next day, for the Duke's two nephews who were to fight on his side were not yet arrived.

They came that evening; the Duke made such account of them that he thought Olivas could not produce their peers. They went before the King. Olivas defied the Duke, who demanded battle, three to three. Then Don Galvanes, who was at the feet of the King, rose, and called his nephew Agrayes, and said to Olivas, Friend, we promised to be on your side if need was: now then let the battle be. When the Duke saw them, he remembered how they had rescued the Damsel whom he would have burnt, and he was somewhat abashed. They armed themselves, and entered the place appointed for such trials; one party through the one gate, the other on the opposite side. From the Queen's window Olinda overlooked the lists, and seeing Agrayes about to fight her heart failed her; and Mabilia and Oriana were greatly grieved for the love they bore to him and Galvanes. The lists were cleared: the King withdrew from them, and the champions ran their encounter. Agrayes and his Uncle dismounted their enemies, and broke both their lances. Olivas made the Duke fall on his horse's neck, but received a deep wound himself, and the Duke recovered his seat. Agrayes rode at him, and laid on him a heavy load of blows, heartily hating him for his great discourtesy and falsehood; but one of the dismounted Knights struck at the Prince's horse, and buried the sword in his flank: the horse fell, and the Duke and his Nephew both assailed Agrayes as he lay upon the ground. Don Galvanes, closely busied with his antagonist, saw nothing of this. At that hour all who loved Agrayes were in great consternation; Amadis yearned to be among them, for he greatly feared his cousin's death; the three Damsels above were well nigh desperate, and it was pitiful to behold Olinda, what she suffered. Howbeit, Agrayes got on his feet, and with the good sword of Amadis, which he wielded, laid lustily about him. Ah, God, cried Galaor aloud, what is Olivas about this while! better that he had never borne arms, if he fails at a time like this! But Galaor knew not what sore agony Olivas suffered; for he had such a wound, and bled so fast, that it was a wonder how he kept his seat. He saw the peril of Agrayes, and heaving a deep sigh, as one whose heart did not fail him though his strength was failing, he cried, Oh God, let me help my good friend before my soul depart! and then, feebly as he could, he laid hand to sword and turned upon the Duke, and his spirit kept him up. Agrayes was now left man to man, and he remembered that his Lady saw him, and he laid on so furiously that his friends trembled lest his strength and breath should fail him; but this was his custom, and if his strength had been equal to his great courage, he would have been one of the best Knights in the world; but even as it was he was right good, and of great prowess. Anon he had cut through armour and flesh in sundry places, and left his foe quivering with death, at the same moment when Olivas, fainting for loss of blood, fell from his horse. The Duke not seeing how Agrayes had fared, turned upon Galvanes; Agrayes leaped upon Olivas's horse, and rode to his Uncle's assistance: he smote the Duke's Nephew upon the helmet, so that the sword stuck there; and plucking it away, he burst the lacings, and left him bareheaded to the wrath of Galvanes, while he turned upon the Duke. Presently Galvanes having finished his enemy, attacked the Duke on the other side, but his horse being wounded fell and bruised him, so that man to man were left. Still were all the beholders right glad; but above all Don Guilan, who hoped to see the Duke slain, for the love he bore to his wife. The Duke was flying, Agrayes reached the rim of his shield, the sword went in, the Duke threw off the shield from his neck, and still fled; then turned, while Agrayes was recovering his sword, and struck twice at him. The Prince, as soon as his weapon was free, requited him with a blow on the left shoulder that went through harness and flesh and bone, down to the ribs. The Duke fell, but hung in the stirrup, and the horse dragged him out of the lists, and when he was picked up his head was found dashed to pieces by the horse's heels. Agrayes forthwith alighted, and ran to his uncle, and asked how he fared. Bravely, quoth Galvanes, God be thanked! but I am right sorry for Olivas, for methinks he is dead. They then cast the two nephews out of the lists; then went to Olivas, and found that he had just opened his eyes, and was asking to be confessed. Galvanes looked at his wound: take heart, cried he, it is not in a dangerous place! Sir, replied Olivas, my heart and all my limbs are dying away; I have been sore wounded ere now, but never was in such weakness. They disarmed him, and the fresh air was of service, and the blood somewhat ceased. The King sent a bed whereon to remove him, and skilful surgeons dressed his wound, and said that though it was very deep, by God's help they could heal it.

The Queen then sent Grumedan to bring Brandalisa to court, and, with her, her niece Aldeva: Thereat was Don Guilan well pleased, and in a month they arrived, and were honourably welcomed. So the fame of King Lisuarte went abroad, and in half a year it was a marvel how many Knights came from foreign parts to serve him, whom he rewarded bountifully, hoping by their aid not only to preserve his own kingdom, but to conquer others, that in old times had been subject and tributary to Great Britain.

CHAPTER 41.

This history has related to you how Amadis promised Briolania to revenge her father's death, and how she gave him a sword, and that when in his combat with Gasinan he broke the sword, he gave the pieces to Gandalin's care: You shall now hear how the battle was performed, and what great danger he underwent because of that broken sword, not from any fault of his own, but for the ignorance of his dwarf Ardian.

Amadis, now recollecting that the time was come to perform his promise, acquainted Oriana, and requested her leave, though to him it was like dividing his heart from his bosom to leave her; and she granted it, albeit with many tears, and a sorrow that seemed to presage what evil was about to happen. Amadis took the Queen's leave for form's sake, and departed with Galaor and Agrayes. They had gone about half a league, when he asked Gandalin if he had brought the three pieces of the sword which Briolania had given him, and finding he had not, bade him return and fetch them. The Dwarf said he would go, for he had nothing to delay him; and this was the means whereby Amadis and Oriana were both brought into extreme misery, neither they nor the Dwarf himself being culpable.

The Dwarf rode back to his master's lodging, found the pieces of the sword, put them in his skirt, and was retiring, when, as he passed the palace, he heard himself called. Looking up, he saw Oriana and Mabilia, who asked him why he had not gone with his master. I set out with him, said he, but returned for this; and he showed her the broken sword. What can your master want a broken sword for? quoth Oriana. Because, said the Dwarf, he values it more than the two best whole ones, for her sake who gave it him.—And who is she—The Lady for whom he undertakes this combat, and though you are daughter to the best King in the world, yet, fair as you are, you would rather win what she has won, than possess all your father's lands.—What gain so precious hath she made? perchance she hath gained your master?—Yes, she has, his whole heart! and he remains her Knight to serve her! Then, giving his horse the lash, he gallopped away, little thinking the wrong he had done. Oriana remained pale as death; she burst into bitter reproaches against the falsehood of Amadis, and wrung her hands, and her heart was so agitated that not a tear did she shed. It was in vain that Mabilia and the Damsel of

Denmark strove to allay her rage with reasonable words: as passionate women will do, she followed her own will, which led her to commit so great an error, that God's mercy was necessary to repair it.

The Dwarf rejoined his master, and showed him the pieces of his sword, but Amadis asked him no questions, and he said nothing of what had passed. Presently they met a Damsel, who asked whither they were going.—Along this road.—I advise you to leave it.—Why?—Because no Knight hath taken it for fifteen days but he hath been either slain or wounded. And who hath done all this mischief? quoth Amadis.—The best Knight in arms that I have ever seen. Damsel, said Agrayes, you must shew us this Knight.—He will shew himself so soon as you enter the forest. The Damsel then followed them; they looked all round the forest in vain, till, as they were at the other side thereof, they saw a Knight of good stature completely armed, on a roan horse, holding a lance, and a Squire by him with four other lances. He speaking to his Squire, the man laid the lances against a tree, and came up to the Knights.—Sirs, yonder Knight sends to inform ye that he hath kept this forest for fifteen days against all Knights Errant with fair fortune, and for the pleasure of the joust hath yet stayed a day and a half longer than his time appointed; he says, that if it please you to joust with him he is ready, but there shall be no sword combat, for in that he hath done much evil against his own will, and will avoid it henceforth if he can. Agrayes had taken his helm and thrown the shield round his neck, while the Squire was speaking: tell him to defend himself! quoth he. They ran their race; their spears brake, and Agrayes was dismounted, and his horse ran loose, whereat he was greatly ashamed. Galaor took his arms to avenge him; the lances were broken: their bodies met with such force, that Galaor's horse, being the weaker and more weary, fell and threw him, and then ran away. Amadis seeing this, blessed himself: in truth, said he, the Knight may well be praised, for he hath proved himself against two of the best in the world; but as he went on to take his turn he found Galaor on foot, with his sword in hand defying the Knight to battle, but the Knight laughed at him; and Amadis said, brother, do not chafe yourself; it was the covenant that there should be no sword-battle. Then he bade the stranger defend himself, and they ran at each other: their spears flew up in splinters; they came against each other, shield and helmet; the horse fell with Amadis, and the horse broke his shoulder; the Knight of the forest was dismounted, but he held the reins, and lightly took the saddle again. Quoth Amadis, you must joust again, for this encounter was equal, we both fell. I do not chuse to joust again, said he. Amadis replied, Knight, you do me wrong. Right yourself when you can! said the other: I am bound no farther, as I sent to tell you! and then he gallopped away through the forest.

Amadis leapt upon Gandalin's horse, and told his companions to follow him as fast as they could to find that Knight, for they were all greatly abashed. Quoth the Damsel, it will be a foolish quest: all the Knights of King Lisuarte's household would fail to find him without a guide. My friend, said Galaor, belike you know who he is, and where to be found? If I do, quoth she, I mean not to tell you, for I would bring no harm to so good a man. Ah, Damsel, said Galaor, by the faith you owe to God, and by the thing in the world which you love best, tell me what you know of him. She answered, I care not for these conjurings, and will not discover him for nothing. Ask what you will, quoth Amadis.——Tell me your name, and promise me each a boon hereafter, when I shall demand it. They in their earnestness promised. When she heard the name of Amadis, she exclaimed, God be praised, for I was seeking you!—And wherefore?—You shall know when it is time; but tell me, have you forgot your promise to the daughter of the King of Sobradisa, who let loose the lions to save you? I am now going, replied Amadis, to perform the battle. Why then, quoth she, would you turn astray to follow this Knight, who is not so easy to find as you imagine, when your day is appointed for the combat? She says true, Sir brother, said Galaor: go you with Agrayes upon this business; I will follow the Knight with this Damsel, for I shall never have joy till I find him, and I will join you in time for the battle if it be possible. In God's name! cried Amadis, but tell us, Damsel, the name of the Knight.——I know it not, yet once I was a month with him and saw never else such deeds of arms; but I can show where he is to be found. Then Galaor departed with her.

Amadis and Agrayes proceeded till they came to the castle of Torin, the dwelling of that fair young Damsel, who was now grown so beautiful that she appeared like a bright star. What think you of her? said Amadis. Agrayes answered, if her Maker designed to make her beautiful, he has most perfectly accomplished his will. They were disarmed, and mantles given them, and they were conducted into the hall. But when Briolania saw Amadis how young he was, for he was not twenty, and how beautiful, for even the scars in his face became him, and of what fair renown he was, she thought him the best Knight in the world, and greatly affected him; so that when by his help she had recovered her kingdom, she would have given him herself and that, but Amadis told her right loyally how he was another's.

CHAPTER 42.

Four days Galaor rode with the Damsel, and so wrathful was he for this fall that whatever Knight encountered him in that time felt the effects, and many were slain for the act of another. At length they saw a fair fortress, built above a vale; the Damsel told him there was no other place near where he could lodge that night, and they made up to it. At the gate they found many men and Dames and Damsels, so that it seemed to be the house of a good man, and among them was a Knight of seventy years, with a cloak of scarlet skin, who courteously bade him welcome. Sir, quoth Galaor, you welcome us so well, that, tho' we found another host, we would not leave your hospitality. Then were they led into a hall, and supper was given them right honourably; and, when the cloths were removed, the old Knight went to Galaor and asked him if the Damsel was to be his bedfellow. He replied, no; and two Damsels then conducted her to her chamber, while he was shewn a rich bed for himself. Here rest yourself, said his host: God knows the pleasure I have in entertaining you, and all Errant Knights, for I myself have been one, and have two sons who are the like, but both now are badly wounded, for there came by a Knight who dismounted them both, and they greatly ashamed of their foil rode after him, and came up to him by a river as he was about to cross it in a boat; and they would have made him do battle with the sword, since they knew how he could joust. The Knight, who was in haste, would have declined the battle, but my sons prevented him from entering the boat. A Lady who was in the boat then said to them, that they were discourteous in detaining her Knight against her will; but they said, he must needs do battle. Let it be, then, said the Lady, that he shall fight with the better of you twain, and if he conquer him that shall suffice. Not so, they answered; if one failed, the other would prove his fortune. The Knight then grew angry, and cried, come both, since you will not let me proceed! and one after the other he sent them from their horses, utterly confounded; then crossed the river and went his way. I went afterwards to bring home my sons, for they were sorely wounded: you shall see with what wounds, such as never before were given by any Knight. He then sent for the armour which they had worn, and it was so cut through with the sword that Galaor greatly marvelled, and asked what arms the Knight bore.—A vermilion shield with two grey lions, and another on his helmet, and he rides a roan horse. Know you who he is? cried Galaor. No, said the old Knight. It is the same Knight whom I am seeking, quoth Galaor, and, if I find him, I will revenge your two sons and myself, or die. Sir friend, quoth his host, I would counsel you to forbear the attempt, for as for what my sons have suffered they brought it on themselves; and then he bade him good night.

The next morning Galaor and his guide departed; they crossed the river in the boat, and proceeding about five leagues came to a fortress. Wait for me a little, said the Damsel; I will be here presently: and she entered the castle. Presently she returned, bringing with her another Damsel and ten Knights on horseback; and that other Damsel, who was passing fair, said to Galaor, Sir, my Cousin tells me you are in quest of the Knight who bears two grey lions in a vermilion shield, that you may know who he is; but I tell you that you cannot learn by force, for there is no Knight like him in all the islands, and he will neither tell you nor any other for three years, unless it be forced from him. Damsel, said Galaor, I shall not cease my enquiry, and would rather learn his name by force than by other means. Since that be so, said she, within three days I will bring you to him, at my Cousin's request. They set forth, and by vespers time came to an arm of the sea that clipped round an island, so that there was full three leagues of water to cross; a bark was ready at the harbour, but before they entered it an oath was demanded, that there was only one Knight in company. Why is this oath required? said Galaor. The Damsel replied, the Lady of the island will have it so; when one Knight has crost over, no other is suffered to come till the first return, or is slain.——Who is it that kills or conquers them?——The Knight whom you are seeking; he has been here half a year, and by this occasion: a turney was held here by the Lady of the island, and another Dame of great beauty; this Knight came hither from a foreign land, and being on her side won the victory. Whereat she was so pleased, that she never rested till she had won him for her paramour; but because he is desirous of seeking adventures, the Lady, to detain him with her, invites Knights to joust against him. If by chance they are slain, they are there interred; otherwise, they are sent back, and he gives their arms and horses to his mistress. She is a full fair Lady, and her name Corisanda; the island is called Gravisanda. How came he, said Galaor, to keep the forest? It was a boon asked of him by a Damsel, said she, tho' his mistress hardly permitted him to perform it.

By this they had reached the island; the night was some way advanced, but it was clear moonlight, the Damsel had two tents pitched beside a little brook, and there they supped, and rested till the morning. Galaor would fain have shared the Damsel's tent, but to that, albeit, she thought him the fairest of all Knights and much delighted in his conversation, she would not consent. In the morning they set forward, and he asked his guide if she knew the Knight's name?——Neither man nor woman in all this land know it, except his mistress. Then was Galaor the more curious that one of such worth in arms should so conceal himself. Presently they saw a castle on a height,

surrounded for a league on all sides by a rich plain. In that castle, quoth the
Damsel, is he whom you seek. Having advanced farther, they found a stone
pillar curiously wrought, and a horn upon it. Sound that horn, said she,
and you shall presently see the Knight. Galaor blew the horn, and forthwith
there came certain men from the castle, and pitched a tent in the meadow
before the gate, and then there issued out ten Dames and Damsels, and in
the midst of them one richly clad, who was the Lady of the rest. Why does
the Knight tarry? quoth Galaor, who saw all this. The Damsel answered,
he will not come till the Lady send for him. I beseech you then, said he, go
to her and request her to summon him, for I have much to do elsewhere and
cannot tarry. When the Lady heard this errand, what! cried she, holds he
our Knight so cheap that he already thinks of doing ought elsewhere? he will
depart sooner than he thinks, and more to his cost. Then she turned to her
man: go, call the strange Knight. Anon he came from the castle, armed and
afoot; his men led his horse, and carried his shield and lance and helmet, and
he went straight to his mistress. You see a foolish Knight yonder, said she,
who thinks lightly to take his leave of you: I desire you would make him know
his foolishness! and then she embraced, and kissed him. All this made Galaor
the more angry.

The Knight mounted, and slowly rode down the height. Galaor was ready
as soon as he saw him in the level, and bade him defend himself: they ran at
each other; both lances were broken, both shields pierced, both Knights deeply
wounded. Don Galaor drew his sword: the stranger said to him, Knight, by
the faith you owe to God, and to the thing you love best, let us joust once
more! You conjure me so, said Galaor, that I will do it, but I am sorry my
horse is not so good as yours, else we would joust till one of us fell, or till all
your lances were broken! The Knight made no answer, but called to his Squire
for two lances, and sent the one to Galaor. Again they encountered: Galaor's
horse came on his knees and tottered, and was almost down; the stranger lost
both his stirrups, and was fain to hold round the neck of his horse. Galaor
spurred up his and had now sword in hand; thereat the stranger, somewhat
abashed, exclaimed, you are desirous to do combat with the sword; certes, I
fear it rather for you than for myself: if you do not believe me, you shall see.
Do your worst! quoth Galaor: I will either die, or revenge those whom you
left in the forest. Then the stranger recollected that it was he who had defied
him on foot, and he answered him angrily, revenge yourself if you can, but I
rather think you will carry back one shame upon another.

The Ladies, seeing how gallantly they had jousted, thought they would
then have accorded, but when they saw the sword-battle, they were greatly
amazed at the fury with which it was begun. Such mortal blows they gave
each other, that the head was often made to bow upon the breast, and the
steel [50:A]arches of the helmets were cut through, and their trappings, and
the sword went through the linings and was felt upon the head; and the field
was strewn with the fragments of their shields and their broken mail. This

continued long, till each wondered that his antagonist could hold out. Galaor's horse at last began to fail him, and could scarcely move, whereat he waxed exceeding wroth, thinking that only this delayed his victory, for the stranger could lightly come on, and withdraw again from his blows. Galaor, when indeed he did reach him, made him feel the sword, but his horse tottered as if he had been blind, and he began to fear his own death more than he had ever done before in any battle, save in that with his brother Amadis, for from that he never expected to leave off alive. Next to Amadis, he thought this the best Knight he had ever encountered, albeit he doubted not of conquering him, were it not for the fault of his horse. Being in this strait, he called out. Knight! either finish the battle on foot, or give me another horse, or else I will slay yours, and that villainy will be your fault. Do your worst! replied the stranger: the battle shall not be delayed; it is a great shame that it hath lasted so long. Look to your horse then! quoth Galaor. The Knight rode close to him, fearing for his horse; so close, that Galaor caught him with both arms, and at the same instant spurred his own horse violently, and they both fell upon the ground, each holding his sword, and there they struggled for some time before they released each other. But, when they rose, they attacked again so furiously as if the battle were but then beginning; there was not a moment's respite, now that they could freely close or strike. As the fight continued Galaor perceived he was gaining the better, for his enemy's strength evidently weakened: Good Knight! quoth he, hold a while! whereat the other paused, being indeed in need of rest. You see, quoth Galaor, that I have the better of the battle; tell me your name, and why you so carefully conceal yourself, and I will acquit you from the combat and shall receive great pleasure; but unless you do this I will not leave you. Certes, quoth the Knight, I shall not leave off with these conditions: I never found myself so hardy in any battle as in this, and God forbid that any single Knight should ever know me, except to my great honour. Be not rash, cried Galaor; by my faith I swear never to let you go till I know who you are, and why you conceal yourself. God never help me, quoth the stranger, if ever you learn it from me: I will rather perish in battle than tell it, except to two Knights, to whom, tho' I know them not, I neither could nor ought to deny any thing. Who are they whom you value so much? quoth Galaor. Neither shall you know that, replied the stranger, because it seems that it would please you. Certes, rejoined Galaor; I will know what I ask, or one of us, or both, shall die. I am not averse to that, quoth his enemy. Then they renewed the combat with full fury; but the stranger waxed weaker, his armour was every where laid open and streaming with blood, till at last the Lady of the Island ran like one frantic to Galaor, and cried, hold, Knight! would the bark had been sunk that brought thee hither! Lady, said he, if it offends you that I am avenging myself, and one who is better than myself, the fault is not mine. Offer him no more harm, quoth she, or you shall die by the hands of one who will have no mercy. He answered, I know not how that may turn out, but I will not leave him till I know what I have asked.—And what is that?—His name, and why he conceals it? and who the two Knights are whom he esteems above the rest of the world. She answered, A curse upon him who taught you to strike, and upon you who have learnt so well! I will tell you: his name is Don Florestan; he conceals himself because he hath two brothers in this land of such passing worth in arms, that, albeit you have proved his prowess, he dares not make himself known to them, till, by his fame, he is worthy to join them; and these two Knights are in the household of King Lisuarte, the one is called Amadis, the other Don Galaor, and they are all three sons of King Perion. Holy Mary! cried Galaor, what have I done? and then he presented his sword to Florestan: good brother, take my sword, and the honour of the battle!—Are you my brother?—I am your brother Don Galaor. Then Florestan fell on his knees before him, saying, Sir, pardon me! for this offence that I have committed in combatting against you, was caused by no other reason than that I durst not name myself your brother, as I am, till I had somewhat resembled you in prowess. Galaor raised him up, and took him in his arms, and wept over him for joy, and for sorrow to see him so sorely wounded.

But the Lady beholding all this was greatly rejoiced. Sir, quoth she, if you gave me great anguish you have repaid it with double pleasure. They were then both carried into the castle and laid in bed, both in one apartment, and Corisanda, being skilful in chirurgery, looked to their wounds herself with great care; for she knew that if the one died, the other would die also for pure sorrow, and her own life would be doubtful if Florestan were in great danger.

FOOTNOTES:

[50:A] Cortando de los yelmos los arcos de azero con parte de las faldas dellos, assi qui las espadas descendian a los almofares, y las sentian en las cabeças.

CHAPTER 43.

This valiant and hardy Knight, Don Florestan, you should know how and in
what land he was begotten, and by whom. Know then that when King Perion,
being a young man and of good heart, sought adventures, he passed two years
in Germany, doing great deeds in arms, and as he was returning with great
glory to his own land, he lodged one day with the Count of Selandia, where
he was right worshipfully entertained, and at night he was shewn to a rich
bed, and there being weary with his journey fell asleep. Ere long he felt a
Damsel embracing him, and her mouth joined to his; and, waking thereat,
was drawing back, but she cried out, how is this, Sir? would you rather be
alone in the bed? The King then looked at her by his chamber-light, and
saw the fairest woman that ever he saw: tell me, quoth he, who you are?
She answered, one that loves you, and gives you her love.—First tell me your
name?—Why do you distress me with the question?—I must know.—I am
the Count's daughter. Then the King said, it becomes not a woman of your
rank to commit this folly: I tell you I will not do this wrong to your father.
Ah, quoth she, ill betide those who praise your goodness! you are the worst
man in the world, and the most discourteous! what goodness can there be in
you when you thrust away a fair Lady of such lineage? King Perion answered,
I shall do that which is to your honour and my own, not what would injure
both. Then, quoth she, I will do that which shall grieve my father more, than
if you consent to my will! and she leapt up and took King Perion's sword, that
same sword which was laid in the ark with Amadis, and unsheathed it, and
placed the point against her heart:—Will not my father grieve more for my
death? When the King saw that, he was greatly astonished, and he sprung
from the bed, crying, hold! I will perform your will! and he snatched the
sword from her, and that night she became pregnant. On the morrow Perion
departed, and never saw her more.

She, so long as she could, concealed her situation, and when the time drew
nigh contrived to go visit her Aunt, with one Damsel; but as she was passing
through a forest her pains came on her, and she alighted from her palfrey,
and there brought forth a son. The Damsel seeing her in this plight, put the
baby to her breast. Now, Lady, said she, the same courage that you showed in
sinning, show now in supporting yourself till I return; and then she mounted

her palfrey, and rode on as fast as she could to the Aunt's castle, and told her all that had happened. The Dame was greatly troubled, yet delayed not for that to succour her, but went forthwith with a litter, wherein she used to visit her brother to shade her from the sun; and when she saw her niece she alighted, and wept with her, and had her placed with the infant in the litter, and taken by night into the castle, and enjoined secrecy to all who were with her. So the mother returned after her recovery to the Count's castle, and nothing was known of what had passed, and the boy was educated till he was of eighteen years, a braver youth, and better limbed than any other in the district; and the Dame his Aunt seeing this gave him horse and arms, and took him to the Count to knight him, who knew not that he whom he was knighting was his own grandson.

As they were returning, the Dame told him the secret of his birth, and said that he ought to go seek his father and make himself known to him. Certes, Lady, quoth he, I have often heard of King Perion, but never thought he was my father; but by the faith I owe to God, and to you who have brought me up, neither he nor any one else shall know who I am, till they can say that I am worthy to be the son of so good a man. Then taking his leave, he went with two Squires to Constantinople, where he heard there was a cruel war; there he remained four years, and did such deeds in arms as never Knight had wrought before in those parts, so that at the end of that time he determined to go and discover himself to his father. But as he drew nearer France, he heard the fame of Amadis and Galaor, who were now beginning to work wonders, so that he changed his first intention, and resolved to gain more honour in Great Britain, where there were more good Knights than in any part of the world, and that he would not make himself known till his prowess had given him sufficient renown: in which mind he continued till his combat with Galaor, as you have heard.

Amadis and Agrayes remained five days at the castle of Torin; then all things being prepared, they set forward with Briolania and her aunt, who took with them two damsels and five serving-men, on horseback, and three palfreys laden with apparel, for Briolania went in black, and would wear nothing else till her father's death was avenged. As they began their journey Briolania requested a boon of Amadis, and her Aunt another of Agrayes; the which they granted, without knowing what it might be: they then demanded, that, let what would happen, the Knights should not leave the road, that so their present quest might not be interrupted. Much did they repent their promise, and great shame did they endure thereby, for in many places was their succour needed, and rightly might they have bestirred themselves if they had been at liberty. Thus they travelled twelve days before they entered the kingdom of Sobradisa; it was night when they reached it: they left the high road, and struck by a by-way for three leagues; and then, great part of the night being past, they came to a little castle, where a Lady dwelt named Galumba, who had served in the court of the King Briolania's father. She right joyfully admitted them, and set supper before them, and provided their night's entertainment; and the next morning asked the Aunt whither they were going. A joyful woman was she, hearing that those Knights were going to revenge her Master's death; but I fear, said she, lest that traitor should destroy them by some deceit: for that reason, said the old Lady, am I come to consult with you. Leave it to me, quoth Galumba. Then she took ink and parchment, and wrote a letter, and sealed it with Briolania's seal, and gave it to a Damsel, and directed her what she should do. The Damsel mounted her palfrey, and rode on till she came to the great city of Sobradisa, from whence the whole kingdom took its name. She went directly to the palace of Abiseos, and rode through the gate, being richly apparelled. The Knights came around to assist her to dismount; but she said, no, she would not alight till the King saw her, and commanded her so to do. They then took her bridle, and led her into a hall where the King was, with his sons and many other Knights, and he bade her alight if she had any thing to say. She answered, I will, Sir, on condition that you protect me, and that I shall suffer no injury for any thing that I may say against you, or against any other here. The King assured her that she should be under his protection and royal faith, and bade her deliver what she was come to say. Upon that she alighted, and said, Sir, I bring a message which must be delivered in the presence of all the chiefs of your realm: summon them, and it shall be made known. Quoth Abiseos, it is as you would wish: they are already in my court, and have been assembled on business these six days. Call them together, said she. Forthwith they were summoned, and being all met, the Damsel then said, King, Briolania, she whom you disherited, sends you this letter, to be read before this assembly. When Abiseos heard the name of his niece he was touched with shame, remembering the wrong he had wrought her; yet, the letter was openly read, which was to give credit to the Damsel's words. To this he only replied, that they were not to believe what the Damsel might say on Briolania's behalf: but the people of the realm who were there present were moved with great compassion at the name of their lawful Lady, who was so unjustly dispossessed, and they besought God secretly that he would no longer suffer so great a treason to remain unpunished. Give your errand, quoth the King. Sir King, said the Damsel, it is true that you killed the father of Briolania, and have disherited her of her kingdom; and you have often declared, that you and your sons would justify what you have done by force of arms. Briolania now sends to say, that if you hold your word she will bring here two Knights who will undertake the battle in her cause, and make you know your treason and great tyranny. When Darasion, the eldest of the sons heard this, he arose in great anger, being of a hot nature, and without his father's permission replied, Damsel, if Briolania has these Knights, I promise the combat for myself, and for my father and brother; and, if I do not perform this, I promise before all these Knights to give my head to her, that she may take it in requital of her father's. Certes Darasion, answered the Damsel, you answer like a Knight of great courage, yet may I doubt your words to proceed from choler, for I see you are enraged; but if you will obtain from the King an assurance of your words, I shall think they proceed from that great worth and hardihood which are in you. What would you have? quoth he. Cause the King, she replied, to give our Knights assurance that, for any mishap which you may receive in the battle, they shall sustain no injury from any in this land, nor be meddled withal but by you three: give them this safe conduct, and they will be here within three days. Darasion knelt down before his father;—you see, Sir, what the Damsel requests, and what I have promised; and, because my honour is yours, let it be granted, else they will without danger have put us to shame, for we have always avowed that if any one attainted your deeds we would justify it in battle; and even without the promise we ought to accept the defiance, for they tell me these Knights are some of King Lisuarte's rash household, whose pride and folly makes them magnify their own worth and despise all others. The King, albeit he felt himself guilty of his brother's murder, and dreaded the battle, yet, because he loved his son as he did himself, gave the safe conduct as the Damsel had demanded, the hour appointed by the Most High being come. The Damsel having accomplished this, said, hold yourselves ready, for to-morrow the Knights will be here. And then she mounted her palfrey, and departed.

Much were the Ladies and the Knights rejoiced at the success of her embassy. When Amadis heard that Darasion held them as fools, because they were of King Lisuarte's household, he grew angry, and exclaimed, there are those in that household who could easily break his pride, and his head too! but, when he had said this, he was ashamed that he had been so mastered by anger. Briolania, who could not keep her eyes off him, observed this, and said, you cannot, Sir, either say or do any thing against those traitors which they have not deserved, and worse: have pity on me, since you know my father's murder, and my wrongs: my trust is in God and in you. Amadis, whose heart was submiss to virtue and all gentleness, moved with pity for that fair Damsel, answered, if God be so pleased, Lady, I ween that ere to-morrow night your sorrow will be turned into joy. Then Briolania would, for thankfulness, have humbled herself to have kissed his feet, but he drew back abashed, and Agrayes raised her up. They determined to set forward by day-break, and hear mass at the chapel of the Three Fountains, which was half a league from Sobradisa.

That night they made good cheer, and Briolania, who talked much with Amadis, was oftentimes moved to offer marriage to him, but seeing his frequent reveries, and the tears that sometimes fell down his cheeks, which she knew proceeded from no fear in his brave heart, she suspected that he loved elsewhere, and so refrained. At dawn they all departed; and, arriving at the Three Fountains, heard mass from the good Hermit, who hearing wherefore they were on their way, besought God to speed them well in the battle, as he knew their cause was right. There they armed themselves all save the head and hands, and so proceeded to the city. Without the walls they found King Abiseos and his sons, and a great company attending them: the people all flocked towards Briolania, whom in their hearts they loved, thinking her their rightful and natural Lady. Amadis led her bridle, and uncovered her face,[65:A] that all might see her how beautiful she was: she was weeping, and the multitude blessed her in their hearts, and prayed that she might now be restored to her rights. Abiseos dissembled a feeling from which neither his ambition nor his wickedness could shield him, and seeing how the people flocked round Briolania, he exclaimed, fools, I see how you rejoice in her sight! but it is to your honour and safety that a Knight like me should protect you, not a weak woman; who in so long a time has only been able to get these two Knights for her champions; whom, because they are thus deceitfully brought to their death, or dishonour, I cannot forbear to pity. These words so kindled the indignation of Amadis, that blood seemed starting from his eyes; he rose in his stirrups that all might hear him, and answered, King Abiseos, I well see how the coming of Briolania troubles you, because you have murdered her father, who was your King and brother: if there be yet virtue enough in you to resign to her what is her own, I will excuse the battle, that you may have leisure for repentance, that, though you have lost your honour in this world, you may save your soul. Before the King could reply, Darasion exclaimed, Thou foolish Knight of King Lisuarte's court! I never thought I could endure to hear a speech like thine: come on! and if your heart fails, you cannot fly where I cannot reach you with such a vengeance, that none can behold it without compassion. Arm thyself, traitor, and do battle! quoth Agrayes. Darasion answered, say what thou wilt now! presently I will send thy tongue without thy body to King Lisuarte's court, as a warning to all such fools! Then they armed themselves; and Amadis and Agrayes laced on their helmets, and took their shields and spears, and entered the place which had been of yore marked out for such trials. Dramis, the second son, who was so good a Knight that no two Knights of that country could keep the field against him, said to his father, Sir, where you and my brother are present, I might well be excused from speaking; but now I have to act with that strength which I have received from God and you. Leave that Knight who has reviled you to me: if I do not slay him with the first lance-thrust, may I never again bear arms! or if it be his good fortune that the spear does not strike right, the first blow with the sword shall do it. There were many who heard this speech, and did not think it vain boasting, he was of such exceeding strength. Darasion looked round the lists: how is this? quoth he; ye are but two! hath the heart of the third failed him? call him to come directly, for we will not tarry. Trouble not yourself about the third, said Amadis, you will presently wish the second away: now look to your defence!

They placed their shields before them, and gave their horses the rein. Dramis ran right at Amadis, and pierced his shield and broke his lance against his side; but Amadis smote him so roughly, that the spear went through his shield, and, without piercing his breast-plate, burst his heart within him, and he fell like the fall of a tower. In God's name, cried Ardian the Dwarf, my Master's deed is better than his word! The other twain ran at Agrayes: he and Darasion broke their lances upon each other, and both kept their seats. Abiseos failed in his course; he saw Dramis on the ground, and in great grief, albeit he did not suppose him to be dead, ran full at Amadis, and pierced his shield, and broke the lance in his arm, so that all thought he could not continue the battle. Well may you think how Briolania felt at that; her heart sunk, and the sight of her eyes failed her, and without support she would have fallen from her palfrey. But he, who was not to be dismayed by such wounds, graspt well that good sword which he had so lately recovered from Arcalaus, and struck Abiseos upon the helm; through helm it went, and slanted down the head, and pierced into the shoulder; a slant wound, but so staggering that Abiseos tottered on his seat, and fell, half senseless. Then he of Gaul rode up to Darasion, who was close engaged with Agrayes:—now Darasion, you had rather the second were absent, than that the third were come! Agrayes cried out to him to hold:—Cousin, you have done enough, leave me this man who has threatened to cut out my tongue. Amadis did not hear him; he had made a blow which sliced off a part of the shield, and came through the pummel of the saddle to the horse's neck; but Darasion, as he past, ran his sword into the belly of Amadis's horse; the horse instantly ran away; the reins broke in the rider's hand, and Amadis seeing that he had no remedy, and that he should be carried out of the lists, struck the beast between the ears with his sword, and split his head; the fall bruised him sorely, but he arose, and turned to Abiseos.

At this time Agrayes had driven his sword into Darasion's helmet, so that he could not recover it. Darasion had forced it from his hand, and was driving at him. Agrayes grappled him; they fell together and struggled on the ground. Abiseos came up, and was lifting the skirts of his armour to thrust his sword into him. Amadis came up in time. The King was compelled to look to his own safety; he lifted his shield, the blow dashed shield against helmet, and made him reel. Agrayes and Darasion had loosed each other: Agrayes caught up Darasion's sword; Darasion plucked the other from his helm, and ran towards his father. Amadis saw that Agrayes was all bloody from a wound in his neck, and fearing it was mortal, he cried, leave them to me, good cousin, and rest yourself! I have no wound, quoth Agrayes, to keep me from aiding you: see if it be so! Have at them, then! cried Amadis; but the fear he felt for his cousin gave him such anger, that presently his enemies, their armour all hacked, and their flesh too, began to turn here and there disorderly, and with the fear of death. So it continued till the hour of tierce, when Abiseos, seeing death before him, lifted his sword in both hands, and ran desperately at Amadis, and gave him a blow, such as might not be looked for from a man so wounded: it cut away the brim of the helmet, and the shoulder mail and a part of the flesh with it. Amadis felt it sorely, and did not delay to give him his wages: he struck his shoulder, and lopt off that arm with which he had murdered his own king and brother; arm and shoulder he lopt off, and cried, that arm brought thee by treason to the throne, and it now brings thee to death and the depth of hell! The King had fallen in the pangs of death. Amadis looked round him, and saw that Agrayes had smitten off the head of Darasion. Then the people of the land went joyfully to kiss the hand of Briolania their [70:A]Lady.

The conquerors dragged their enemies out of the lists. Amadis, though he was much wounded, would not disarm himself till he knew if there were any to gainsay Briolania's right. But one of the chiefs of the realm, by name Goman, came before him with an hundred men of his lineage and household, and they declared that they had only endured the usurpation of Abiseos because they had no remedy: now God had delivered them, they were in that loyalty and vassallage which they owed to Briolania. Within eight days all the kingdom came joyfully to do homage to her. Amadis meantime was laid in bed, and that fair Queen never left him but when she went to sleep herself. Agrayes, who was dangerously wounded, was put under the care of a skilful man, who suffered none to approach him, that he might not speak, for the wound was in his throat.

FOOTNOTES:

[65:A] *Quitole los antifazes.* She was muffled in the Moorish manner, not veiled.

[70:A] There follows in the original a page of advice to all wicked kings and rulers.

CHAPTER *44.*

Don Galaor and Florestan remained in the castle of Corisanda till their wounds were well healed, then took they their departure; but Corisanda made such sorrow that it was pitiful to see her, albeit Florestan comforted her, and assured her of his speedy return. They crossed to the mainland, and proceeded towards Sobradisa, hoping to arrive there before the battle. Brother, quoth Florestan, as they rode along, grant me a boon for courtesy. Sir, and good brother, cried Galaor, is it a thing that I shall repent? You will not repent it, said Florestan.—Ask it then; for what I can grant without shame, I shall grant with good will.—I ask then, that you will attempt no combat in this journey till I have tried my fortune. Certes, quoth Galaor, I repent. Not so, replied Florestan, for if there be any worth in me, it is to your honour as well as to mine. Four days they rode without adventure: on the fifth at evening they came to a Tower. A Knight, who stood at the court-gate, courteously invited them for the night; and there were they worshipfully entertained. The Knight their host, was a fair Knight and a wise, and of goodly stature; but oftentimes he appeared so lost in thought and sadness, that the brethren asked each other what it might mean, and Don Galaor at last said to him, Sir, methinks you are not so chearful as you should be! if your sadness is for any cause which our aid can remedy, tell us, and we will do your will. Many thanks, replied he of the Tower: I believe you would do so like good Knights; but my sadness proceeds from the force of love, and I will not tell you more now, for it would be to my own great shame. The hour of sleeping came on; their host went to his apartment, and the brethren remained in a handsome chamber where there were two beds. In the morning he rode to bear them company, but unarmed; and, that he might see whether they were such in arms as their appearance bespoke them, he led them not along the high road, but through bye ways, till they came to a place called the fountain of the Three Elms, for there were three great and lofty Elm-trees above the fountain. Three fair Damsels and well apparelled, were by the fountain, and there was a Dwarf aloft in the trees. Florestan went first and saluted them gently, as a courteous man, and one who had been gently bred. God save you, Sir Knight, quoth the one; if you are as brave as you are handsome, God hath gifted you well. Damsel, he replied, if my beauty pleaseth you, my courage would please you more if it were put to proof. You answer well, quoth she: see now, if your courage be enough to carry me from hence.—Certes, quoth Florestan, little goodness is enough for that; since it is your pleasure, I will do it.—He then bade his Squires place her upon a palfrey which was tied to one of the Elms: when the Dwarf, who was sitting up in the tree, cried out aloud, Come forth, Knights, come forth! they are carrying away your mistress! At these words a Knight, well armed and on a great horse, came up from the valley, and cried out to Florestan, Knight! who bid you lay your hands upon that Damsel? I do not think she can be yours, replied Florestan, seeing of her own will she desired me to carry her hence. The Knight answered, though she consent, I do not; and I have defended her against better than you.—I know not how that may be, but unless you act up to your words, carry her away I will!—Learn first what the Knights of the Valley are, and how they defend their mistresses! With that they ran at each other, and Florestan smote his shield so strongly against his helmet that the laces brake, and the helmet came off. The Knight could not keep his seat; he fell upon his sword, and broke it in two. Florestan turned his horse and pointed his lance at him:—you are dead, unless you yield the Damsel! I yield her, quoth he, and cursed be she, and the day wherein I first beheld her, for she made me commit so many follies that at last I have destroyed myself. Florestan left him, and went to the Damsel, saying, you are mine! You have well won me, quoth she, and may do with me as you please. Let us go then! said he; but one of the other Damsels then said to him, Sir Knight, you are parting good company; we have been a year together, and it grieves us to be separated. Said Florestan, if you chuse to go in my company I will take you also, otherwise you must be separated, for I will not leave so fair a Damsel as this. And if she be fair, quoth the Damsel, neither do I esteem myself so ugly, but that Knight should venture something for me also; but I believe you are not of that temper. What! cried he, think you that I would leave you here for fear? so help me as I would have done so only to respect your free will, but you shall see. He bade the Squires place her also on her palfrey, and the Dwarf, who sate up aloft, cried out again for help.

Presently there came another Knight from the valley, and said to Florestan, Don Cavalier, you have won one Damsel, and, not content with her, you would carry off another; you must, therefore, lose both, and your head too; for it is not fit that a Knight of such degree as you should have in your keeping a Damsel of such rank. You praise yourself bountifully, quoth Florestan; yet had I rather have two Knights of my kin for my helpers than thee! I neither regard thee nor them, said the Knight: you have won this Damsel from him who could not defend her; if I conquer thee, she shall be mine; if the victory is yours, you shall take the other whom I defend. Content, quoth Florestan. Defend yourself now, if you can! said he of the valley; and they ran their encounter. The Knight pierced through Florestan's shield, and broke his lance against the strong mail. Florestan failed in the race; ashamed at that, when the Knight had taken from his Squire another lance, he ran again, and pierced the shield of his antagonist and the arm that held it, and drove him back upon the crupper of his horse; the horse reared and threw him, and, the ground being hard, he neither moved hand nor foot. Damsel, said Florestan, you are mine; for methinks your friend can neither help you nor himself. So it seems, quoth she.

Florestan looked at the other Damsel, who now remained alone by the fountain, and saw that she was very sad. Damsel, said he, if it please you, I will not leave you here alone. She did not answer him, but said to his host, Go from hence, I counsel you! you know that these Knights are not enough to protect you from him who will presently be here, and, if he take you, you are sure to die. I will see what may happen, he answered, my horse is swift, and my Tower at hand. Ah, said she, take care of yourself; ye are but three, and you unarmed, and you well know that is nothing against him. When Florestan heard this, he became more desirous to carry away that Damsel, and see him whom she praised so greatly. So he had her also placed on her palfrey; and the Dwarf, who sate up aloft, said, Don Cavalier, in an ill hour are you so bold: here comes one who shall take vengeance for all! and then he shouted out, help! help, Sir! you linger too long! Presently there came another Knight from the same valley; his armour was inlaid with gold, and he rode upon a bay horse, big enough for a giant. Two Squires came after him, armed with corselets and morions like serving men, and each carried a huge battle-axe in his hand, in the use of which weapon their master prided himself. He cried out to Florestan, stay, Knight, and seek not to fly, for it will not save you: die you must, and it is better die like a brave man, than like a coward! When Florestan heard himself threatened, he waxed wonderous angry, and cried out, come on, wretch and rascal, and clumsy[78:A] fool! So help me God, as I fear thee no more than a great cowardly beast. Ah, quoth the Knight, how it grieves me that I cannot wreak sufficient vengeance upon thee! would that the best four of thy lineage were here, that I might cut off their heads with thine! Protect yourself from one, cried Florestan, you may dispense with the rest. Then, being both greatly incensed, they ran at each other, and the shields and the mails of both were pierced with the violence of the encounter: the large Knight lost both his stirrups, and was fain to save himself by clinging round his horse's neck. Florestan, as he past on, caught at one of the battle-axes, and plucked it with such force from the Squire who held it, that both the man and his horse were brought to the ground. The Knight of the Valley had recovered his seat, and was ready with the other battle-axe, and Florestan made at him with equal arms: both struck at once, each on the helmet of his enemy; the axes went in three fingers' depth. Florestan bowed his face upon his breast with the weight of the blow: the Knight fell upon the neck of his horse, and the axe, being fast in the other's helmet, slipt from his hand; before he could raise himself, Florestan smote him as he lay between the helm and gorget, so that his head fell at the horse's feet. This done, he turned to the Damsels. Certes, good Knight, quoth the first of them, I once thought that not ten such as you could have won us.

The young Knight, their host, then came up to Florestan, and said, Sir, I love this Damsel dearly, and she loves me. It is a year since this Knight whom you have slain hath forcibly detained her, so that I could not see her: now, that I may receive her from your hands, I beseech you refuse me not. My host, quoth Florestan, of a truth I will right gladly aid you, if it be as you say; but against her will I will yield her to none. Ah, Sir, cried the Damsel, this is with my will! I beseech you give me to him: he is my true love. Florestan answered, in God's name, dispose of yourself as you like best! and she went joyfully to her true love. Galaor then gave his horse to their friend, and took the bay horse of the dead Knight, which was the handsomest he had ever seen, and then they separated. The two Damsels whom Florestan had won, were young and fair; he took the one to himself, and gave the other to Galaor: I give you to this Knight, said he, and command you to do as he pleases. What! quoth she, do you give me to this Knight, who has not the heart of a woman? who stood by and saw you in such danger, and did not help you? Damsel, answered Florestan, by my faith to God and to you, I swear that I give you to the best Knight whom I know in the world, except it be Amadis my Lord. The Damsel then looked at Galaor, and seeing him so handsome, and so young, she marvelled at his worth, and granted him her love. That night they had their lodging at the house of a Lady, sister to their last night's host. On the morrow they resumed their road, and said to their fair friends, we have a long journey to perform thro' foreign lands, where you would endure many hardships in following us: tell us where you would like best to go, and there we will conduct you. They replied, that their Aunt had a castle four days journey on that road whither they would go. As they proceeded, Galaor asked his Damsel how she came into the power of those Knights. She answered, that great Knight who was slain loved the Damsel who went with your host, but she hated him. He took her by force, for he was the best Knight in all these parts, and none could gainsay him, yet would she never yield him her love; and he, for the affection he bore her, withheld from offering her any wrong; and he said to her, My fair friend, great reason is it that I should be loved by you, being the best Knight in the world. Now I will do this for your sake: there is a Knight who is called the best that ever was, Amadis of Gaul by name, and he slew my cousin Dardan, in King Lisuarte's court; I will find him, and cut off his head, and then shall I inherit all his renown. Till I do this, I will give you two of the fairest Damsels in all this land for your companions, and they shall have the two best Knights of my lineage for their friends; and you shall every day be taken to the fountain of the Three Elms, where many Errant Knights pass, that you may see brave jousting, and learn to love me as I love you. He then took us by force, and gave us to his kinsmen, and thus had we past a year, till Don Florestan broke the bonds. That Knight, quoth Galaor, had a haughty mind: what was his name?

Alumas, she answered; and, if it had not been for his exceeding pride, he was of great prowess. Thus they proceeded till they reached the Lady's castle, who thankfully entertained them, because they had delivered her nieces from Alumas and his kinsmen, who had forcibly and dishonourably detained them.

Galaor and Florestan proceeded till they reached the kingdom of Sobradisa, and there heard the joyful tidings of what their brother and Agrayes had done. They hastened to the city, and went immediately to the palace, where Amadis and his cousin, now whole of their wounds, were conversing with the new Queen. Amadis, from the Damsel who had guided Galaor, knew who they were, and went to welcome Florestan with tears of joy, embracing and kissing him who would have knelt before him. But when Briolania saw four such Knights in her palace, and recollected how powerful she now was, and how lately she had lived, not without fear, in a single castle, she knelt down, and thanked the Most High for the mercy he had vouchsafed her. Of a truth, Sirs, said she, these changes are the work of him, before whom the mightiest are nothing; but for this dominion, and this wealth, which we suffer so much anxiety and trouble to gain, and having gained, to keep; would it be better, as being neither certain nor durable in themselves, and as things superfluous and destructive to the body, and moreover to the soul,—would it be better to reject and abhor them? Certainly I say, no: and affirm, that, when they are gained with a good conscience, and justly administered, we may enjoy from them comfort and pleasure and joy in this world, and everlasting glory in the next.

Here endeth the First Book of the noble and virtuous Knight, Amadis of Gaul.

FOOTNOTES:

[78:A] Ven cativa cosa, y mala, y fuera de razon, sin talle. The language of vituperation is not easily translatable.

AMADIS of GAUL. Book the Second.

CHAPTER 1.

There was a King in Greece married to the sister of the Emperor of Constantinople, by whom he had two fair sons, especially the elder, named Apolidon, who in his days had no equal for strength of body and courage of heart. He having a subtle genius, which is so seldom found with valour, gave himself to the study of the sciences and of all arts, so that he shone among those of his own time like the Moon among the stars; especially he excelled in necromancy, whereby things that appear impossible are done. The King his father was very rich in treasure, but poor in life, by reason of his great age; and seeing himself at the point of death, he commanded that the kingdom should be given to Apolidon, as his eldest son, and his books and treasures to the other. The younger was not contented with this, and told his father so with tears, and complained that he was disherited; but the old man, not knowing what to do, wrung his hands for pure sorrow. Then that famous Apolidon, seeing his father's grief and the littleness of his brother, bade him take comfort, for he would accept the books and treasure, and relinquish the kingdom to his brother. Whereat the father gave him his blessing with many tears. So Apolidon took his inheritance, and fitted out certain ships, manning them with chosen Knights, and set forth into the sea, trusting himself to Fortune, who seeing his great obedience to his father, and how he had thrown himself upon her mercy, resolved to requite him with glory and greatness. A fair wind carried him to the empire of Rome, where Siudan was then Emperor, at whose court he abode some time, doing great feats in arms, till there grew a true affection between him and the Emperor's sister, Grimanesa, who then flourished among all other women for beauty. So it was that as he was loving, even so was he loved, and as their loves might no other ways be indulged, they left Rome together, and set sail in Apolidon's fleet, and sailed till they came to the Firm Island. There Apolidon landed, not knowing what country it was, and pitched a tent upon the shore, and placed a couch there for his Lady, who was weary of the sea. Presently there came down a fierce Giant, who was Lord of the island, with whom, according to the custom of the place, Apolidon was to do battle for the preservation of his Lady and himself, and his company. It ended in such sort that the Giant lay dead on the field, and Apolidon remained master of the island. When he had seen its strength, he neither feared the Emperor of Rome, whom he had offended, nor all the world besides; and there he and Grimanesa, being greatly beloved by the islanders, whom he had delivered from their oppressor, dwelt in all happiness for sixteen years. During that time many rich edifices were made, as well with his great treasures, as with his surpassing wisdom, such as it would have been difficult for any Emperor or King, how rich soever, to have completed. At the end of that time the Emperor of Greece died without an heir, and the Greeks, knowing the great worth of Apolidon, and that by his mother's side he was of the blood and lineage of the Emperors, elected him with one common consent to rule over them. He, albeit he was enjoying all possible delights in his own island, yet, with Grimanesa's consent, accepted the Empire; but she, before they left the island where she had enjoyed such rare happiness, requested her husband that he would work such a means by his great knowledge, that that island might never be possessed, except by a Knight as excellent in arms and loyal in love as himself, and by a Dame resembling her in beauty and truth.

Then Apolidon made an arch at the entrance of a garden, wherein there were all kind of trees, and also four rich chambers, but it was so surrounded that none could enter, except by passing under the arch, over which he placed the Image of a man made of copper, holding a trumpet in his mouth as if he would wind it. And in one of the chambers within he placed two figures, in the likeness of himself and his Lady, the countenances and the stature like unto them, so true that they seemed alive, and near them he placed a bright stone of jasper; and, about the distance of half a cross-bow shot, he made a [87:A]perron of iron. Henceforward, said he, no man or woman who hath been false to their first love shall pass here, for yonder Image shall blow from that trumpet so dreadful a blast with smoke and flames of fire, that they shall be stunned and cast out as dead. But if Knight, or Dame, or Damsel come, worthy by virtue of true loyalty to finish this adventure, they shall enter without let, and the Image shall make a sound so sweet that it shall be delightful to hear, and they shall see our images, and behold their own name written in the jasper. Grimanesa afterwards ordered some of her Knights and Ladies to make trial, and then the Image blew the dreadful blast with smoke and flames of fire; whereat Grimanesa laughed, knowing them to be in more dread than danger. But yet, my Lord, quoth she, what shall be done with that rich chamber wherein we have enjoyed such great contentment? He answered, you shall see. Then he made two other perrons, one of stone, the other of copper: the stone one was placed five paces from the chamber, the copper one five paces farther off. Know now, said he, that henceforth in no manner, nor at any time, shall man or woman enter this chamber, till a Knight come who surpasses me in prowess, or a woman exceeding you in beauty; they shall enter. He then placed these words in the copper perron: Knights shall advance here, each according to his valour; and in the stone perron, he wrote: here none shall pass except the Knight who exceeds Apolidon in prowess. And over the door of the chamber he wrote: He who surpasses me in prowess shall enter here, and be Lord of the island. And he laid such a spell, that none could approach within twelve paces of the chamber round about, nor was there any entrance but by the perrons.

Then he appointed a Governor to rule the island, and collect the revenues, which were to be reserved for the Knight who should enter the chamber; and he commanded that all who failed in attempting to pass the Arch of Lovers, should, without ceremony, be cast out of the island; but such as passed through were to be entertained and served with all honour. And farther, he appointed that all Knights who attempted the adventure of the Forbidden Chamber, and did not pass the copper perron, should leave their arms there; but from those who advanced any way beyond it, only their swords should be taken. They who reached to the marble perron should leave only their shields, and if they penetrated beyond that, but failed to enter the chamber, they should lose only their spurs. From the Dames and Damsels who failed, nothing was to be taken, only their names should be placed upon the castle-gate, and an account how far they had advanced. Apolidon then said, when this island shall have another Lord, the enchantment shall be dissolved, and all Knights may freely pass the perrons and enter the chamber; but it shall not be free for women, till the fairest shall have come, and lodged in the rich chamber with the Lord of the island. These enchantments being thus made, Apolidon and his wife entered their ships, and passed over into Greece, where they reigned during their lives, and left children to succeed them.

FOOTNOTES:

[87:A] *Padron* is the Spanish word: the English version renders it pillar, but the word means more; there must be a roof and a flooring. Our market-crosses would be called *padrones*. *Perron* is used in the English Amadis of Greece.

CHAPTER 2.

While Amadis remained with his comrades at the court of Sobradisa, his thoughts were perpetually fixed upon his Lady Oriana; and, so thoughtful was he, and so often, both sleeping and waking, was he in tears, that all saw how he was troubled, yet knew they not the cause, for he kept his love silent, as a man who had all virtues in his heart. At length, not being able to support a longer absence, he asked permission of the fair young Queen to depart, which she not without reluctance having granted, loving him better than herself, he and his brethren and their cousin Agrayes took the road towards King Lisuarte. Some days had they travelled when they came to a little church, and entering there to say their prayers, they saw a fair Damsel, accompanied by two others, and by four Squires, who guarded her, coming from the door. She asked them whither they went. Amadis answered, Damsel, we go to the court of King Lisuarte, where, if it please you to go, we will accompany you. Thank you, quoth the Damsel, but I am faring elsewhere. I waited, because I saw you were armed like Errant Knights, to know if any of you would go and see the wonders of the Firm Island, for I am the Governor's daughter, and am returning there. Holy Mary! cried Amadis, I have often heard of the wonders of that island, and should account myself happy if I might prove them, yet till now have I never prepared to go! Good Sir, quoth she, do not repent of your delay; many have gone there with the same wish, and returned not so joyfully as they went. So I have heard, said Amadis: tell me, would it be far out of our road if we went there?—Two days journey.—Is the Firm Island then in this part of the sea, where is the enchanted Arch of True Lovers, under which neither man nor woman can pass that hath been false to their first love? The Damsel answered, it is a certain truth, and many other wonders are there. Then Agrayes said to his companions, I know not what you will do, but I will go with this Damsel, and see these wonderful things. If you are so true a lover, said she, as to pass the enchanted Arch, you will see the likenesses of Apolidon and Grimanesa, and behold your own name written upon a stone, where you will find only two names written besides, though the spell hath been made an hundred years. In God's name let us go, quoth Agrayes, and I will try whether I can be third. With that, Amadis, who in his heart had no less desire and faith to prove the adventure, said to his brethren, we are not enamoured, but we should keep our cousin company who is, and whose heart is so bold. Thereto they all consented, and set forth with the Damsel. What is this island? said Florestan to Amadis, tell me, Sir, for you seem to know. A young Knight whom I greatly esteem, replied Amadis, told me all I know; King Arban of North Wales: he was there four days, but could accomplish none of the adventures, and so departed with shame. The Damsel then related the history of the enchantments, which greatly incited Galaor and Florestan to the proof.

So they rode on till sunset, and then entering a valley, they saw many tents pitched in a meadow, and people sporting about them, and one Knight, richly apparelled, who seemed to be the chief. Sirs, quoth the Damsel, that is my father: I will go advertise him of your coming, that he may do you honour. When he heard of their desire to try the enchantment, he went on foot with all his company to welcome them, and they were honourably feasted and lodged that night. At morning they accompanied the Governor to his castle, which commanded the whole island, for at the entrance there was a neck of land, only a bow-shot over, connected with the main land, all the rest was surrounded by the sea; seven leagues in length it was, and five broad, and because it was all surrounded by the sea, except where that neck of land connected it with the continent, it was called the Firm Island. Having entered, they saw a great palace, the gates whereof were open, and many shields hung upon the wall; about an hundred were in one row, and above them were ten, and above the ten were two, but one of them was in a higher niche than the other. Then Amadis asked why they were thus ranked. The Governor answered, according to the prowess of those who would have entered the Forbidden Chamber; the shields of those who could not enter the perron of copper, are near the ground; the ten above them are of those who reached it; the lowest of the two passed that perron, and the one above all reached to the marble perron, but could pass no farther. Then Amadis approached the shields to see if he knew them, for each had its owner's name inscribed; the one which was the highest of the ten bore a sable lion, with argent teeth and nails, and a bloody mouth, in a field sable: this he knew to be the shield of Arcalaus. Then he beheld the two uppermost; the lower bore, in a field azure, a Knight cutting off the head of a Giant; this was the shield of King Abies of Ireland, who had been there two years before his combat with Amadis: the highest had three golden flowers in a field azure: this he knew not, but he read the inscription, This is the shield of Don Quadragante, brother to King Abies of Ireland. He had proved the adventure twelve days ago, and had reached the marble perron, which was more than any Knight before him had done, and he was now gone to Great Britain to combat Amadis, in revenge for his brother's death. When Amadis saw all these shields, he doubted the adventure much, seeing that such Knights had failed.

They went out from the palace towards the Arch of True Lovers. When they came near, Agrayes alighted and commended himself to God, and cried,

Love, if I have been true to thee, remember me! and he past the spell; and, when he came under the arch, the Image blew forth sweet sounds, and he came to the palace, and saw the likeness of Apolidon and Grimanesa, and saw also the jasper-stone, wherein two names were written, and now his own the third. The first said, Madanil, son of the Duke of Burgundy, atchieved this adventure: and the second was, this is the name of Don Bruneo of Bonamar, son to Vallados, Marquis of Troque: and his own said, this is Agrayes, son to King Languines of Scotland. This Madanil loved Guinda, Lady of Flanders. Don Bruneo had proved the enchantment but eight days ago, and she whom he loved was Melicia, daughter to King Perion, the sister of Amadis.

When Agrayes had thus entered, Amadis said to his brethren, will ye prove the adventure? No, said they, we are not so enthralled that we can deserve to accomplish it. Since you are two, then, quoth he, keep one another company, as I, if I can, will do with my cousin Agrayes. Then gave he his horse and arms to Gandalin, and went on without fear, as one who felt that never in deed or in thought had he been faithless to his Lady. When he came under the arch, the Image began a sound far different and more melodious than he had ever before done, and showered down flowers of great fragrance from the mouth of the trumpet, the like of which had never been done before to any Knight who entered. He past on to the Images, and here Agrayes, who apprehended something of his passion, met him and embraced him, and said, Sir, my Cousin, there is no reason that we should henceforth conceal from each other our loves. But Amadis made no reply, but taking his hand, they went to survey the beauties of the garden.

Don Galaor and Florestan, who waited for them without, seeing that they tarried, besought Ysanjo, the Governor, to shew them the Forbidden Chamber, and he led them towards the perrons. Sir brother, said Florestan, what will you do? Nothing, replied Galaor: I have no mind to meddle with enchantments. Then amuse yourself here, quoth Florestan, I will try my fortune. He then commended himself to God, threw his shield before him, and proceeded sword in hand. When he entered the spell, he felt himself attacked on all sides with lances and swords, such blows and so many that it might be thought never man could endure them; yet, for he was strong and of good heart, he ceased not to make his way, striking manfully on all sides, and it felt in his hand as though he were striking armed men, and the sword did not cut. Thus struggling, he passed the copper perron, and advanced as far as the marble one, but there his strength failed him, and he fell like one dead, and was cast out beyond the line of the spell. When Galaor saw this he was displeased, and said, however little I like these things, I must take my share in the danger! and bidding the Squires and the Dwarf to stay by Florestan, and throw cold water in his face, he took his arms and commended himself to God, and advanced towards the Forbidden Chamber. Immediately the unseen blows fell upon him, but he went on, and forced his way up to the marble perron, and there he stood; but, when he advanced another step beyond, the blows came on him so heavy a load, that he fell senseless, and was cast out like Florestan.

Amadis and Agrayes were reading the new inscription in the jasper, This is Amadis of Gaul, the true lover, son to King Perion,—when Ardian the Dwarf came up to the line, and cried out, Help! help, Sir Amadis, your brothers are slain! They hastened out to him, and asked how it was.—Sir, they attempted the Forbidden Chamber, and did not atchieve it, and there they lie for dead! Immediately they rode towards them, and found them so handled as you have heard, albeit some little recovering. Then Agrayes, who was stout of heart, alighted and went on as fast as he could to the Forbidden Chamber, striking aright and aleft with his sword, but his strength did not suffice to bear the blows, he fell senseless between the perrons, and was cast out as his cousins had been. Then Amadis began to curse their journey thither, and said to Galaor, who was now revived, Brother, I must not excuse my body from the danger which yours have undergone. Galaor would have withheld him, but he took his arms, and went on, praying God to help him. When he came to the line of the spell, there he paused for a moment, and said, O Oriana, my Lady, from you proceeds all my strength and courage! remember me now at this time, when your dear remembrance is so needful to me! Then he went on. The blows fell thick upon him and hard till he reached the marble perron, but then they came so fast as if all the Knights in the world were besetting him, and such an uproar of voices arose as if the whole world were perishing, and he heard it said, if this Knight should fail, there is not one in the world who can enter. But he ceased not to proceed, winning his way hardly, sometimes beaten down upon his hands, sometimes falling upon his knees; his sword fell from his hand, and, though it hung by a thong from the wrist, he could not recover it, yet holding on still he reached the door of the chamber, and a hand came forth and took him by the hand to draw him in, and he heard a voice which said, Welcome is the Knight who shall be Lord here, because he passeth in prowess him who made the enchantment, and who had no peer in his time. The hand that led him was large, and hard, like the hand of an old man, and the arm was sleeved with green sattin. As soon as he was within the chamber it let go his hold, and was seen no more, and Amadis remained fresh, and with all his strength recovered; he took the shield from his neck and the helmet from his head, and sheathed his sword, and gave thanks to his Lady Oriana for this honour, which for her sake he had won. At this time they of the castle who had heard the voices resign the lordship, and seen Amadis enter, began to cry out, God be praised, we see accomplished what we have so long desired. When his brethren saw that he had atchieved that wherein they had failed, they were exceedingly joyful, because of the great love they bore him, and desired that they might be carried to the chamber; and there the Governor with all his train went to Amadis, and kissed his hand as their Lord. Then saw they the wonders which were in the chamber, the works of art and the treasures, such that they were amazed to see them. Yet all this was nothing to the chamber of Apolidon and Grimanesa, for that was such, that not only could no one make the like, but no one could even imagine how it could be made; it was so devised, that they who were within could clearly see what was doing without, but from without nothing could be seen within. There they remained some time with great pleasure; the Knights, because one of their lineage was found to exceed in worth all living men, and all who for a hundred years had lived: the islanders, because they trusted to be well ruled and made happy under such a Lord, and even to master other lands. Sir, quoth Ysanjo, it is time to take food and rest for to-day: to-morrow, the good men of the land will come and do homage to you. So that day they feasted in the palace, and the following day all the people assembled and did homage to Amadis as their Lord, with great solemnities and feasting and rejoicing.[101:A]

You have heard in the first part of this great history, how Oriana was moved to great anger and rage by what the Dwarf had said to her concerning the broken sword, so that neither the wise counsels of Mabilia nor of the Damsel of Denmark aught availed her. From that time she gave way to her wrath, so that wholly changing her accustomed manner of life, which was to be altogether in their company, she now forsook them, and for the most part chose to be alone, devising how she might revenge herself for what she suffered, upon him who had caused her sufferings. So recollecting that she could by writing make him sensible of her displeasure, even at a distance, being alone in her chamber, she took ink and parchment from her coffer, and wrote thus:

My frantic grief, accompanied by so great a reason, causes my weak hand to declare what my sad heart cannot conceal against you, the false and disloyal Knight, Amadis of Gaul; for the disloyalty and faithlessness are known which you have committed against me, the most ill-fortuned and unhappy of all in the world, since you have changed your affection for me, who loved you above all things, and have placed your love upon one who by her years cannot have discretion to know and love you. Since then I have no other vengeance in my power, I withdraw all that exceeding and misplaced love which I bore towards you; for great error would it be to love him who has forsaken me, when in requital for my sighs and passion I am deceived and deserted. Therefore, as the wrong is manifest, never appear before me! for be sure the great love I felt is turned into raging anger. Go, and deceive some other poor woman as you deceived me with your treacherous words, for which no excuse will be received, while I lament with tears my own wretchedness, and so put an end to my life and unhappiness.

Having thus written, she sealed the letter with the seal of Amadis, and wrote on the superscription, I am the Damsel wounded through the heart with a sword, and you are he who wounded me. She then secretly called a Squire, who was named Durin, and was brother to the Damsel of Denmark, and bade him not rest till he had reached the kingdom of Sobradisa, where he would find Amadis; and she bade him mark the countenance of Amadis while he was reading the letter, and stay with him that day, but receive no answer from him, if he wished to give one.

FOOTNOTES:

[101:A] The Spanish Writer moralizes here a little upon the mutability of fortune.

CHAPTER 3.

Durin, in obedience to the command of Oriana, presently departed, and hasted so well that on the tenth day he arrived at Sobradisa, where he found the new Queen Briolania, whom he thought the fairest woman, except Oriana, that ever he had seen; and learning from her that Amadis had departed two days before, he followed him, and reached the Firm Island just as Amadis was passing under the Arch of True Lovers, and so he beheld how the Image did more for him than ever it had done for any other. And though he saw Amadis after he came forth to his brethren, yet he did not speak with him, nor give him the letter, till after he had entered the Forbidden Chamber, and been received by all as Lord of the island. This he did by Gandalin's advice, who, knowing the letter to be from Oriana, feared that it might cause his Master either to forslow or fail in the atchieving of so great an enterprise, for he would not only have left off the conquest of the Firm Island, but also of the whole world, to fulfil what she had commanded; but, when every thing was finished, Durin went before him, and Amadis took him apart from his brethren and from all others into a garden, and asked him if he came from the court of King Lisuarte, and what tidings. Sir, said he, the court is as when you left it: I come from thence by the command of my Lady Oriana; by this letter you will know the cause of my coming. Amadis took the letter, and he concealed the joy that was in his heart, that Durin might know nothing of his secret; but his grief he could not conceal when he had read those strong and bitter words, for neither his courage nor reason could support him then, for he seemed struck with death. When Durin saw him so disordered, he cursed himself and his ill fortune, and death, that had not overtaken him on the way. Amadis, for he could not stand, sate down upon the grass, and took the letter which had fallen from his hands, and, when he saw the superscription, again his grief became so violent that Durin would have called his brethren, but feared to do so, observing what secrecy Amadis had chosen. Presently Amadis exclaimed, O Lord, wherefore does it please thee that I should perish, not having deserved it! and then again, Ah, truth, an ill guerdon dost thou give him who never failed thee! Then he took the letter again, saying, you are the cause of my unhappy end; come here, that it may be sooner! and he placed it in his bosom. He asked Durin if he had aught else to say; and hearing that he had not, replied, well then thou shalt take my answer. Sir, quoth he, I am forbidden to receive any.—Did neither Mabilia nor thy sister bid thee say any thing?—They knew not my coming: my Lady commanded me to conceal it from them.—Holy Mary help me! I see now my wretchedness is without remedy. He then went to a stream that proceeded from a fountain, and washed his face and eyes, and bade Durin call Gandalin, and bid him bring Ysanjo the Governor; and he said to the Governor, promise me, as you are a loyal Knight, to keep secret all that you shall see till after my brothers have heard mass to-morrow; and the same promise he exacted from the two Squires. Then he commanded Ysanjo to open privately the gate of the castle, and Gandalin to take his horse and arms out, privately also. This done they left him, and he remained alone, thinking upon a dream which he had dreamt the last night, wherein it seemed, that being armed and on horseback he was on a hill covered with trees, and many persons round about him making great joy; when a man from amongst them presented him a box, saying, Sir, taste what I bring you; which he did, and it was exceeding bitter; and therewith feeling himself cast down and disconsolate, he loosed the reins of his horse, and let him go whither he would; and he thought that the mirth of all around him was changed into such sorrow as was pitiful to behold; but his horse carried him far away from them, and took him through the trees to a rocky place surrounded with water; and then it seemed in his dream that he left his horse and arms, as if by that he would have had rest, and there came to him an old man in a religious habit, and took him by the hand as if he had compassion, and spoke to him in a language which he did not understand, whereupon he awoke. Upon this dream Amadis now mused, thinking that he now found it true.

Then hiding his face from his brethren, that they might not see his trouble, he went to the castle-gate, which the sons of Ysanjo had opened. Come you with me, said Amadis to the Governor, and let your sons remain here, and keep this matter secret. So they went to the foot of the rock, where there was a little chapel, and Gandalin and Durin went with them. There he armed himself, and asked the Governor to what saint that chapel was dedicated.—To our Lady the Virgin, who hath wrought many miracles here. Hearing this, Amadis went in and knelt down, and said, weeping, Our Lady Virgin Mary, the consoler and helper of those that are afflicted, I beseech you to intercede with your glorious Son, that he may have mercy on me; and, if it be your will not to help me in my body, have mercy on my soul in these my last days, for other thing than death I do not hope. He then called Ysanjo, and said, promise as a loyal Knight to do what I shall direct! and turning to Gandalin, he took him in his arms and wept abundantly, and held him somewhile, for he could not speak. At length he said, my good friend Gandalin, you and I were nursed by the same milk, and our lives have been past together, and never have I endured hardship and danger in which you had not your part also. Your father took me from the sea when I was so little, being only that night's child, and they brought me up as a good father and mother bring up their beloved son; and you, my true friend, have always thought how to serve me, and I have hoped in God that he would one day enable me to requite thee; but now this misery, which is worse than death, is come upon me, and we must part, and I have nothing to leave thee, except this island: I therefore command Ysanjo and all others, by the homage which they have done to me, that so soon as they shall know my death they take thee for their Lord. The Lordship shall be thine, but I enjoin that thy father and mother enjoy it while they live, and afterwards it shall remain to thee. This I do for what they did for my childhood, for my ill fortune will not suffer me to do what they deserve, and what I desire. He then told Ysanjo to take from the rents of the island, which had accumulated, enough to build a monastery by that chapel, in honour of the Virgin Mary, and to endow it for thirty friars. But Gandalin cried out, Sir, you never yet had trouble wherein I was separated from you, nor shall it be now; and if you die, I do not wish to live: and I want no honours or lordships; give it to your brethren, I will not take it, and I do not want it. Hold thy peace, for God's sake, quoth Amadis, and say no such folly to displease me. My brethren are of such worth that they can gain lands for themselves, and to bestow on others. Then he said to Ysanjo, it grieves me, my friend Ysanjo, to leave you before I could honour you according to your deserts; but I leave you with those who will do it. Ysanjo answered, let me go with you, Sir, and suffer what you suffer. Friend, answered Amadis, it must be as I say; God only can comfort me! I will be guided by his mercy, and have no other company. He then said to Gandalin, if thou desirest knighthood, take my arms; for, since thou hast kept them so well, it is right they should be thine. I shall little need them: if not, my brother Galaor shall knight thee. Tell him this Ysanjo, and serve and love him as thou hast me, for I love him above all my lineage, because he is the best, and hath ever been humble towards me. Tell him, too, that I commit Ardian the Dwarf to his care. They for great sorrow could make him no answer. Then Amadis embraced them, and commended them to God, saying that he never thought to see them more, and he forbade them to follow him; and with that spurred his horse and rode away, forgetting to take either shield, or helmet, or spear. He struck into the mountain, going whither his horse would. Thus he kept till midnight, being utterly lost in thought; the horse came then to a little stream of water, and proceeded upward to find a place so deep that he could drink thereat. The branches struck Amadis in the face, and so recalled him to himself, and he looked round, and seeing nothing but thickets, rejoiced, thinking that he was hidden in that solitude. So he alighted, and fastened his horse to a tree, and sate upon the green herb by, and wept till his head became giddy, and he fell asleep.

CHAPTER 4.

Gandalin and his companions remained by the chapel, looking after Amadis as he rode so fast away: then Gandalin, who was passionately weeping, cried out, I will follow and carry his arms to him, although he hath forbidden me! And I, quoth Durin, will bear you company for this night. So they left Ysanjo, and getting to horse, rode after him, coasting here and there about the wood, till fortune brought them so near the place where he was lying, that his horse scented theirs, and began to neigh. Then they knew that he was near, and Gandalin alighted, and went quietly through the shrubs till he saw his Master sleeping by the fountain. The Squire then took his horse and led it where he had left Durin, and taking off the bridles from all the horses that they might browze the green boughs, they remained still. It was not long before Amadis awoke, for his sleep was restless: he rose, and looked round: the Moon was almost down, but it was yet some time till day; then he lay down again, and broke out into pitiful lamentations for his evil fortune.

The two Squires heard all he said and were greatly moved thereat, yet durst they not appear before him. Presently there came up a Knight singing along the way, and, when he was near the place where Amadis lay, he exclaimed, Love, love, I thank thee for exalting me above all other Knights! giving me good first, and better afterwards. You made me affect the fair Queen Sardamira, thinking to secure her heart by the honour which I should bear away from this land; and now, for my greater happiness, you make me love the daughter of the greatest King in the world, the fair Oriana, who hath no peer on earth: you make me love her, and you give me strength to serve her. Saying this, he drew from the wayside to a great tree, whereunder he meant to wait for day-break. Then said Gandalin to his comrade, stay here while I go see what Amadis will do. He went towards the fountain, but Amadis had risen and was seeking his horse; and seeing Gandalin dimly in the night, he cried out, who goes there? tell me, I beseech thee?—Gandalin, Sir! who is going to bring you your horse.—Who bade thee follow me against my command? you have displeased me: give me my horse and go thy way, and tarry not here, unless thou wouldst have me slay thee and myself. Sir, cried Gandalin, for God's sake no more of this! did you hear the foolish words of a Knight hard by? And this he said to make him angry, that he might forget his displeasure for a while. Amadis answered, I heard him, and therefore want my horse to depart.—How! is this all you will do?—What wouldst thou more?—That you should fight with him, and make him know his folly.——Fool that thou art! I have neither heart, nor strength, nor spirit! having lost all in losing her from whom all came: she gave me courage, and hath taken it away: the most caitiff Knight in Great Britain might slay me now. Sir, said Gandalin, for God's sake speak lower, that Durin may not hear this, for he has heard all that the Knight said.—What! is Durin here?—We came together: I think he tarries to see what you will do, that he may report it to her who sent him. I am vexed at what you tell me, quoth Amadis; but his spirit arose, knowing that Durin was there, and he said, give me my horse then, and guide me to the Knight. He mounted and took his arms, and Gandalin led him where the Knight sate under a tree, holding his horse by the bridle. You Sir Knight, quoth Amadis, who are enjoying yourself, rise, and let us see if you can maintain the love of which you boast. The Knight arose, and cried, who are you who question me? you shall see how I maintain it, if you dare do battle with me, for I will strike terror into thee, and all who are scorned by Love. I am one of those, quoth Amadis: Love hath foully requited me: I tell thee this, Sir Lover, where I have found one truth in him, I have found seven lies. Come, and maintain his justice: let us see if he has gained more in you than he has lost in me! and, as he spake these words, his anger kindled, feeling how unjustly his Lady had abandoned him. The Knight mounted and took his arms, and said, You Knight, whom Love has justly forsaken, because you were not worthy to serve him, get you gone! I am offended even at the sight of you. And he would have rode away, but Amadis cried out, What, Knight! do you defend your love only with words, and ride off like a coward? How! quoth he: I was leaving thee for contempt, and thou callest it fear! thou art very desirous of thy own hurt: defend thyself now if thou canst! They ran against each other, and both shields were pierced, but the Knight was thrown down: he kept the reins, and mounted again lightly. Quoth Amadis, If you do not defend Love better with the sword than with the lance, you will be a bad champion. The Knight made no reply, but struck at him in great fury: the sword fell on the rim of the shield, and entered in aslant, and he could not pluck it out. Amadis stood in his stirrups, and gave him a blow on his head, and cut away the trappings of his helmet and the skin of his head, and the sword held on and came upon the neck of the horse, so that he fell dead, and the rider senseless. Amadis waited a minute, thinking that he had slain him; then seeing him recover, he said, Knight, what Love has gained in you, and you in him, you may both enjoy: I leave you. So departing from him, he called Gandalin, and seeing Durin there, he said to him, friend Durin, my sorrow hath no equal, and my grief and recollections are intolerable: it is better that I should die: pray God it may be soon! Go, with good fortune! Salute for me, Mabilia, my good cousin, and the Damsel of Denmark, thy sister; and tell them, if they grieve for me, that I perish more undeservedly than ever Knight perished; and tell them that I sorely regret that those who have loved me so much, and done so much for me, have never had their guerdon! Durin stood weeping before him, and could make no reply. Amadis embraced him, and he commended him to God, and kissed the skirts of his armour and departed. By this it was day-break: Amadis said to Gandalin, if you chuse to go with me, attempt not to disturb me in whatever I say or do: if you will not obey this, go back. He promised obedience. Then Amadis gave him his arms, and bade him pluck the sword from the shield and give it the Knight, and so they rode on.

CHAPTER 5.

This wounded Knight was Patin, brother to Don Sidon, who was then Emperor of Rome; he was the best Knight in all those lands; and therefore greatly feared throughout the empire. The Emperor was very old, and had no son, therefore all thought this brother should succeed him. He loved Sardamira, Queen of Sardinia, who was a fair and comely Damsel, and being niece to the Empress had been brought up in the court; and he had so far profited by his service, that she had promised him, if ever she married, to marry him. El[119:A] Patin upon this grew more presumptuous, though his natural arrogance was enough; and he said to her, I have heard that King Lisuarte hath a daughter who is renowned over all the world for her beauty. I will go to his court, and say she is not so fair as you, and this I will maintain against the two best Knights who dare undertake her cause. They say there are Knights there of great worth in arms, but if I do not conquer them in one day, I will that King Lisuarte do cause my head to be cut off! The Queen answered him, do not do this; for, if that Princess be fair, it impaireth not the beauty which God hath bestowed upon me, if beauty there be; and, methinks, you might with more reason and less pride prove your prowess in some other cause, for this enterprize is not becoming a man of so high a rank, and moreover it is unreasonable and arrogant, and you cannot expect it to come to a good end. Come what will, quoth he, I will do it, to prove that you, who are the fairest Lady in the world, have the best Knight for your servant. So he took his leave, and with rich arms and ten Squires passed over into Great Britain, and went directly to where King Lisuarte was, who seeing him so accompanied thought him to be some great personage, and courteously welcomed him. When he was disarmed, all that saw his great stature judged him to be of great courage. Lisuarte then asked him who he was. He answered, King, I will tell you, for I do not come to your house to conceal myself, but to make myself known. Know, then, that I am El Patin, brother to the Emperor of Rome, and so soon as I see the Queen, and your daughter Oriana, you shall know the cause of my coming. When the King heard that he was a man of so high rank, he embraced him and said, Good friend, much are we pleased with your coming, and you shall see the Queen and her daughter and all others of my house, when it pleaseth you. Then he placed him at his own table, and they were feasted in a manner befitting the table of such a personage. El Patin looked round him, and when he saw so many Knights he was astonished, and began to hold the household of his brother, the Emperor, as nothing. Don Grumedan took him to his lodging, by the King's command, and did him much honour. The next day after mass, the King took with him El Patin and Don Grumedan, and went to the Queen, who received him honourably, and made him sit before her and near her daughter. Now Oriana's beauty was much impaired by reason of her great trouble of mind, yet when El Patin saw her he marvelled greatly, and thought that they who praised her had not mentioned half her beauty, and his heart was entirely changed from the purpose with which he had come, and wholly bent to obtain her. Wherefore calling to mind his own high birth and great qualities, and moreover that he should one day possess the empire, he thought that if he demanded her in marriage she would not be refused him. So taking the King and Queen apart, he said, I come hither to request the marriage of your daughter, for your worth and for her beauty: if I sought others of her rank, I could obtain them, seeing what I am, and what I expect to be. The King answered, we thank you much for what you say, but the Queen and I have promised our daughter not to give her in marriage against her consent: we must talk with her, before we can answer you. This the King said that he might not offend him, but in his mind he was resolved not to give her to him, or to any other who would carry her out of the land which she was to inherit. El Patin was satisfied with this, and waited five days, expecting a favourable answer; but the King and Queen, thinking it folly, had said nothing to Oriana. Then El Patin asked the King how the business went on. He answered, I do what I can, but it is necessary that you should speak to my daughter, and request her to obey my commands. El Patin went to the Princess, and said, Lady Oriana, I wish to ask a thing of you which will be much to your honour and profit. What thing is that? quoth she.—That you will do the will of your father. She knowing not for what reason he spake, replied, that shall I right willingly, being sure it will be as you say. Then Patin was full joyful, thinking he had won her, and said, I will go through this land seeking adventures; before long you will hear such things of me, as will make you with more reason grant what I require. And this also he said to the King, telling him that he would see the wonders of his land. The King replied, you have it in you to do this; yet would I dissuade you, for in this land you will find many great and perilous adventures, and many strong and hardy Knights, practised in arms. I like this, quoth El Patin: if they are strong and hardy, I am neither weak nor faint, as my deeds shall show. So he departed, right joyful at Oriana's answer, and for this joy he was singing as you have heard, when his ill fortune led him where Amadis was making moan; and this is the reason why that Knight came from so far a land.

Durin departed from Amadis when it was clear day-light, and he passed by El Patin, who had taken off the piece of his helmet that was left, and had his face and neck all bloody. He seeing Durin, said to him, Good child, so may God make you a good man as you tell me if there be any place near where I may have remedy for my wound. Yes, quoth he, but all there are so afflicted that they will hardly attend to you.——For what cause?——For the loss of a good Knight, who hath won that lordship, and seen the likenesses and secrets of Apolidon, which none other could ever do, and he is departed in such sorrow that nothing but his death is looked for.——Methinks you speak of the Firm Island?——I do.——What! hath it found a a master? certes I am heartily sorry, for I was going there myself to prove the adventure and win the Island. Durin laughed, and answered, Truly, Sir Knight, if there be no more prowess in you than you have just now manifested, you would have gained little honour! El Patin raised himself as well as he could, and tried to catch his bridle, but Durin turned aside. Tell me, said he, what Knight is he that hath won the Firm Island?——Tell me first who you are?——I am El Patin, brother to the Emperor of Rome.——God-a-mercy! quoth Durin, your birth is better than your prowess or your courtesy. Know that the Knight you ask about is the same who hath just now left you: by what you have seen you may judge that he is worthy of what he hath won. So he went his way, and took the straight road to London, greatly desirous to tell Oriana all that he had seen of Amadis.

FOOTNOTES:

[119:A] The article is uniformly prefixed to his name, except where he is first mentioned. In our language it is only used where the name is a family or clan appellation: The Plantagenet, the Douglas, the Graham.

CHAPTER 6.

Ysanjo, according to his promise, revealed nothing concerning Amadis till after mass the next day. Then, when his brethren and his cousin enquired for him, he said, arm yourselves, and I will tell you his commands. And, when they were armed, Ysanjo began to weep passionately, and exclaimed, O Sirs, what a grief and a misery is come upon us, that we should lose our Lord so soon! Then he told them all that Amadis had said, and how he besought that they would not seek him, for they could not help his ill, and that they should not grieve for his death. Holy Mary! cried they, the best Knight in the world is about to perish! but we will seek him, and, if we cannot with our lives help him, we will bear him company with our deaths. Ysanjo then told Galaor his brother's request that he would make Gandalin a Knight, and take the Dwarf into his service: this he delivered weeping, and they weeping also heard it. The Dwarf for pure grief was beating his head against a wall; but Galaor caught him up and said, Ardian come with me, since thy Master has so commanded, and my lot shall be yours. The Dwarf answered, Sir, I will follow you, but not as my Master, till we know some certain tidings of Amadis. Forthwith they went to horse, and all three hastened along the road which Ysanjo pointed. All day they rode on, meeting no one of whom they could ask tidings, till they came where El Patin lay wounded beside his dead horse: his Squires had found him, and were cutting down boughs and poles to make him a litter, for he was exceeding faint with loss of blood, so that he could not answer them, but made sign that they should speak to his Squires, and they replied, that their Lord had sped so ill in an encounter with the Knight who had won the Firm Island. Good Squires, know you which way he went?——No; but before we came up to this place we met an armed Knight in the forest, upon a stout horse, and he was weeping and accusing his fortune: a Squire behind him carried his arms; the shield had two lions azure in a field or., and the Squire was lamenting also. That is he! cried they; and they pushed on with great speed till they came out of the forest upon a great plain, where there were many roads in every direction, so that they knew not which way to take; therefore they agreed to separate, and meet at the court of Lisuarte upon St. John's day, that if by then they had been unsuccessful in their search, they might consult anew how to find him. There then they embraced and separated, each earnestly bent on his quest, but in vain; for, when Amadis reached the open country, he took none of those roads, but struck aside along a glen, and thence made into the mountain.

He rode on lost in thought, suffering his horse to chuse the path. About noon the horse came to some trees that grew beside a mountain-stream, and then stopt, being weary with the heat and with the toil of last night. Here Amadis recollected himself and looked round, and was pleased to see no signs of a habitation: he alighted and drank of the brook. Gandalin came up, and turning the horses to feed came to his Master, whom he found more dead than alive; and, not daring to disturb him, he lay down before him. Amadis continued in this mood till sunset, then rising, he struck his foot against Gandalin: art thou sleeping? quoth he. No, replied Gandalin, but I am thinking upon two things which concern you, the which, if it please you to hear, I will speak: if not, I will be silent. Amadis answered, go saddle the horses, and let us begone: I do not chuse to be found by those who seek me. Sir, said Gandalin, you are in a solitary place, and your horse is so weary that, unless you allow him some rest, he cannot carry you. Amadis replied, weeping, do what you think best: whether I stay or go, there is no rest for me! Then Gandalin looked after the horses, and returned to his Master, and begged him to eat of a pasty which he had brought, but he would not. Sir, said he, shall I say the two things whereon I have been thinking? Say what you will, quoth Amadis; I care nothing now for any thing that may be said or done, and wish to live no longer than till I can confess.—Then I pray you hear me, Sir: I have thought much upon that letter which Oriana sent you, and upon the words of the Knight with whom you fought; and seeing how light is the faith of many women, it may be that she hath changed her affections, and so has feigned anger against you, before you discover it. The other thing is, that I believe her to be so good and loyal that she could not have been thus moved, unless some great falsehood had been spoken of you, which she believes and feels in her heart; and, since you know that you have never been false, you should make the truth known, whereby she will repent of what she hath done, and intreat your forgiveness for the wrong, and you will enjoy your former happiness. It is better to take food with this hope, than, by abandoning yourself to despair, to die and lose her, and the glory of this world, and even the other. Hold thy peace, for God's sake! quoth Amadis, for such foolishness and lies as thou hast uttered, are enough to provoke the whole world. Oriana, my Lady, has never done wrong; and, if I perish, it is but reasonable, not for my deserving, but to accomplish her will and command: if I did not know that thou hast said this to comfort me, I would cut off thy head! you have greatly displeased me: never say the like to me again! He then turned away in anger, and walked along the side of the stream.

But Gandalin, who for two days and a night had not slept, was overcome with heaviness, and at length fell asleep. When Amadis saw this, he saddled his horse, and hid Gandalin's saddle and bridle among the bushes, that he might not be able to find them; and, taking his arms, he struck into the wildest part of the mountain. All night he went; and the next day till vespers, then he came to a plain at the foot of a mountain: there were two high trees there that grew over a fountain, and there he went to give his horse drink, for they had found no water all that day. When he came up to the fountain, he saw an old man in a religious habit, who was giving his ass water; his beard and hair were grey, and his habit was very poor, being made of goat's hair. Amadis saluted him, and asked him if he was a Priest. The good man answered, he had been one forty years. God be praised! quoth Amadis: I beseech you for the love of God stay here to-night, and hear my confession, of which I am in great need. In God's name! said the old man. Then Amadis alighted, laid his arms upon the ground, and took the saddle from his horse and let him feed; and he disarmed, and knelt before the good man, and began to kiss his feet. The good man took him by the hand and raised him, and made him sit by him, and, beholding him well, he thought him the goodliest Knight that ever he saw, but he was pale, and his face and neck were stained with tears, so that the old man had great pity, and said, Sir Knight, it seems that you are in great affliction: if it be for any sin that you have committed, and these tears spring from repentance, in a happy hour came you here! but if it be for any worldly concerns, from which by your youth and comeliness it seems you cannot be removed, remember God, and beseech him of his mercy to bring you to his service. He then raised his hand and blessed him, and bade him relate all the sins he could call to mind. Hereon Amadis began the whole discourse of his life, without letting any thing pass. The good man then said, seeing that you are of such understanding, and of so high a lineage, you ought not to despair and cast yourself away for any thing that may befall you, much less for the action of a woman, for they are as easily won as lightly lost. I counsel you to lay aside such folly, for the love of God, to whom it is displeasing, and even for worldly reason, for man ought not to love where he is not beloved. Good Sir, replied Amadis, I am now in such extremity that I cannot live any long time: I beseech you, by that God whose faith you hold, take me with you for the little while I have to live, that I may have comfort for my soul. My horse and arms I need no longer: I will leave them here, and go with you on foot, and perform whatever penitence you enjoin. If you refuse, you will sin before God, for else I shall wander and perish in this mountain. When the good man saw him thus resolute, he said to him, with a heart wholly bent to his good, Certes, Sir, it becomes not a Knight like you to abandon himself as if he had lost the whole world, by reason of a woman: their love is no longer than while they see you with their eyes, and hear such words as you say to them, and that past, presently they forget you; especially in those false loves that are begun against the Lord: the same sin which makes them sweet at first, gives them a bitterness in the end, as you experience. But you who are of such prowess, and have such power, you who are the true and loyal protector of such as are oppressed, great wrong would it be to the world if you thus forsake it. I know not what she is who hath brought you to this extremity, but if all the worth and beauty of the sex were brought together in one, I know that such a man as you ought not to be lost for her. Good Sir, quoth Amadis, I ask not your counsel upon this, where it is not wanted; but, for my soul's sake, I pray you take me in your company, for else I shall have no remedy, but to die in this mountain. The old man hearing this, had such compassion on him that the tears fell down his long white beard. Sir, my son, said he, I live in a dreary place, and a hard life; my hermitage is full seven leagues out at sea, upon a high rock, to which no ship can come except in summer time. I have lived there these thirty years, and he who lives there must renounce all the pleasures and delights of the world, and all my support is the alms which the people of the land here bestow upon me. I promise you, said Amadis, this is the life I desire for the little while I shall live, and I beseech you, for the love of God, let me go with you. The good man, albeit against his will, consented; and Amadis said, now, Father, command me what to do, and I will be obedient. The good man gave him his blessing, and said vespers, and then taking bread and fish from his wallet, he bade Amadis eat; but Amadis refused, though he had been three days without tasting food. You are to obey me, said the good man, and I command you to eat, else your soul will be in great danger if you die. Then he took a little food; and when it was time to sleep, the old man spread his cloak and laid him down thereon, and Amadis laid himself down at his feet.

The most part of the night Amadis did nothing but turn from side to side, but at last being sore wearied he fell asleep, and in that sleep he dreamt that he was fastened in a dark chamber, where there was no light at all, neither could he find any way to come out thereof, whereat he greatly lamented; then he thought that his cousin Mabilia and the Damsel of Denmark came to him, and there was a sun-beam before them which dispelled the darkness, and they took him by the hand, saying, Come forth, Sir, to this great palace. And he thought that he was right joyful; and going out he saw his Lady Oriana surrounded with a great flame of fire, whereat he cried out, Holy Mary, help her! and ran through the fire to save her, feeling no hurt, and took her in her arms and carried her into a garden, the greenest and pleasantest that ever he had seen. At the loud cry which he made the good man awoke, and took him by the hand, asking him what he ailed? Sir, said he, I felt such pain in my sleep that I was almost dead. So it seemed by your cry, said the old man, but it is time to set out; then he got upon his ass. Amadis would have walked by him, but the good man with great entreaty made him mount his horse, and so they fared on together.

As they went, Amadis besought him to grant one boon, which should be no-ways hurtful, the which the old man granted. I pray you then, said Amadis, that so long as we are together you will not tell any man who I am, nor any thing concerning me, and that you will call me by some other name, not my own; and, when I am dead, you tell my brethren of me, that they may take my body into their country. Your life and death, said the good man, are in the hands of God, so talk no more of this, he will help you if you know and love and serve him as you ought; but tell me, by what name will you be called?—Even by whatever it shall please you.—So the old man, seeing how fair he was, and in how forlorn a condition, replied, I will give you a name conformable to your appearance and distress, you shall be called Beltenebros. Now Beltenebros being interpreted, signifyeth, the Fair Forlorn. The name pleased Amadis, and he admired the good sense of the old man in chusing it; so by this name he was long known, till it became as renowned as that of Amadis. Thus communing they reached the sea-side just as the night closed in; there they found a bark, wherein the good man might cross to his hermitage. Beltenebros gave his horse to the mariners, and they gave him in exchange a cloak of goat skin, and a garment of coarse grey woollen. They embarked, and Beltenebros asked the good man what was his own name, and the name of his abode. They call my dwelling-place, said he, the Poor Rock, because none can live there without enduring great poverty: my own name is Andalod. I was a clerk of some learning, and spent my youth in many vanities, till it pleased God to awaken me, and then I withdrew to this solitary abode: for thirty years I have never left it, till now that I went to the burial of my sister. At length they reached the Rock and landed, and the mariners returned to the main land. Thus Amadis, now called Beltenebros, remained on the Poor Rock, partaking the austerities of the hermit, not for devotion, but for despair, forgetful of his great renown in arms, and hoping and expecting death,—all for the anger of a woman!

When Gandalin awoke in the mountain, he looked round him, and seeing only his own horse, started up, misdoubting what had happened; he called aloud, and searched among the shrubs in vain, he could find neither Amadis nor his horse. Then, knowing that Amadis was departed, he turned to his horse to ride after him, but the saddle and bridle were gone! upon that he cursed himself and his evil fortune, and the day wherein he was born, going from one place to another, till at length he espied the harness, and immediately set out on pursuit. Five days he rode on, sleeping in desert places, enquiring at every habitation for his Master. On the sixth, chance led him to the fountain where Amadis had left his armour. Here he beheld a tent, in which were two Damsels: he alighted, and asked them if they had seen a Knight who bore two lions azure in a golden field. They answered that they had not seen him, but such a shield and the whole harness of a Knight, they had found beside that fountain. When Gandalin heard this, he tore his hair, and exclaimed, Holy Mary, help me! my Master, the best Knight in the world, is dead or lost! how badly have I served you, my Lord! and now with reason ought I to be hated by all men, and the earth ought not to suffer me upon her, since I have left you at such a time! You were he who succoured all, and now all have forsaken you! the world and all in it have abandoned you!

and I, caitiff wretch, and more wretched than all that ever were born, have left you in your death! And with that, for excess of passion, he fell down. The Damsels shrieked out, Holy Mary, help! the Squire is dead! and they ran to him, and flung water in his face, but it was long before they could recal him to his senses. Good Squire, they cried, be not desperate for a thing which is not certain: you had better seek him till you learn whether he be alive or dead: good men ought to bear up against sorrow, not to die in despair. Gandalin took heart at their words, and resolved to seek his Master as long as he lived. Ladies, said he, where did you see these arms?—We will tell you willingly: we were in the company of Don Guilan the Pensive, who delivered us and twenty other Knights and Damsels from the prison of Gandinos the ruffian, behaving himself there so valiantly that he hath destroyed the wicked customs of the castle, and constrained the Lord thereof to swear never more to maintain the same. We came with Guilan to this fountain four days ago, and when he saw the shield for which you enquired, he was very sorrowful, and alighting, said, the shield of the best Knight in the world should not lie thus! and with that, weeping sorely, he hung the shield upon this tree, and bade us keep it while he rode to seek him whose it was. We set up our tents here, and Guilan sought for him three days without success: yesterday he returned, and this morning, giving his own arms to his Squires, he girded on the sword and took the shield, saying, By God, shield, thou makest a bad exchange, in losing thy master to go with me! He told us, he would carry the arms to Queen Brisena. We also, and all who were delivered by him, are going to that court, to beg the Queen of her goodness to recompense Don Guilan, as the Knights will beseech the King. Then God be with you! quoth Gandalin. I shall take your advice; and, as the most caitiff and unhappy wretch in the world, go seek for him upon whom my life or death depends.

CHAPTER 7.

On the tenth day after he had left Amadis in the forest, Durin reached London, and, alighting at his own lodging, went straight to the Queen's palace. So soon as Oriana saw him, her heart throbbed violently, so that she could not calm it, and she went into her chamber and lay down upon the bed, bidding the Damsel of Denmark go for her brother, and bring him to her secretly. The Damsel returned with Durin, and leaving him with her mistress, went out to Mabilia. Now, friend, said Oriana, tell me where you have been, and where you found Amadis, and what he did when he read my letter, and if you have seen Queen Briolania: tell me every thing. Then Durin related how he had followed Amadis from Sobradisa to the Firm Island, and arrived there just as Amadis was passing under the Arch of True Lovers, under the which none might pass that had been false to his first love. How, cried she, dared he prove that adventure, knowing that he could not accomplish it? It did not turn out so, replied the Squire; he accomplished it with more loyalty than any other had ever there displayed, and was received with more honour, and such signs as had never been seen before. When Oriana heard this, her joy was very great, that that which had occasioned her great anger was thus disproved. He proceeded with his tale, how Amadis had won the Forbidden Chamber. Hold! quoth she, and she lifted up her hands and began to pray God that she might one day be in that Chamber with him who had worthily won it. Now, quoth she, tell me what did Amadis when you gave him the letter? The tears came into Durin's eyes. Lady, I advise you not to ask, for you have done the worst cruelty and devilry that ever Damsel committed. Holy Mary! cried Oriana, what art thou saying? I say, repeated Durin, that you have unjustly destroyed the best and truest Knight that ever woman had, or will have to the end of the world. Cursed be the hour in which such a thing was devised, and cursed be death that did not take me before I carried such a message: if I had known what I carried, I would rather have slain myself than have appeared before him, for you in sending that letter, and I in taking it, have been the cause of his death. Then he related every thing that had passed, and all that Amadis had said, and how he was gone into the mountain to die. While he was relating these things, all Oriana's anger was gone, and her shame and anguish became so intolerable, that when he had ceased she could not utter a word, but remained like one who had lost her senses. Durin, albeit that he thought she well deserved this suffering, was yet moved to pity, and he went to Mabilia and his sister, and said to them, go and help Oriana, for, if she hath done wrong, her punishment is come upon her: and he went his way.

They ran to her, and seeing in what state she was, they fastened the door of her chamber, and threw water in her face, and brought her to herself, and she then began to lament what she had done, and cry out for death. But those true friends sent again for Durin, and learnt from him all that had past, and then began to comfort her, and they made her write a letter to request his forgiveness, and bid him come with all speed to the castle of Miraflores, there to receive her atonement. This letter the Damsel of Denmark would take and search for him, for she refused no trouble or difficulty for the two persons in the world whom she loved best; and, because Amadis in his sorrow had talked so much of Gandales, they thought he might be with him; and they agreed, as a pretext for her going there, that she should carry gifts to the Queen of Scotland, and tidings of her daughter Mabilia. Oriana therefore told her mother they were about to send the Damsel, and Brisena approving thereof, sent also presents from herself. This being settled, the Damsel, in company with her brother Durin, and Enil, a nephew of Gandales, rode to a port called Vegil, which is in that part of Great Britain towards Scotland, and embarking there, in seven days they came to the town called Poligez, in Scotland. From thence they proceeded to the castle of Gandales; him they met going to the chace, and saluted him; and he, perceiving that the Damsel was of a foreign land by her speech, asked her from whence she came. I am the messenger, quoth she, of some Damsels who love you much, and who have sent gifts to the Queen of Scotland.——Good Damsel, and who are they?——Oriana, daughter of King Lisuarte, and Mabilia, whom you know. Then Gandales joyfully bade them welcome, and took them to his castle. As they were conversing, the old Knight enquired for his foster son, Amadis. At this the Damsel was grieved, perceiving that he was not there as they had hoped; but, not to distress Gandales by the truth, she only answered that he was not yet returned from Sobradisa. We thought, said she, that he would first accompany his cousin Agrayes here, to see you and the Queen his aunt; and I bring letters to him from Queen Brisena and his other friends, which he would be right glad to receive. This she said, that if Amadis were there in secret, he might be induced to see her. She remained with Gandales two days, then proceeded to the Queen.

CHAPTER 8.

Don Guilan the Pensive proceeded with the arms toward the court of Lisuarte. He always carried the shield of Amadis round his neck, except when he was constrained to fight, and then he took his own. So as he rode, two nephews of Arcalaus met him and knew the shield, and attempted to force it from him, saying they would take that shield, or the head of him who carried it, to their uncle. When Guilan knew of how bad a race they were, he cared the less for them, and gave them both battle. They were strong Knights, and both younger men than he; he, nevertheless, was a valiant man and tried in arms, so that he slew one, and drove the other to flight. That evening he took up his lodging in the house of a Knight whom he knew, who welcomed him gladly, and gave him another lance, for his own was broken in the encounter. He continued his way till he came to a river called Guinon, which was a great water, and over it was a wooden-bridge, just so broad that one horseman might come and another go. At one end of the bridge was a Knight who wished to pass; he bore a shield vert, with a bend argent, whereby Guilan knew him to be his cousin Ladasin. On the other side was a Knight who kept the passage; he rode a large bay horse, and did bear in his shield argent a lion sable: this Knight called out aloud to Ladasin, You must joust, Knight, if you would pass. Your joust shall not prevent me, quoth Ladasin. They ran at each other upon the bridge, and Ladasin and his horse fell into the river. There would Ladasin have perished, by reason of the weight of his arms, and the height whence he had fallen, if by good hap he had not caught the boughs of some willows, by which he got to the bank. Don Guilan ran to his help, and with the aid of his Squires got him out of the water. Cousin, said he, you would hardly have been saved without these boughs: all Knights should avoid to joust upon these bridges, for they who keep them have their horses practised to the place, and rather by that, than by their own prowess, win the honour. I would rather turn out of the way and go round, if this had not happened to you, but now I must try to revenge you. By this, Ladasin's horse had got upon the opposite bank, and the Knight bade his servants lead him to the castle, which was a strong and pleasant fortress, built in the river, and the way to it was by a bridge of stone. The Knight was ready at the bridge-end. Don Guilan gave the shield of Amadis to his Squire, and took his own, and they met together upon the bridge with a most rude encounter. The Knight was unhorsed and fell into the water; Guilan also was dismounted, and his horse went over, but he saved himself by clinging to the planks. The Knight got upon Guilan's horse, and so to shore, while Guilan's Squires took the bay courser for their master. Don Guilan presently saw the Knight of the bridge shaking off the water, and holding the bridle: give me my horse, said he, and let me depart. How! quoth he, think you to escape so lightly with this?—Quoth Guilan, have we not performed the custom? The battle is not yet over, cried the Knight, because we both fell: we must decide it with the sword. Perforce must I fight? cried Guilan: is not the wrong done already enough, for bridges should be free for every passenger? Will you, nill you, quoth he of the bridge, you shall feel how my sword can cut. He then sprung upon Guilan's horse, without setting his foot in the stirrup, and placed himself right in the road. Don Cavalier, tell me, said he, before we fight, if thou art of Lisuarte's country or court?—Why ask you?—I wish it pleased God, that I had King Lisuarte here as I have thee, by my head his reign should be finished. Certes, quoth Guilan, you have now given me a good will to fight with thee, which before I had not: I am of his household, and, if it be in me, you shall never more do him disservice. Before noon, quoth the Knight, you shall carry my message to him, and I will tell you who I am, and what present I will send him: my name is Gandalod, son to Barsinan, Lord of Sansuena, he whom King Lisuarte slew in London. The presents you shall carry him, are the heads of four of his Knights, whom I hold prisoners in yonder tower: the one is Giontes his nephew, and thy own right hand, which I mean to cut off and tie round thy neck. Don Guilan laid hand to sword; you have boasting enough, if that were all that were needed.

Then began so fierce a battle, that Ladasin and the Squires thought even the conqueror could not escape with life; but they were both hardy Knights, and their armour of excellent temper, and they knew how to defend themselves. Now when their fight was at the hottest, they heard the winding of a horn from the top of the tower. Gandalod knew not what it could mean, and Guilan thought it was a signal for succour to his enemy; therefore they both more eagerly bestirred themselves to end the battle. Gandalod grappled with him, and they both fell; then was the fight closer and more dangerous, but Guilan had the advantage; it was evident that his antagonist waxed weary and weak, and at length, by a well driven blow, Don Guilan lopt off his right arm. He shrieked out, and turned to fly to his tower, but Guilan reached him, plucked the helmet from his head, and bade him chuse instant death, or to present himself with his presents, but in another guise, to King Lisuarte. I will rather trust his mercy, quoth Gandalod, than be slain here outright.

Don Guilan then took horse, and rode with Ladasin towards the tower, where there was a great uproar. The Knights had broken from their prison and seized arms, and one of them it was who wound the horn, and now they had won the castle; the gate was opened, and the servants and one Knight came flying out: they called out to Ladasin and Guilan to kill those villains, and particularly the Knight: three of the men escaped them, but the Knight they took. Then said Guilan to them, Sirs, I cannot tarry, but my cousin Ladasin shall keep you company; let the castle be kept for me, and do you carry this Knight and Gandalod to King Lisuarte for his judgment. Then he gave his own shield, which was much battered, to his Squire, and took that of Amadis, and as he hung it round his neck the tears came. They knew the shield, and hearing how Don Guilan had found it, were sorely troubled, thinking that some great mishap had befallen Amadis. So he proceeded to the court, and all that saw the shield crowded round him; and the King said, for God's sake, Don Guilan, tell us what you know of Amadis. I know nothing of him, Sir, quoth he, but how I found the shield I will declare before the Queen. So he was taken to the Queen, and he knelt before her weeping, and told her how he had found the arms of Amadis, and sought for him three days in vain. Knowing, said he, the value of that good Knight, and that it was his desire to employ it till death in your service, I have brought you these arms, in testimony of the duty which I do owe both to you and to him. Let them be placed where all may see them; there may be some among the many strangers who come here, who may know some tidings of their master, and they will be memorials to all who follow arms, that they may take example by his great chivalry. Greatly was the Queen distressed at this, and Lisuarte also, and all the court; but Oriana could not remain there, and she went to her bed, and bitterly reproaching her own folly, wished for death. Albeit Mabilia did somewhat cheer her with a hope that the Damsel of Denmark might find him and repair all.

The Knight and Damsels whom Don Guilan had released, soon arrived, and the two Damsels who had seen Gandalin, and they related what lamentation a Squire had made over the arms. Presently after came Ladasin, and the Knights who led Gandalod prisoner; and when Lisuarte heard what cruelties he had purposed, he said to him, here I slew thy father for the great treason which he committed against me, and here thou shalt die for that which thou didst purpose to commit. So he commanded him, and the Knight his follower, to be thrown from the Tower, before which Barsinan had been burnt.

CHAPTER 9.

Beltenebros and the Hermit were one day sitting on the stone-bench by the door of their chapel, when the old man said, I pray you, son, tell me what it was that made you cry out so in your sleep, when we were by the fountain of the plain? That shall I willingly, father, he replied, and I beseech you tell me what you understand by it. Then he related to him the manner of his dream, only the names of the women, those he did not tell. The good man mused for a while, and then said, with a cheerful countenance, Beltenebros, you have given me great pleasure by this account, and you also have great reason to rejoice. The dark chamber, in the which you thought yourself to be, and from whence you could not get out, signifieth this great tribulation which you now endure. The Damsels who opened the door, are those friends who continually solicit your cause with her whom you love so much, and they will succeed so well as to withdraw you from this place. The sun-beam which went before them, is the joyful news that they are to send you here; and the fire, wherein you saw your Lady enveloped, is the great pain of love which she suffers for you as well as you for her: from that fire you delivered her, that is, from the pain which your presence will remove; and the pleasant garden is a sign of great happiness, wherewith you shall pass your lives. Truly, I know a man of my habit should not discourse of such things as these, yet it is more for God's service to speak the truth that may comfort you, than to conceal it, seeing your desperate state.

Beltenebros knelt down and kissed the old man's hands, thanking God for having given him such a friend in his need, and praying with tears that he would mercifully be pleased to accomplish the words of that holy man his servant. Then he besought him to tell the interpretation of the dream he had dreamt before Durin gave him the letter, which when the Hermit had heard, he answered, This I can show you clearly, for it is all accomplished. The place overshadowed with trees, was the Firm Island, and the people who made such great joy about you, signified the great pleasure of the Islanders in gaining you for their Lord. The man who came to you with the box of bitter electuary, was the messenger of your Lady, for the bitterness of her words, you, who have proved them, can best tell; and you laid aside your arms. The stony place amidst the water, is this Poor Rock; and the religious man who spoke to you in an unknown tongue, am I, who tell you the holy word of God, which before you neither knew nor thought of.

Verily, said Beltenebros, you tell me the truth of this dream, for these things have all come to pass, and therefore great cause have I to hope for the future. Yet was not this hope so great or so certain as to remove his sorrow, for he would often sit with his eyes fixed upon the ground, remembering what he had been, and his life would have been endangered by exceeding melancholy, had it not been for the counsel of that good man. And sometimes, to take him away from that pensiveness, the Hermit would make him go with two nephews that kept him company there, to angle in a little stream hard by, where they caught plenty of fish.

Here Beltenebros dwelt in penitence and great grief, and he past the night most frequently under some large trees in the garden near the chapel, that he might there lament, without the knowledge of the Hermit or the boys; and calling to mind the great wrong he endured, he made this song in his passion:

Sith that the victory of right deserved By wrong they do withhold for which I served; Now sith my glory thus hath had a fall, Glorious it is to end my life withall. By this my death, likewise my woes release, My hope, my joy, my inflamed love doth cease. But ever will I mind my during pain, For they, to end my glory and my gain, Myself have murdered, and my glory slain.[156:A]

He had passed one night as usual under these trees, when towards morning he heard certain instruments touched so sweetly, that he took great delight in hearing them, and marvelled what it might be, knowing that in that place there dwelt none else than the Hermit and his nephews. He rose, and went softly towards the sound, and saw that there were two Damsels by a fountain, who, tuning their voices to their lutes, did sing a most pleasant song. He stood awhile listening, then advanced, and said, God save you, gentle Damsels, but your sweet music has made me lose my matins! They wondered who he should be, and said to him, tell us, friend, for courtesy, what place is this where we have landed, and who are you who speak to us? Ladies, he replied, they call it the Rock of the Hermitage, because of the Hermit that dwells here. As for me, I am a poor man who bear him company, doing great and hard penance for the sins that I have committed. Then said they, friend, is there any house here where our Lady could rest for two or three days? for she is very sick: she is a Lady of high rank and wealth, whom love hath greatly tormented. Beltenebros answered, here is a little cabin, it is very small, in which I lodge: if the Hermit pleases, you shall have it, and I will asleep abroad in the field, as I often use to do. For this courtesy the Damsels heartily thanked him. By this the day began to break, and Beltenebros saw under some trees the Lady of whom they spake, lying upon a rich bed; four armed Knights and five serving men, who attended her, were sleeping on the shore, and a well appointed ship rode at anchor. The Lady was young and beautiful, so that he took pleasure in beholding her.

Beltenebros then went to the Hermit, who was robing himself to say mass. Father, said he, there are strangers here: it will be well to wait mass for them. So they both went out from the chapel. The Knights and serving-men were carrying the sick Lady towards them, and her Damsels were coming with her, and they asked the Hermit if there was any house wherein they could place her. He answered, here are two cabins: I live in the one, and by my will never woman shall enter that. This poor man, who makes his penitence here, lodges in the other, and I will not remove him against his will. To this Beltenebros replied, Father, you may well give them that, for I will rest under the trees, as I often do. They then entered the chapel to hear mass; but the sight of Knights and Damsels reminded Beltenebros of what he had been, and of his own Lady, and renewed in him his exceeding sorrow, so that he sobbed aloud, and kneeling down at the altar, besought the Virgin Mary to help him in his affliction. The Knights and Damsels, who saw how he wept, held him for a man of good life, and marvelled how he could employ his youth and beauty in that desert place, for any sin that he could have committed, seeing that the mercy of God may be obtained in all places alike, by such as truly repent. As soon as mass was ended, they carried the Lady into his cabin, and laid her in her rich bed, and she lay there weeping and wringing her hands. The Damsels went for their lutes to solace her, and Beltenebros asked them wherefore she appeared so distressed. Friend, said they, this Lady hath great possessions, and is of high rank and beautiful; though her sorrow doth now diminish her fairness, and we will tell you the cause of her sorrow, tho' it should not be told to others. It is excessive love that afflicts her: she is going to seek him whom she loves at the court of King Lisuarte, and God grant that she may find him there! When he heard the house of King Lisuarte mentioned, and that the Lady was sick of love, the tears came into his eyes, and he said, I pray you, Ladies, tell me the name of the Knight whom she loves. They answered, he is not of this country, but is one of the best Knights in the world, excepting only two who are of the greatest renown.—By the faith you owe to God, I beseech you tell his name, and the name of those other two.—We will tell you, on condition that you in return tell us if you be a Knight, as you seem by every thing, and likewise what is your name. I am content, said he, that I may know what I ask.—Know then, the Knight whom our Lady loveth, is Don Florestan, brother to the good Knight Amadis of Gaul, and to Don Galaor, and son of King Perion of Gaul and the Countess of Selandria. Now, quoth he, you tell me truly of his goodness, for you cannot say so much good of him as he deserveth.—Do you then know him?—It is not long since I saw him in the house of Briolania, for I saw the battle there of Amadis and his cousin Agrayes against Abiseos and his sons; after which Florestan arrived there, and I heard Don Galaor speak great things of his prowess, for they say he fought with him.—Yes, replied the Damsels, it was in that battle they knew each other, and then Florestan went away.—What! is this the Lady of the island where that battle was fought?—The same.—Her name is Corisanda. I do not now grieve for her so much, for he is so gentle and of such disposition, that well I know he will do whatever is her pleasure. Now then, said the Damsels, tell us who you are. Gentle Damsels, replied he, I am a Knight who have had more pleasure in the vanities of the world than falls to my lot now, for which I am now suffering, and my name is Beltenebros. God's mercy upon you! said they: we must now go play to our Lady.

After they had sung to her awhile, they told her what Beltenebros had said of Florestan. Ah, call him here, cried she, he must be some good man, since he knows Don Florestan. They brought him to her. These Damsels, said she, tell me that you have seen and that you love Don Florestan: by the faith you owe to God, tell me all you know concerning him. Beltenebros then related how he had gone with his brethren and Agrayes to the Firm Island, and that he had not seen him since. Tell me, said Corisanda, are you akin to him, for you seem to love him much?—Lady, I love him for his great valour, and because his father knighted me, wherefore I am greatly bound to him and his sons; but I am very sad for the tidings which I heard of Amadis before my coming here.—What are they?—I met a Damsel in a forest by the way side, singing a sweet song, and I asked her who had made it. She answered, a Knight, to whom God give more comfort than he had when that was made, for by the words it seemed he had suffered great wrong in love, and complained heavily. I stayed two days with the Damsel till I had learnt it. She told me that Amadis did show it her, and that he wept at the time and was in great misery. I beseech you, quoth Corisanda, teach it to my Damsels, that they may sing and play it to me. That will I, said he, for your own sake, and for his sake whom you love; albeit that is no time for singing, nor for aught that is matter of joy. He then went with the Damsels to the chapel, and showed them the song which he had made: his voice was of rare sweetness, and now his melancholy made it more soft and in unison; and the Damsels learnt the song, and did sing it to their Lady, who took great pleasure to hear them. Corisanda remained there four days; on the fifth she took leave of the Hermit, and asked Beltenebros if he should remain there long? Lady, till I die, he replied. Then she entered her ship, and made voyage to London.

Lisuarte and the Queen received her in a manner suitable to her high rank, and lodged her in the palace, and the Queen asked her if she had any suit to Lisuarte, that, if so, she might further it. My Lady, said Corisanda, I thank you for the favour; but my coming is to seek Don Florestan, and because tidings from all parts reach this court, I will remain here some time till I hear news of him. Good friend, replied Brisena, that may you do so long as you think good; at present we have no other news of him, than that he is gone in search of his brother Amadis, who is lost, we know not for what cause; and she then related how Guilan had found the arms. Hearing this, she began to weep, and say, O Lord God, what will become of my Lord and friend Don Florestan! for he so loves that brother, that, if he finds him not, he also will become desperate, and I shall never see him more! The Queen having great pity, consoled her, and Oriana, who was by, hearing the love she bore to the brother of Amadis, had the greater desire to honour her, and accompanied her to her chamber, and learnt from her all her love. Thus talking with her and Mabilia of sundry things, Corisanda related how she had been upon the Poor Rock, and found a Knight there doing hard penance, who had taught her Damsels a song made by Amadis in his affliction, and the words, she said, were very sad. My good friend and Lady, quoth Mabilia, beseech you let your Damsels sing it! I desire much to hear it, seeing it was made by that Knight, my cousin. The Damsels then sung the song, which it was a pleasure to hear, and yet so sorrowful that it made those sad who heard it. But Oriana, who understood the complaint, could no longer abide there for the shame of the tears that she felt flowing, and she went to her chamber. Mabilia therefore said to Corisanda, I see Oriana is unwell; she hath for courtesy remained here longer than she should: I must go and assist her; but tell me what manner of man was he whom you saw upon the Poor Rock of the Hermitage, and what did he know concerning Amadis? She then told her how they had found him, that she had never seen a man so comely in grief and being wasted, nor one of such manners in poverty, nor a man so young of such discourse and reason. Mabilia forthwith went joyfully to her friend's chamber. He who asks news, said she, sometimes learns more than he expects: the melancholy man who lives upon the Poor Rock, and calls himself Beltenebros, by all that I can learn from Corisanda, must be Amadis. Oriana lifted up her hands, O Lord of the World, grant that it be true! Dear friend, tell me what to do, for I have neither sense nor judgment: unfortunate wretch, who by my own folly and intemperate passion have lost all my happiness! Mabilia turned away her face, that the tears might not be seen: we must wait for the Damsel's return, said she; if she should not find him, leave it to me: I am sure he is this Beltenebros.

FOOTNOTES:

[156:A] This is the version in the English translation from the French: the matter is preserved, the manner lost. The poem is curious from its age; it is printed with these marks:

Pues seme niega victoria

dojusto mera deuida

alli do muere la gloria - (: · :)

es gloria morir la vida.

Y con esta muerte mia

moriran todas mis daños, - (: · :) - (: · :)

mi esperanza y mi porfia

el amor y sus engaños;

mas quedara en mi memoria

lastima nunca perdida, - (: · :)

que por me matar la gloria,

me mataron gloria y vida.

CHAPTER 10.

Ten days that Damsel of Denmark remained in Scotland, not so much for pleasure, as because she had suffered much from the sea, and for the ill success of her search, and she feared that to return, when she had sped so ill, would be the death of her mistress. At length she took her leave, and receiving presents from the Queen of Scotland to Queen Brisena and Oriana and Mabilia, she embarked for Great Britain, not knowing what other course to pursue; but that Lord of the World, who to those that are utterly without hope or remedy shows something of his power, that we may know it is he that helpeth us and not our own wisdom, he changed her voyage, to her own great fear, and the fear and sorrow of all in the ship; for the sea began to rage, and such a tempest arose, that the sailors lost all power over the ship, and all knowledge of their course, and the ship was driven whither the winds would, they that were in her having no hope of life. At last one morning they came to the foot of the Poor Rock; some of them knew the place, and said that Andalod the Hermit lived there, which, when the Damsel heard, she ordered them to put to land, that being rescued from such a danger, she might hear mass from that holy man, and return thanks to the Virgin Mary for the mercy which her glorious Son had shown them.

Beltenebros was sitting at this time by the fountain under the trees, where he had passed the night, and he was now so reduced that he did not expect to live fifteen days. What with weeping, and with the wasting away of sorrow, his face was more deadly pale than sickness could have made it, and so worn down and wan that no one could have known him. He saw the ship, and the Damsels and two Squires landing; but his thoughts being wholly bent upon death, the things that once gave him pleasure, as in seeing strangers that he might help them if they needed succour, now had become hateful. So he rose and went into the chapel, and told the Hermit that there were strangers landed and coming up; and then he knelt before the altar, and prayed God to have mercy upon his soul, for he was soon going to his account. The Hermit vested himself to say mass, and the Damsel with Durin and Enil entered. After she had prayed, she uncovered her face. Beltenebros rose from his knees, and seeing her and Durin, the shock was so great that he fell down senseless. The Hermit thought him dead, and exclaimed, Ah, Lord Almighty, why has it not pleased thee to have pity upon him who might have done so much in thy service! and the tears fell fast adown his long white beard. Good Damsel, said he, let these men help me to carry him to his chamber, I believe it is the last kindness we can do him. Enil and Durin assisted to lift him up, and they carried him into his chamber, and laid him upon a poor bed, and neither of them knew him.

After the Damsel had heard mass, she resolved to make her meal ashore, for she was weary of the sea. So by chance she asked who that poor man was, and what sore sickness afflicted him.—He is a Knight, who liveth here in penance. He is greatly to be blamed, quoth she, to chuse so desert a place. It is as you say, replied the Hermit, for he has done so for the foolish vanities of the world, more than for the service of God. I will see him, said the Damsel, since you tell me he is a Knight, perhaps there may be something in the ship which would relieve him.—That you may do, but he is so near his end, that I believe Death will ease you of that trouble. Beltenebros was lying upon his bed, thinking what he should do: if he made himself known, that would be breaking his Lady's command, and, if he did not, he should remain without any hope or possible remedy; but he thought to disobey her will would be worse than death, and so determined to be silent. The Damsel came to the bedside, and said, Good man, I learn from the Hermit that you are a Knight, and because Damsels are beholden to all Knights for the dangers they encounter in our defence, I resolved to see you, and leave with you any thing which is in the ship that may contribute to your health. He made her no answer, but sobbed with such exceeding passion, that she thought his soul was departing; and because the room was dark, she opened a shutter for the light, and drew near to see if he were dead. They looked at each other some time, and the Damsel knew him not. At last, she saw a scar in his face: it was the mark of a wound which Arcalaus had given him with his lance, when Oriana was rescued; then, tho' before she had no suspicion, she knew that this was Amadis.—Ah, Holy Mary, help me! you are he, Sir! and she fell with her face upon the bed, and knelt down, and kist his hands. Now, Sir, said she, your compassion and pardon are needed for her who has wronged you, for, if her unjust suspicion have reduced you to this danger, she herself with more reason passes a life more bitter than death. Beltenebros took her in his arms, and held her awhile, having no power to speak. She then gave him the letter: your Lady sends you this, and she bids you, if you are the same Amadis, whom she loves so well, to forget the past, and come to her in the castle of Miraflores, and there receive her atonement for your wrongs, which excessive love occasioned. Amadis kissed the letter, and placed it upon his heart, saying, Heart, take thy remedy, for there was none other that could save thee! This was the letter:

If great faults committed by enmity, when humbly acknowledged, deserve pardon, what shall we say to those which proceeded from excess of love? Not that by this do I deny, my true friend, that I deserve exceeding punishment, for neither having considered your truth, that had never before failed, nor my own mind in how passionate a state it was. I pray you receive this Damsel as coming from one who humbly confesseth her fault, and who will tell you the wretchedness which she endures who requests your pity, not because she deserves it, but for your comfort, as well as her own.

Such joy had Beltenebros at this letter, that he was lost even as in his past sorrow, and tears that he did not feel ran down his cheeks. It was agreed between them, that the Damsel should give out how she took him aboard for his health sake, because on that Rock he could have no help, and that as soon as possible they should take land, and leave the ship. Beltenebros then told the Hermit by what happy chance the Damsel had found him, and besought him that he would take charge of the Monastery that was to be built by his command at the foot of the rock of the Firm Island. This the old man promised, and Beltenebros then embarked, being known of none but the Damsel.

They soon landed with the two Squires, and left the mariners. Presently they found a pleasant place upon the side of a brook, with many goodly trees, and there they resolved to rest, because Beltenebros was so weak; and there, if it had not been that the absence of his Lady afflicted him, he would have passed the pleasantest life, and best for his recovery that might be, for under those trees where the brook-springs arose, they had their meals, and there was their tent for the night. There related they to each other all that had past, and a pleasure was it now to him to talk over his misery. Ten days they remained, and in that time he so regained strength, that his heart felt its old inclination for arms. He made himself known to Durin there, and took Enil for his Squire, who knew not whom it was that he served, but was well content with him for his gentle speech. Hence departing, in four days they reached a nunnery; there they determined that he and Enil should abide, while the Damsel and her brother went to Miraflores. She then gave Beltenebros money to buy horses and armour, and for his wants; and she left behind her part of the Queen of Scotland's presents, that she might send Durin for them as if they had been forgotten, and so he might bring news.

CHAPTER 11.

After their year's vain search, Agrayes, Galaor, and Florestan, met at the place appointed, which was a chapel half a league from London. Gandalin came with Florestan, and, when he found no tidings of his Master, he said to them, that they should leave their lamentation and begin their search again, remembering what Amadis would have done for them if they had been in like case. So they determined to enter the court, and, if they learnt nothing there, to set out again upon their quest; and they wept to think how happily they had accomplished all adventures that had befallen them, and yet had failed to find him whom they sought.

Then having heard mass at the chapel, they rode towards the city. It was St. John's day, and presently they met King Lisuarte riding out with all his Knights in honour of that holy day, because the Saint was so great a Saint, and also because on that day he had been made King. When he saw three Errant Knights approaching, he drew nigh to welcome them. Great joy was there when they unhelmed, and at first Lisuarte thought Florestan was Amadis, for he much resembled him; but Gandalin and the Dwarf, when they beheld this meeting, wept with great grief. The news soon spread: greatly was Corisanda rejoiced thereat, and Olinda, the gentle friend of Agrayes, who knew how he had past under the Arch of True Lovers. Mabilia, in joy for her brother's coming, went for Oriana, who was sitting sorrowfully at her chamber-window, reading. She answered, weeping and sighing as if her heart-strings would have broken, how can I go? do you not see my face and eyes, how they show that I have been weeping? and how can I see those Knights, in whose company I was wont to see Amadis: it is better to die! Mabilia comforted her how she could:—the Damsel might yet bring tidings. Nay, quoth Oriana, if these Knights have failed, who have sought him so far and so long, how shall she succeed? a woman! and seeking him but in one place? But she may induce him to discover himself, said Mabilia, for she carries comfort to him, and knows the secret of his love, which they did not. So she cheared her, and made her wash her eyes, and called Olinda to go with them to the Queen. Look, quoth the King to Galaor, how ill your friend Oriana is! I grieve to see her thus, replied he: reason is it that we should try to help her health by our services. My good friend, Galaor, said she, God it is who heals sickness and sorrow, and if it pleaseth him he will me, and recover your brother Amadis, whom you have lost, and whom we all lament. Anon an outcry was heard without, for Gandalin and the Dwarf seeing their Master's shield where it was hung, began to lament aloud, and the Knights were comforting them. What! cried Lisuarte, is Gandalin here? Florestan answered, I met him two months ago seeking for his Master, and made him bear me company. I hold Gandalin, said the King, to be one of the best Squires in the world, and we ought to comfort him. So he rose, and went out to him. When Oriana heard the name of Gandalin, and the lamentation that he was making, she grew pale, and would have fallen, but Galaor and Florestan caught her. Mabilia, who knew the cause, ran to her, and put her arms round her neck. Good and true friends, then said Oriana to the two brethren, if I do not show you what honour I ought and desire to show, I pray you impute it to its true cause, this sore illness! and then she went to her chamber. Dear friend, said she to Mabilia, since we entered this city of London, I have never been without some cause of sorrow: let us go to Miraflores, that is a delightful place, and there I can have the comfort of solitude. We will ask your parents' permission, said Mabilia, and there the Damsel of Denmark will find us, and there you may the more freely see him, when he shall be found. Ah, quoth Oriana, let us lose no time!

This castle of Miraflores was about two leagues from London, a little place, but the pleasantest abode in all that land, for it was in a wood by the side of a mountain, surrounded with orchards and gardens that abounded with fruits and flowers, and there were fountains in the courts canopied with trees, that all the year round bore flower and fruit. The King one day had taken the Queen and Princess there when he was hunting, and because the Princess was much pleased with the place, he gave it her for her own. About a bow-shot from the gate was a nunnery, which she had founded, and there were nuns in it of holy life. So that night she asked permission of Lisuarte and her Mother to retire there, which was readily granted.

The King being at table with Agrayes and his cousins, said to them, I trust we shall have good news of Amadis, for I have sent thirty Knights of the best of my household to seek him, and, if they fail, take you as many as you will and seek him; but I beseech you do not depart till after a battle which has been appointed between me and King Cildadan of Ireland, who is a King renowned in arms, and has married the daughter of King Abies, whom Amadis slew. The battle is to be an hundred against an hundred, and the quarrel this: That kingdom has been obliged to pay tribute to the Kings of Great Britain: Cildadan demands battle on condition, that, if he be conquered, the tribute shall be doubled; but, if he succeed, the country shall be freed therefrom. I trow he will need all his Knights and friends! The three companions, albeit loth to have their search delayed, yet could they not refuse to stay and share the peril. After the cloths were removed, Florestan bade Gandalin go to Mabilia, who wished to see him. He went accordingly, and, when they saw each other, they both wept. Ah, Lady, quoth he, what great wrong hath Oriana done to you and to your lineage, in depriving you of the best Knight in the world! and what wrong hath she done to him, who never erred against her in deed nor word! Ill hath God bestowed such beauty and such goodness, when this could be in her! and yet none hath lost so much by it as herself! Say not thus, Gandalin! cried Mabilia, what she did was from exceeding love, and in the belief that he was loving another. And then she related all that had been said by Ardian concerning the broken sword. O God! quoth Gandalin, where were all your understandings? he would have buried himself alive for her displeasure! and she believed this! and thus is the best Knight in the world destroyed! Oriana had listened to all this: she came forward as if she had heard nothing; and weeping, so that hardly could she speak, she said, O Gandalin! God preserve and bless you, as you shall do what you ought! Lady, said he, in tears also, what do you command me? Kill me! cried she, for I killed your master, and you should revenge his death, as he would have revenged your's! And then she fell senseless.

The King bade Grumedan accompany his daughter to Miraflores, and see that there were serving-men left there, and porters for the gate, and all things needful. Early the next morning they set out, and when Oriana saw the place, how fresh it was with flowers and roses, and the water-pipes and fountains, her mind felt greatly comforted. The keys of the castle and of the garden-gates were every night to be carried by the porters to the Abbess Adalasta, that she might keep them securely. I have desired to have the keys by day, said Oriana to Mabilia, that Gandalin may get another set made, so that if by good fortune Amadis should come, we may admit him by the postern-door thro' the garden; and there Oriana determined to remain till she saw Amadis, or till she died in that solitude. Her apartments were full pleasant, and before the chamber-door there was a little court wherein three trees grew, that quite shadowed it; and there they took their pleasure, but with great anxiety expected the Damsel of Denmark and her tidings. The next day the Porter came and said, a Squire asked for Mabilia. Let him in, quoth Oriana; it is Gandalin, a right good Squire, who was brought up with us, and is the milk-brother of Amadis, whom God preserve from harm! God preserve him, indeed! cried the Porter, for great loss to the world would it be if such a Knight were to perish. Lo now! said Oriana to her friend, as the Porter went away, how Amadis is loved by all, even by these simple men! and I who was so loved by him, I have been his death! Herewithal Gandalin entered, and Oriana making him sit by her side, related how she had sent the Damsel of Denmark to seek Amadis, and what she had written to him: think you, Gandalin, said she, that he will forgive me? You little know his heart, Lady, quoth the Squire; by God for the least word in the letter he will come: if you bade him, he would bury himself alive under the earth,—how much sooner will he come at your command! And the Damsel of Denmark will sooner find him than all the persons in the world; for, if he hid himself from me, he will not show himself to any other. And you, Lady, should take comfort with this hope, lest he should find your beauty so altered when he comes, and fly from you. What, Gandalin! seem I so ugly? quoth she, being well-pleased at his words. You seem so to yourself, said he, that you thus hide yourself where none may see you. I do it to this end, said Oriana, that, when thy master cometh, if he would fly, he may not be able. She then showed him the keys, and bade him get others made like them, that when his master came they might admit him at their pleasure.

Gandalin took the keys to London, and returned that same night with others so exactly like them, that there was no difference, except that these were new and the others old. Here they are! cried Mabilia, showing them to Oriana: come, we have supt, and all the people are at rest! let us try them. They took hand, and went in the dark to the posterns that opened from the castle into the garden. When they were near the first, Oriana cried, I cannot go on, I am dying with fear! Fear nothing! quoth Mabilia, laughing as she spake, when I am here to protect you, for I am cousin to the best Knight in the world, and am going on his service. Oriana could not but smile. I will take courage, and trust in your prowess in arms. Come on boldly, quoth Mabilia, and see how I finish the adventure! if I fail, I swear for one whole year never to hang shield from my neck, nor gird on a sword. In this merry mood she opened the first postern, and presently the other with as little difficulty, and then they were in the garden. How will he get over the wall? cried Oriana. At yonder corner, replied Mabilia, there must be a piece of wood laid on the other side, and we will give him our hands here. You must perform this labour, for it is you who will be paid for it. Oriana at this took hold of her cousin's coif and threw it on the ground, and they stood laughing for some time, then returned and fastened the gates, and went to rest. As Oriana lay down, Mabilia cried, I wish that poor wretch were here who is now despairing! eat, cousin! and sleep, that you may recover your beauty, as Gandalin advised!

CHAPTER 12.

King Lisuarte was at table; the cloths were removed, and Galaor, Florestan, and Agrayes, were about to take their leave and conduct Corisanda to her island, when there came a strange Knight into the palace, all armed except his head and hands, and with him two Squires, and he carried in his hand a letter sealed with five seals, which on his knees he presented to the King, saying, let this be read, and then I will say for what I am come. Lisuarte saw that it was a letter of credence, and bade him speak his errand. Then said the Knight, King, I defy thee on the part of Famongomadan, the Giant of the Boiling Lake; Cartadaque, his nephew, Giant of the Defended Mountain; and Madanfabul, his marriage-brother, the Giant of the Vermillion Tower; and for Quadragante, brother of King Abies, and Arcalaus the Enchanter: they tell thee that thy death, and the death of all who call themselves thine is in their hands, for they are coming against thee on King Cildadan's side. Howbeit, if thou wilt give thy daughter Oriana to Madasima, the fair daughter of Famongomadan, to be her damsel and servant, they will not injure thee, nor be thine enemies, but will give her in marriage when it is time to Basagante, Madasima's brother, who doth well deserve to be Lord of her and thy land. Therefore, King, look to thy choice! such peace, or such war! Lisuarte smiled when he began to reply, as one who set at nought the defiance. Knight, said he, better is a dangerous war, than a dishonourable peace: a bad account should I render to Him, who hath placed me in this high rank, if for lack of heart I should so shamefully debase it! Tell them I would rather chuse war with them all the days of my life, and death in that war at last, than consent to the peace they offer! Tell me where I may send a Knight to carry them this answer? They may be found, replied the Embassador, in the Boiling Lake, which is in the Isle of Mongaza. I know not the manner of these Giants, quoth Lisuarte, whether a Knight can go amongst them safely? That, replied he, doubt not; where Don Quadragante is present, no wrong can be committed: I will be his warrant. In God's name! said Lisuarte, now tell me who you are?—Landin, the son of Quadragante's sister. We are come to revenge the death of King Abies of Ireland, and greatly it grieves us that we cannot find him who slew him, neither know we whether he be alive or dead. Quoth Lisuarte, I would you did know him to be alive and well! all would then be right. I know wherefore you say thus, replied Landin; you think him the best Knight living, but, be I what I may, you shall find me in the battle with King Cildadan, and see what I can do against you. I had rather have you in my service, answered Lisuarte; but there will not be wanting those who will oppose you there.

Meantime Florestan's anger was rising. Knight, said he, I am a stranger in this country, and not vassal to the King, so that there is no quarrel between us for what you have said to him, nor do I undertake it because there are many Knights in his household. But, you say, you seek for Amadis, and cannot find him; that I believe is not to your loss! but if it please you to do battle with me, who am Don Florestan, his brother, let it be with this condition: if you are conquered, you shall give over the pursuit of vengeance; if I am slain, your wrath will in part be satisfied, for whatever sorrow you feel for the loss of King Abies, that and much greater would Amadis endure for my death. Landin replied, Don Florestan I perceive you have a heart for battle, but I cannot satisfy you now, being bound to return with this embassy on an appointed day, and also having pledged myself to undertake no enterprize before the battle; but, if I come from that field alive, I will meet you in the lists. Landin, quoth Florestan, you answer like a good and honourable Knight, as you are bound to do; let it be as you have said. And he gave his gloves in gage to the King, and Landin gave the lappets of his armour; and the day for their combat was fixed for the thirtieth after the battle. Lisuarte then sent a Knight called Filispinel with Landin to carry his reply, and they departed together.

When they were gone, the King said to Galaor, and Florestan, and their cousin Agrayes, you shall see something that will please you! and he sent for his daughter Leonoreta to come with her little damsels and dance before him, as she used to do; a thing which he had never ordered, since the news that Amadis was lost. She came, and the King said to her, Daughter, sing now the song which Amadis, being your Knight, made for your love. So the child and the other young damsels began to sing.

Leonor, sweet Rose, all other flowers excelling, For thee I feel strange thoughts in me rebelling.

I lost my liberty when I did gaze Upon those lights which set me in a maze, And of one free am now become a thrall, Put to such pain thou serv'st thy friends withal; And yet do I esteem this pain a pleasure, Endured for thee whom I love out of measure. Leonor, sweet Rose, all other flowers excelling, For thee I feel strange thoughts in me rebelling.

I little joy in any other's sight, My heart is thine, thyself my chief delight. But yet I see the more that I do love, More smart I feel, more pain, more grief I prove. Well! let Love rage, though he be angry ever, I'll take my loss for gain, though I gain never. Leonor, sweet Rose, all other flowers excelling, For thee I feel strange thoughts in me rebelling.

And though to you I manifest my woes, My martyrdom, my smart, another knows; One unto whom I secretly invoke, Who is the cause of this my fire, my smoke. She hath a salve to cure my endless grief, And only she may yield me some relief. Leonor, sweet Rose, all other flowers excelling, For thee I feel strange thoughts in me[188:A] rebelling.

You should know by what occasion Amadis made this song for the Princess Leonoreta. One day, as he was talking with Queen Brisena, Oriana, Mabilia, and Olinda, told Leonoreta to go and ask Amadis to be her Knight, and that he would then serve her and no one else. The little girl went to him, and did so; and Amadis, smiling, took her in his arms, and placed her on the estrado. Since you would have me be your Knight, said he, give me some jewel in token that you hold me for yours; and then she took from her head a gold clasp set with gems, and gave it him. All began to laugh at seeing how verily she believed the jest, and Amadis, being thus chosen her Knight, made for her this song. And when she and her damsels sung it they were dressed alike, having garlands on their heads, and garments of the same costliness and fashion as Leonoreta wore. She was a fair princess, albeit not so fair as Oriana, who had no peer, and afterwards she became Empress of Rome, and her twelve little damsels were all daughters of Counts and noble chiefs. So having sung their song, they knelt before Lisuarte, and then returned to the Queen.

Galaor and Florestan and Agrayes then asked the King permission to guard Corisanda home. He took them aside and said, Friends! there are no other three in the world in whom I have the same confidence as in you. This battle is to be the first week in August, and you hear who are coming against me, and they will bring others with them, who are brave and terrible in arms, and are also of the nature and blood of the Giants: therefore, I request you not to undertake any adventure that may delay you from being there to aid me, for with your aid, and the justice of my cause, I trust in God, my enemies, powerful as they are, will be put to shame. Sir, said they, this command was not needed: as Errant Knights, our wish is to be in danger, to be where, being conquerors, we may win the renown which we seek; or, if conquered, come to the end for which we were all born: we will presently return. So they took their leave, and departed with Corisanda.

Gandalin, who saw them depart, went to Miraflores, and related to Oriana and Mabilia all that had past. Now, quoth Oriana, is Corisanda in all happiness, for she hath with her Don Florestan, whom she loves. God ever continue her joy! for she is a good Lady. And then she herself began to weep, and cry, Lord God, let me see Amadis again, if it be but for a day!—Gandalin greatly pitied her, but he affected anger, and said, Lady, you will make me stay away from Miraflores, for here are we looking for good tidings, and you will make us thus unhappy! Oriana wiped away her tears: Do not reproach me, Gandalin! I would do otherwise if I could; but, whatever semblance I should put on, my heart is always weeping! But tell me, what will become of the King my father, since Amadis will not be in the battle? He cannot so have hidden himself, replied Gandalin, that such news should not reach him; and though you have forbidden him your sight, yet he may be present there, thinking then to merit pardon for a fault which he never committed, nor thought to commit. While they were thus communing, a little girl came running in, Lady, here is the Damsel of Denmark, and she brings noble presents for you! At this her heart trembled, and sunk within her, so that she could not speak, and she was altogether so agitated as one who expected life or death from the messenger who was coming. Mabilia answered for her: tell the Damsel to come to us alone, that we may speak with her in private. This she said that there might be none to witness Oriana's agitation; but she herself and Gandalin were dismayed, not knowing what was to come. The Damsel entered with a chearful countenance, and kneeling before Oriana gave her a letter; here, Lady, are tidings of joy! I have fulfilled all your commands: read, and see if Amadis have not written it with his own hand. The letter fell from Oriana's hand, she trembled so with exceeding joy: she opened it, and found in it the ring which she had sent by Gandalin to Amadis, the day whereon he fought with Dardan at Windsor, the which she knew well and kissed it many times, and said, blessed be the hour in which thou wert made, that art transferred with such joy from one hand to another! So when she had read the letter, and blest God with lifted hands for his mercy, she made the Damsel relate how she had found him. Greatly were they pleased at her wisdom in leaving a part of the presents with Amadis; now then, said they, produce the rest before those who are here, and say how you have forgotten the others, that we may send for them.

They showed Durin to what part of the garden-wall he was to bring Amadis, and he kissed Oriana's hands for sending him upon this errand, which might atone for what unwittingly he had carried before. It was agreed that Mabilia should publicly ask him to go; but he feigned himself little contented at the bidding, and said, angrily, to Mabilia, for you, Lady, I will go, but not for the Queen or Oriana, for I have had great hardships in this journey for their pleasure. Friend Durin, said Oriana, you should not upbraid us with your services, so that we shall not thank you for it. Your thanks, replied he, I believe will be worth about as much as my service! however, said he to Mabilia, since you desire it, I will set out to-morrow. He then took leave, and went with Gandalin to the town to sleep; and Gandalin bade him remember him to his cousin Enil, and tell him, said he, to come and see me as soon as he can, for I have much to say to him, and request him while he continues with that Knight, to see if he can learn any news of Amadis. This he said that Amadis might be the better disguised, and that he might not want a pretext to send Enil away. So Durin mounted his palfrey the next morning and departed.

FOOTNOTES:

[188:A] The song of Amadis has suffered much in this second translation, this "shadow of a shade."

VILLANCICO.

Leonoreta, fin roseta, blanca sobre toda flor, fin roseta, no me meta en tal cuyta vuestro amor.

Sin ventura yo en locura me meti; en vos amar es locura que me dura, sin me poder apartar, o hermosura sin par, que me da pena y dulzor, fin roseta, no me meta en tal cuyta vuestro amor.

De todas las que yo veo no desseo servir otra sino a vos; bien veo que mi desseo es devaneo, do no me puedo partir, pues que no puedo huyr de ser vuestro servidor, no me meta, fin roseta en tal cuyta vuestro amor.

Aunque mi quexa parece referirse a vos senora, otra es la vencedora, otra es la matadora, que mi vida desfallece, aquesta tiene el poder de me hazer toda guerra; aquesta puede hazer, sin yo selo merecer, Que muerto biva so tierra.

CHAPTER 13.

While Beltenebros remained in the Nunnery, his health and strength recovered, and he sent Enil to the next town to get arms made for him, a green shield with as many golden lions as it could hold, and to buy him a horse, and a sword and breast-plate, the best he could find. In twenty days all was ready, as he had ordered it, and at the end of that time Durin arrived. Beltenebros was right glad to see him, and asked him before Enil how the Damsel was, and wherefore he had returned. Durin answered, that the Damsel commended herself to him, and had sent for two jewels which she had left in her bed; and then he delivered to Enil the bidding of his cousin Gandalin. Who is Gandalin? said Beltenebros. A Squire, my cousin, replied Enil, who long time served a Knight called Amadis of Gaul. Then Beltenebros took Durin apart to walk with him, and heard the message of Oriana, and also how his brethren were to be in the battle with Cildadan, and of the defiance that Famongomadan had sent, and how he had demanded Oriana to be serving-damsel to his daughter, till he should give her in marriage to his son. When he heard this, his flesh shook with exceeding anger, and he resolved in himself, so soon as he had seen his Lady, to undertake no adventure till he had found Famongomadan, and fought with him a combat to the utterance for what he had dared propose.

That night Beltenebros took leave of the Nuns, and early the next day, armed in his green armour, he set forth, and Enil with him carrying his shield and helmet and lance. The day was clear, and he feeling himself in his strength and once more in arms, began to manage his horse so skilfully that Enil said to him, I know not, Sir, what the strength of your heart may be, but I never saw a Knight appear so well in arms. The worth, quoth Beltenebros, lies in a good heart, not in a good appearance! happy dole hath he whom God has gifted with both! You have judged the one, judge the other as you shall see it deserves when put to proof. Seven days they travelled without adventure, and Beltenebros, as he drew nearer, wore his helmet that he might not be known. On the eighth, as they were passing the foot of a mountain, they met a Knight upon a large bay horse, so huge in stature that he appeared to be a Giant, and two Squires carrying his arms. He cried out with a loud voice to Beltenebros, Stop, Sir Knight, till you have told me what I want to know! Beltenebros looked at the stranger's shield, and seeing three golden flowers in a field azure, he knew it was Don Quadragante, for he had seen a like shield in the Firm Island, hanging above all the others, as his who had approached nearest the Forbidden Chamber. Yet, remembering Famongomadan, he would willingly now have avoided battle; as also, because he was on his way to Oriana, and feared lest the great prowess of this Knight should cause him some delay. Howbeit he stopt, and bade Enil give him his arms if they were wanted. God protect you! quoth Enil, he looks to me more like a Devil than a Knight! He is no Devil, quoth Beltenebros, but a right good Knight, of whom I have heard heretofore. By this Quadragante was come up, and said to him, Knight, you must tell me if you belong to the household of King Lisuarte?—Why ask you?—Because I have defied him and all his household, and kill all of them whom I meet. Beltenebros felt his anger rising, and replied, you are one of those who have defied him?—I am; and I am he who will do to him and his all the evil in my power.—And who are you?—My name is Don Quadragante.—Certes, Don Quadragante, notwithstanding your high lineage, and your great prowess in arms, this is great folly in you to defy the best King in the world! they who undertake more than they can effect, are rather rash than hardy. I am not this King's vassal, nor am I of his land, but for his goodness my heart is disposed to serve him, so that I may account myself among those whom you have defied: if you chuse battle with me, you may have it; if not, go your way! I believe Knight, said Quadragante, you speak thus boldly because you know me so little: pray you, tell me your name?—They call me Beltenebros: you will know me by it no better than before, for it is a name of no renown; but, though I am of a far land, I have heard that you are seeking Amadis of Gaul, and, by what I hear of him, it is no loss to you that you cannot find him. What! quoth Quadragante, do you prize him, whom I hate so much, above me? Know, that your death-hour is arrived! take thy arms, and defend thyself if thou canst. I might do it with some doubt against others, he replied, but can have none in opposing thee, who art so full of pride and threats.

Then they ran their course; both felt the shock; the horse of Beltenebros reeled, and he himself was wounded at the nipple of his breast. Quadragante was unhorsed and hurt in the ribs; he rose, and ran at Beltenebros, who did not see him, for he was adjusting his helmet, and he mortally stabbed his horse. Beltenebros alighted, and went against him sword in hand in great anger. There was no courage in this! cried he; your own horse was strong enough to have finished the battle without this discourtesy! The blows fell as thick and loud as though ten Knights had been in combat, for both put forth all their strength and skill, and the fight lasted from the hour of tierce till vespers; but then Quadragante, overcome with fatigue, and with a blow that Beltenebros gave him on the helmet, fell down senseless. Beltenebros took off his helmet to see if he were dead; the air revived him; he placed the sword-point at his face, and said, Quadragante, remember thy soul, for thou art a dead man. Ah, Beltenebros, cried he, for God's sake let me live for my soul's sake!—Yield thyself vanquished, then, and promise to fulfil what I command! I will fulfil your will to save my life, said Quadragante, but there is no reason wherefore I should confess myself vanquished: he is not vanquished, who in his defence hath shown no fear, doing his utmost till strength and breath fail him and he falls; but he who does not do what he could have done, for lack of heart. You speak well, said Beltenebros, and I like much what I have learnt from you: give me your hand and your promise then; and he called the Squires to witness it. You shall go forthwith to the court of King Lisuarte, and remain there till Amadis arrives, and then you shall pardon him for the death of your brother, King Abies; for they by their own will fought in lists together, and such revenge, even among those of meaner degree, ought not to be pursued. Moreover, you shall make null the defiance against King Lisuarte, and not take arms against those who are in his service. All this did Quadragante promise against his will, and in the fear of death. He then ordered his Squires to make a litter, and remove him; and Beltenebros mounting the bay horse of his antagonist, gave his arms to Enil, and departed.

Four Damsels, who were hawking with a merlin, had seen the battle, and they now came up, and requested Beltenebros would go to their castle, where he should be honourably welcomed, for the good will which he had manifested to King Lisuarte. He thankfully accepted their hospitality, being sore wearied with the struggle, and accompanied them. They found no other wound than that upon the nipple of his breast, which bled much; howbeit, in three days he departed. On the second day at noon, from a hill top, he beheld the city of London, and, to the right thereof, the castle of Miraflores, where his Lady Oriana then abode. Here he stood awhile, gazing, and devising how he might dispatch Enil. Do you know this country? said he. Yes, replied Enil; that is London, in the valley.—Are we so near? but I will not go to the court till I have won some renown, and deserve to be there: go you therefore and visit your cousin Gandalin, and there you will hear what may be said of me, and when the battle is to be with King Cildadan.—But shall I leave you alone?— I sometimes go alone; but we will first appoint a place to meet at. They proceeded a little way and saw three tents pitched by a river side, the middle a rich one, and before it there were Knights and Damsels sporting; and he saw five shields at the entrance of one tent, and five at another, and ten armed Knights, therefore he turned aside from the road that he might not joust with them. The Knights called out to him to joust. Not now, said he, for you are many and fresh, and I am alone and weary. I believe, said the one, you are afraid you should lose your horse.—Why should I lose him?—Because he would be won by the man who dismounted you: a likelier chance than that you should win his. Since that is the case, said Beltenebros, I will ride on and secure him while I can; and he continued his course. The Knights cried after him, your arms, Sir Cavalier, are protected better by a smooth tongue than by a stout heart: they will last to be hung over your monument, tho' you should live these hundred years! Think of me as you please, quoth he, your words will not destroy my worth such as it is. I would to heaven you would break one lance with me! cried the Knight; I would not mount horse again for a whole year, if you rode to your lodging this night upon that bay steed! Good Sir, said Beltenebros, that is the very thing I am afraid of, and have therefore got out of the way. Holy Mary, they all exclaimed, what a cowardly Knight! He nothing heeding them, rode on to a ford, at which he meant to cross, when he heard a cry from behind. Stop, Knight! and looking round saw a Damsel following him upon a palfrey richly trappinged. Sir Knight, said she, Leonoreta, daughter to King Lisuarte, is in yonder tent, and she and all her Damsels request that for their sake you will joust with her Knights, a thing you will be more bound to do by this request than by their defiance.—What! quoth he, is the daughter of the Queen there?—Aye, truly!—I should rather do her service myself than commit enmity against her Knights, but at her command I will consent, on condition that they require from me nothing farther than the joust. With this answer the Damsel returned; and Beltenebros took his arms, and rode to an open part of the field to wait for the encounter. The first who came was the one who had such an inclination to win his horse. Beltenebros was pleased that this was the first: he unhorsed him, and bade Enil take his horse, and said, Sir Knight, if you keep your word, you will not have another fall for a whole year, for so you promised unless you won my bay; but he lay groaning, for he had three ribs and a hip broken. Three others shared the same fortune with less hurt; on the last, Beltenebros broke his lance. Enil took their horses one by one, and tied them to the trees, and then Beltenebros would have departed; but he saw another Knight making ready, and a Squire brought him four lances, and said, Sir, Leonoreta sends you these lances, and bids you do your duty with them against the other Knights, since you have overthrown their companions. For her sake, said he, who is daughter to so good a King, I will do what she requires; but for her Knights I would do nothing, for they are discourteous to make Knights who are travelling joust against their will. So he took a lance, and one after the other dismounted all the rest; only the last endured two encounters, and fell not till the third, for he was Nicoran of the Perilous Bridge, and was one of the good jousters in Great Britain. When Beltenebros had finished, he sent all the horses that he had won to Leonoreta, and bade her tell her Knights to be more courteous to strangers, or else to joust better, for they might find a Knight who would make them go afoot. The Knights remained greatly abashed; if Amadis were alive and well, quoth Nicoran, verily I should say this were he, for I know no other who would have left us thus. It is not he, said Galiseo, some of us should have known him, and he would not have jousted with us, being his friends. Giontes, the nephew of King Lisuarte, who was one of them, replied. Would it were Amadis, our dishonour would be well gained! but be he who he may, God prosper him wherever he goes! for he won our horses like a good Knight, and like a good Knight restored them. Curse him, quoth Lasamor, he has broken my hip and my ribs, but it was my own fault.

Beltenebros went on satisfied with his success, and admiring the lance which he held, for it was a good one. About a quarter of a league on, he saw a chapel overbowered with trees, and there he determined to alight for the sake of prayer, and because the great heat and the exercise of jousting had made him athirst. At the chapel-door were three palfreys equipped for women, and two for Squires. He went in, but there was no one there, and commended himself from his heart to God and the Virgin. As he was coming out, he saw the three Damsels and their Squires sitting under the trees beside a fountain, and made up to them that he might drink: but neither of them did he know. Knight, said they, are you of King Lisuarte's household? I would, quoth he, I were so good a Knight as to be approved in such a company: but whither go ye?—To Miraflores, to see our Aunt who is Abbess there, and to see Oriana the Princess; but we are waiting here till the heat of the day be over. In God's name, quoth he, and I will keep you company till it be time to travel: how is this fountain called?—We know not but there is one in yonder valley, by those great trees there, which is called the Fountain of the Three Channels. He knew it better than they, for he had often passed it when hunting, and there he determined to fix a meeting-place with Enil, whom he wished to send away while he went to his Lady.

Presently, while they were thus talking, there came along the road which Beltenebros had passed, a waggon drawn by twelve palfreys, and on it were two Dwarfs who drove. There were many Knights in chains in the waggon, and their shields were hanging at the side, and many damsels and girls among them weeping and lamenting loudly. Before it went a Giant, so great that he was fearful to behold; he rode a huge black horse, and he was armed with plates of steel, and his helmet shone bright, and in his hand he had a boar spear, whose point was a full arm's-length long. Behind the waggon was another Giant, who appeared more huge and terrible than the first. The Damsels seeing them were greatly terrified, and hid themselves among the trees. Presently the Giant who rode foremost turned to the Dwarfs, and cried, I will cut you into a thousand pieces if you suffer these girls to shed their own blood, for I mean to do sacrifice with it to my god, whom I adore. When Beltenebros heard this, he knew it was Famongomadan, for he had a custom to sacrifice damsels to an Idol in the Boiling Lake, by whose advice and words he was guided in every thing, and that sacrifice used to content his god, being the Wicked Enemy who is satisfied with such wickedness. At this time Beltenebros did not wish to encounter him, because he expected to be that night with Oriana, and also because his joust with the ten Knights had wearied him; but he knew the Knights in the waggon, and saw that Leonoreta and her Damsels were there, for Famongomadan, who always took this waggon with him to carry away all he could find, had seized them in their tents shortly after their encounter. Immediately he mounted, and called to Enil for his arms; but Enil said, let those Devils pass by first. Give me! quoth

Beltenebros, I shall try God's mercy before they pass, to see if I can redress this villainy. O Sir, cried the Squire, why have you so little compassion upon your own youth! if the best twenty Knights of King Lisuarte's court were here, they would not venture to attack them. Care not thou for that, replied his Master, if I let them pass without doing my best I should be unworthy to appear among good men: you shall see my fortune. Enil gave him his arms, weeping, and Beltenebros then descended the sloping ground to meet them. He looked toward Miraflores as he went, and said, O Oriana, my Lady, never did I attempt adventure confiding in my own courage, but in you: my gentle Lady, assist me now, in this great need! He felt his full strength now, and all fear was gone, and he cried out to the Dwarfs to stop.

When the Giant heard him, he came towards him with such rage that smoke came through the vizor of his helmet, and he shook his boar-spear with such force that its ends almost met. Unhappy wretch! cried he, who gave thee boldness enough to dare appear before me? That Lord, quoth Beltenebros, whom thou hast offended, who will give me strength to-day to break thy pride. Come on! come on! cried the Giant, and see if his power can protect thee from mine! Beltenebros fitted the lance under his arm, and ran against him full speed: he smote him below the waist with such exceeding force that the spear burst through the plates of steel and ran through him, even so as to strike the saddle behind, that the girths broke, and he fell with the saddle, the broken lance remaining in him. His boar-spear had taken effect upon the horse of Beltenebros, and mortally wounded him. The Knight leapt off and drew his sword. The Giant rose up so enraged that fire came from him, and he plucked the lance from his wound, and threw it at Beltenebros so forcibly that if the shield had not protected his helmet, it would have driven him to the ground; but his own bowels came out with the weapon, and he fell, crying, help, Basagante! I am slain. At this Basagante came up as fast as his horse could carry him: he had a steel axe in his hand, and with this he thought to have cut his enemy in two; but Beltenebros avoided the blow, and at the same time struck at the Giant's horse: the stroke fell short, but the end of his sword cut through the stirrup-leather, and cut the leg also half through. The Giant in his fury did not feel the wound, though he missed the stirrup; he turned and raised his axe again. Beltenebros had taken the shield from his neck, and was holding it by the thongs: the axe fell on it and pierced in, and drove it from his hands to the ground. Beltenebros had made another stroke, the sword wounded Basagante's arm, and, falling below upon the plates of fine steel, broke, so that only the handle remained in his hand. Not for this was he a whit dismayed; he saw the Giant could not pluck his axe from the shield, and he ran and caught it by the handle also; both struggled; it was on that side where the stirrup had been cut away, so that Basagante lost his balance, the horse started and he fell, and Beltenebros got the battle-axe. The Giant drew his sword in great fury, and would have ran at the Knight, but the nerves of his leg were cut through; he fell upon one knee, and Beltenebros smote him on the helmet, that the laces burst and it fell off. He seeing his enemy so near, thought with his sword, which was very long, to smite off his head; the blow was aimed too high, it cut off the whole crown of the helmet, and cut away the hair with it. Beltenebros drew back; the helmet fell over his head upon his shoulders, and Leonoreta and the Damsels, who were on their knees in the waggon praying to God to deliver them, tore their hair and began to shriek and call upon the Virgin, thinking he was surely slain. He himself put up his hand to feel if he were wounded to death, but feeling no harm, made again at the Giant, whose sword falling upon a stone in the last blow had broken. Basagante's heart failed him now, he made one stroke more, and cut him slightly in the leg with the broken sword; but Beltenebros let drive the battle-axe at his head; it cut away the ear and the cheek and the jaw, and Basagante fell, writhing in the agony of death.

At this time Famongomadan had taken off his helmet, and was holding his hands upon his wound to check the blood. When he saw his son slain, he began to blaspheme God and his Mother Holy Mary, saying that he did not so much grieve to die as that he could destroy their monasteries and churches, because they had suffered him and his son to be conquered by one Knight. Beltenebros was then upon his knees returning thanks to God, when he heard the blasphemer, he exclaimed, Accursed of God and of his Blessed Mother! now shalt thou suffer for thy cruelties; pray to thine Idol, that, as thou hast shed so much blood before him, he may stop this blood of thine from flowing out with thy life! The Giant continued to curse God and his Saints; then Beltenebros plucked the boar-spear from the horse's body, and thrust it into the mouth of Famongomadan, and nailed him backward to the earth. He then put on Basagante's helmet that he might not be known, and mounting the other's horse, rode up to the waggon and broke the chains of all who were prisoners therein, and he besought them to carry the bodies of the Giants to King Lisuarte, and say they were sent him by a strange Knight called Beltenebros; and he begged the Princess to permit him to take the black horse of Famongomadan, because it was a strong and handsome horse, and he would ride him in the battle against King Cildadan. The bodies of the Giants were so huge, that they were obliged to bend their knees to lay them in the waggon. Leonoreta and her Damsels made garlands for their heads, and being right joyful for their deliverance entered London singing in triumph. Much was King Lisuarte astonished at their adventure, and the more for Quadragante had already presented himself on the part of Beltenebros, of whom nothing else was known except what Corisanda had related. I would he were among us, said the King, I would not lose him for any thing that he could ask and I could grant.

CHAPTER 14.

Beltenebros having taken leave of the Princess, returned joyfully to the fountain where the Damsels were. He bade Enil go to London, and get him other arms made the same as those he wore, which were now so battered as to be useless, and he was to buy him another sword, and bring them in eight days to the Fountain of the Three Channels. Enil forthwith departed, and the Damsels also taking their leave, rode on to Miraflores, and there told Oriana and Mabilia what great feats they had seen that day atchieved by a Knight called Beltenebros. He meantime struck into the forest, and rode slowly the same way, till he came to a brook winding among the trees, and there, for it was yet early, he alighted and took off his helmet, and drank of the water, and cleansed himself from the sweat of the battle; and there he remained, musing over his past and present fortunes and the strange vicissitudes of life, till night approached; then he made for the castle. Durin and Gandalin met him at the garden-wall, and took his horse. Oriana and Mabilia and the Damsel were on the wall: they gave him their hands: presently he was over, and held Oriana in his arms; but who can tell what joy there then was in embracing and kisses, and the mingling of tears? Mabilia roused them as from a dream, and led them into the castle, and there Beltenebros remained eight days with Oriana in joys dearer to him than even Paradise.

Meantime King Lisuarte was preparing for the battle against King Cildadan, which he much doubted, knowing what Giants and mighty Knights would be with his enemy. Florestan and Galaor and Agrayes were returned, and Don Galvanes Lackland had arrived, and many other good Knights. The whole talk was of Beltenebros, and many said his deeds surpassed those of Amadis; whereat Galaor and Florestan were so enraged, that nothing but their promise to undertake no adventure before the battle, withheld them from seeking him and proving him in mortal combat, but of this they only communed with each other. One day there came into the palace an old Squire with two others, all clad in garments of the same cloth. The old man's beard was shorn, his ears were large, and the hair of his head grey. He, kneeling before the King, addressed him in the Greek language: Sir, the great fame which is gone abroad of the Knights and Dames and Damsels of your court hath brought me hither, to see if I can find among them what for sixty years

I have sought through all parts of the world, and reaped no fruit for my labour. Noble King, if you hold it good, permit that a trial may be made here, which shall not be to your injury nor to the shame of any. All who were present, desirous to see what it might be, besought the King's assent, which he, feeling the like curiosity, readily granted. The old Squire then took in his hand a coffer of jasper, three cubits long and a span wide, its sides being fastened with plates of gold; this he opened, and took out a sword, so strange as the like was never seen; the sheath was of bone, yet green like an emerald, and so clear that the blade of the sword could be seen through, and it was unlike other blades, for the one-half was as bright as it could be, and the other burning red like fire; the hilt was of the same green bone, and the belt also, being made of such small pieces fastened together with gold screws, that it could be girt on like a common belt. This the Squire hung round his neck, and took from the same coffer a head-dress of flowers, the half whereof were as beautiful and fresh as though they had just then been cut from the living stem; the other half so withered and dry, that it seemed they would crumble at a touch. The King asked why those flowers, that all seemed to grow from the same stem, were yet in such different condition, and what was the nature of that strange sword? King, said the old Squire, this sword cannot be drawn from the scabbard, except by the Knight who of all men in the world loveth his Lady best; and as soon as he shall have it in his hand, the half which is now of burning red, shall become clear and bright like the other part, and the whole blade be of one colour; and when this garland of flowers shall be set upon the head of that Lady or Damsel, that with the same surpassing love doth love her husband or friend, the dry flowers shall again become fresh and green. And know, Sir, that I cannot be knighted except by the hands of that true lover, nor take sword except from that loyal Lady; for this, O King, having searched all other courts and parts of the world, I am come hither, after sixty years, hoping that as there is no court of Emperor or King like this, here I may succeed at last. Tell me, said Lisuarte, how is it that the half which is burning red, does not burn the scabbard? You shall hear, quoth the Squire: Between Tartary and India there is a sea so hot, that it boils like water over a fire, and it is all green; and in that sea serpents breed bigger than crocodiles, having wings wherewith they fly, and so venomous that all people run from them in fear; nevertheless, they who at any time find one dead esteem it much, being a thing excellent in medicine. These serpents have one bone reaching from the head to the tail, it is so strong that the whole body is formed upon this one bone, and green as you see it here in this scabbard and hilt and belt, and because it grew in that boiling sea no fire can burn it. Now I will tell you of this garland: the flowers are from trees in Tartary, in an island fifteen miles from the shore; the trees are only two, nor is it known that there are any such in any part elsewhere; but in that sea is a whirlpool, so terrible that men fear to venture to take them, howbeit they that have dared pass and succeeded, sell them for what they will to ask, for this freshness and life-green never fails. Having told you thus much, you shall know who I myself am. I am nephew of the best man of his own time, who was called Apolidon, and who long time dwelt here in your country in the Firm Island. My father was King Ganor, his brother, to whom he gave his kingdom, and my mother, daughter to the King of Panonia, and, when I was of age to be knighted, my father, because of the exceeding love between him and my mother, made me promise to be made Knight by none but the most true Lover in the world, and to receive sword only from the truest Lady. I lightly promised, thinking to accomplish this as soon as I should see my Uncle Apolidon and his Grimanesa; but so it was, that, when I arrived, Grimanesa was dead, and he knowing wherefore I came, greatly pitied me, for it is the custom of my land that no one who is not a Knight can reign therein. So having no remedy to give me then, he bade me return to him at a year's end, and at that time he gave me this sword and garland, telling me by the labour of this search to remedy the folly of such a promise. And now, Sir, I beseech you, as without wrong or shame it may be done, that you and your Knights and the Queen and her Ladies be pleased to make the proof; and if such can be found as shall accomplish it, let the sword and garland be theirs, the profit will be mine, and rest from my weary toil, and the honour yours above all other Princes, that they who could accomplish this adventure were found in your court. The King then said, that Santiago's day was but five days off, and then he had summoned many Knights to be present, wherefore if it pleased him to wait so long, his chance of success would be greater among so many more Knights. This the Squire thought good.

Gandalin was at this time in the court, and heard all that the Squire had said. Forthwith he rode to Miraflores. Beltenebros and Oriana were playing chess in the little court under the trees. When he had related all that had past, and how a day was appointed for the trial, Beltenebros sate musing for a while, lost in thought, till Gandalin and his cousin had left the place, and then, as he looked up, Oriana asked what had made him so deep in thought. Lady mine, quoth he, if by God's help and your's my thought could be accomplished, I should be a happy man for ever. Dear friend, she answered, she who hath made you master of her person will do for you any thing! He took her hands and kissed them often, and said, this is what I have been thinking; that, if you and I could win this sword and garland, our hearts would be for ever at rest, and all those doubts that have tortured us be utterly destroyed. But how can I do this, said Oriana, without great shame and greater danger to myself and to these Damsels, who are privy to our loves? That, replied Beltenebros, may easily be done, you shall go so disguised, and I will obtain such security from the King your father, that we shall be as unknown as before strangers. Then do your pleasure, quoth she, and God prosper it to good! I doubt not to gain the garland, if it is to be won by exceeding love. I will obtain your father's promise, said Beltenebros, that nothing shall be demanded from me against my own consent, and will go completely armed; and you, Lady, shall have a cloak fastened round you, and your face muffled, so that you shall see all, yet no one see you. Let us call Mabilia, cried Oriana, without her counsel I must not adventure. So they called her and Gandalin, and the Damsel of Denmark, and they, albeit they saw great peril, did not gainsay their inclination; and Mabilia said, there was a rich cloak among her mother's presents that the Damsel had brought, which never had been worn or seen in that land. She brought it, and took Oriana apart and dressed her in it, so that when she came out with her gloves on, and her face-cloths,[220:A] no one knew her, though they looked narrowly. Lady mine, cried Beltenebros, I never thought it would give me pleasure not to see and know you! He then bade Gandalin buy the fairest palfrey that could be found in all that country, and bring it at midnight before the day of the adventure, to the garden-wall; and he told Durin to have his horse ready for him this evening, that he might meet Enil, and send him to obtain the security from King Lisuarte.

Beltenebros rode that night through the forest, and at day-break reached the fountain of the Three Channels. Presently Enil came up and brought with him the arms: they were good arms, and pleased him well. He then asked the Squire what news of the court, and Enil told him the talk there was of his prowess, and was about to relate concerning the sword and garland, but Beltenebros said, this I learnt three days since from a Damsel who made me promise to carry her secretly to this proof: this I must do, and will prove the sword myself; but, as you know it is my will not to make myself known to the King nor to any other till my deeds make me worthy, you must return directly and tell the King, that if he will promise and secure us that nothing shall be said or done to us against our pleasure, we will come and try the adventure; and say you, before the Queen and her Ladies, that this Damsel makes me go greatly against my inclination. On the day of the proof, meet me here at dawn, that the Damsel may know if she has this security; meantime I must return to bring her here, for she dwells far off. Beltenebros then took his arms, and while Enil went to the city, lay down by the same brook-side till night, then rode to Miraflores. Durin was ready to take his horse, and his fair friends expected him at the garden-wall. What, Sir Cousin! quoth Mabilia, seeing his arms, you return richer than you went. Do you not understand it? cried Oriana, he went to get arms, that he might free himself from this prison. Thus chearfully they entered the castle, and they gave him food, for he had not eaten the whole day, lest he might be seen.

FOOTNOTES:

[220:A] Antifazes.

CHAPTER 15.

The next day the Damsel of Denmark was sent to London to learn what answer
Enil obtained, and to tell the Queen and her Ladies that Oriana was ill, and
did not rise. It was late before she returned, because the King had gone
forth to meet Queen Briolania, who was come to his court, and brought with
her three hundred Knights to go in search of Amadis, as his brothers might
dispose of them. Twenty Damsels accompanied her, all dressed in mourning
like herself, for in that dress had he found her, and that dress had she worn
when he recovered for her her kingdom, and that she would wear till some
tidings of him were known. Is she so handsome as they say? quoth Oriana.
So save me God, Lady, replied the Damsel, as excepting yourself, I think her
the fairest and most graceful woman that I have ever seen. And it grieved her
much when she heard of your malady, and she bade me say, when it pleased
you, she would come and see you. I should be much pleased, answered Oriana,
for she is the person in the world whom I most wish to see. Honour her well,
said Beltenebros, for she well deserves it, although, Lady, you have suspected
something.—Dear friend, no more of this, I know my thoughts were false.
But this trial, quoth he, will make you more free from this, and me more
subject.—The garland, said Oriana, will prove whether my error proceeded
from excess of love. The Damsel then told them how the King had promised
Enil the security which he required.

They rose at midnight before the day of the proof. Oriana was wrapt
in Mabilia's mantle, and her face muffled, and Beltenebros armed himself in
his new arms. They crossed the wall; Gandalin was there with the horse and
palfrey: they mounted, and rode alone into the forest. Mabilia and the Damsel
of Denmark remained in great fear lest ill should befal; but, when Oriana
found herself in the midst of the forest at night, she was so affrighted that her
whole body trembled and her speech failed, and she began to apprehend that
she might fail to accomplish the adventure, and that if so her lover, who now
trusted in her so fully, would suspect her truth, and then she wished she had
never undertaken the danger. When Beltenebros perceived her agitation, he
said, I would rather have died, Lady, than brought you here, if I had thought
you would have been so terrified; we had better turn back, and he turned his
horse and led her palfrey round. But then Oriana's heart changed, seeing that

so great an adventure would be for her sake foregone, and she said, dear friend do not heed my fears, for I am a woman, and this is a strange place to me; regard only what you, as a good Knight, ought to atchieve. Dear Lady, mine, quoth he, your prudence guides my folly: I can neither do or say other than you command me: so they proceeded, and about an hour before the dawn reached the Fountain. When it was broad day Enil came up. Lady Damsel, said Beltenebros, this is the Squire of whom I spake, let us hear if the King grant your demand. Enil then told them what Lisuarte had promised, and that the proof was to begin immediately after mass. Beltenebros then gave him his shield and spear, the helmet he wore himself; they took the road to London, and in this guise entered the gate. All flocked to see them crying out, this is the good Knight Beltenebros, who sent here Don Quadragante and the giants! This is the prime of all knighthood! Happy the Damsel who comes in his guard! When Oriana heard this she felt a pride to know herself the mistress of him, who, by his great valour, could command all others. Thus they reached the palace, where the King and all his Knights, the Queen and her Ladies, were assembled for the adventure. As soon as their approach was known the King went to receive them at the entrance. They knelt to kiss his hand, but he withdrew it, saying, Good friend, I shall willingly observe your pleasure, for in a short time you have done more for me than ever Knight did for King before. Beltenebros bowed thankfully, but made no answer, and proceeded with his Damsel up to the Queen: But Oriana's flesh quivered with fear, seeing she was before her parents, but her true friend never let go her hand, and so they both knelt before Brisena. The Queen raised them and said, Damsel, I know not who you are, never having seen you; but for the great services which this Knight hath performed, and for your own deserts also, you are both honourably and deservedly welcome. Beltenebros thanked her, but Oriana held down her head as if for humbleness, and made no answer. The King and his Knights then went on one side of the hall, the Queen and her Ladies to the other; but Beltenebros said, that if it pleased the King he would stand apart with his Damsel, and prove the adventure last of all.

Lisuarte then took the sword and drew it a hands breadth, no more. Macandon, the old Squire, said, King, if there be no better lover in the Court than you, I shall depart without my wish, and he thrust the sword back, for so it was to be at every trial; then Galaor essayed, and could only draw it three fingers breadth. Florestan and Galvanes, and Grumedan, and Brandoyuas, and Ladasin, all tried, none so successfully as Florestan, who drew it at a full palm's length. Don Guilan the Pensive was the next, and he drew it half out; had you loved just as much again, said Macandon, you would have won the sword. Others there were who tried and could not move it, and these the old Squire called heretics in love. Then came Agrayes to the proof, he looked at Olinda, and thought surely the sword would be his, for his true and loyal love; he drew it within a hand of the point, and as he still attempted to pluck it forth the burning part of the blade touched his cloak and burnt it; then he retired sufficiently rejoiced that he had so far exceeded all others. Almost Sir Knight, quoth old Macandon, had you been the winner, and I satisfied. Palomir and Dragonis, who had arrived the day before, next essayed, and drew it no farther than Galaor. Knights, quoth the Squire, if you had only as much of the sword as you can draw, you would have but little for your own defence. True, said Dragonis; and if you should be knighted at the end of the adventure, you are not so young but that you may remember the ceremony. At this all laughed, but there remained no more to make the trial; Beltenebros then arose and took his Lady by the hand, and went towards the sword. Sir Stranger, quoth Macandon, this sword will become you better than the one you wear, yet I would not have you be so sure of it as to lay aside your own, for this is to be won by truth of heart, and not by force of arms. But he took the sword, and drew it from the scabbard, and immediately the whole blade became clear and shining with one brightness. When Macandon saw this, he knelt down and said, O good Knight, God give thee honour, for thou hast done great honour to this court! Reason is it that you should be beloved well by your Lady unless she be the falsest and most unreasonable of women. Now then give me the honour of Knighthood, which I may receive from no other hand but yours! and you will give me with it lands and the lordship over many good men. Good friend, replied Beltenebros, let the proof of the garland be made, then I will do with you what can rightly be done. And then he blessed the sword, and laying his own aside, hung it round his neck, and led his Lady back to her station. Great were the praises then which he received for excellence in arms and in love, so that Galaor and Florestan were moved to great anger, for they thought it shame that any other than Amadis should be esteemed above them, and they resolved within themselves that their first business after the battle with King Cildadan should be to fight him, and either die or show to the world the difference there was between him and their brother.

Lisuarte now called upon the Queen and her Ladies to make their proof, without fear, and in the hope of honour; for she who won the garland, if Dame should be more loved and honoured by her husband, if Damsel acquire the praise of loyalty above all. Brisena first placed the flowers on her own head, they did not in the least alter. Queen and Madam, quoth old Macandon, if the King your husband gained little by attempting the sword, it seems you have well requited him; she answered nothing, but drew back greatly abashed. Next was Briolania, that fair Queen of Sobradisa; she, like Brisena, produced no change. Lady and most fair Damsel, cried the Squire, you must be loved before you can love so as to gain the garland; four other King's daughters came on, Eluida and Estrelleta her sister, who was fair and proud, and Aldeva and Olinda the gentle. Upon her head the flowers began to revive so that all thought she would win the praise, but they only began, and when the garland was taken off they withered again as before; more than a hundred other Dames tried, but all with less success than Olinda, and all received their jest from the old Squire. Oriana had felt a fear when Briolania made the proof, and she rejoiced at the failure, lest, had she succeeded, her friend might deem it was for his love, for never had she seen so fair a Damsel, and she thought surely, that if his heart were not won by her, there was no danger of a rival. All others had now failed; she made sign to Beltenebros to lead her up, the garland was placed round her head, and immediately the dry flowers quickened with full freshness and verdure. Excellent Damsel, quoth Macandon, you are she for whom I sought forty years before you were born!

Then the old Squire besought Beltenebros to knight him, and that Damsel to give him a sword. Let it be presently, said Beltenebros, for I cannot tarry. Macandon then put on white garments, and white armour over it like a new Knight, and Beltenebros knighted him according to the manner, and put on his right spur, and Oriana girded on a rich sword which his Squires had brought. The Dames and Damsels laughed at seeing him, and Aldeva said so loud that all heard her. What a fair Child! and he will be a new Knight as long as he lives! How know you that? cried the rest. She answered, because the dress he has now put on will last as long as himself. Gentle Damsels, quoth the old man, I would not exchange my pleasure for your manners; my youth may be ranked with your modesty. The King was pleased at this reply, for he thought their speeches were unseemly.

This done, Beltenebros and his Lady took leave of the Queen; and Brisena said to her daughter, Lady, though it is your pleasure not to be known here, yet I beseech you, when you are returned home, ask of me whatever favour I can grant. I know her Lady, quoth Beltenebros, just as much as you do, though we have been seven days together; but this I can say, that she is fair, and she has locks that need not be thus concealed. Damsel, said Briolania, I know you not: but if your friend love you as you love him, and as he will do if he be wise, love never made a better union. Her words gave pleasure to Oriana; then they took their leave, and mounted, the King and Don Galaor accompanying them; and Beltenebros said to the King, take this Damsel and honour her, Sir, for she well deserves it, having honoured your court. Lisuarte took her bridle, and he went on talking with Galaor, who had little inclination for friendly talk with him, longing to engage him in battle. When they had gone a little way Beltenebros took the bridle from the King, and said, Now, Sir, God be with you, and if it please you that I should be one of your hundred in the battle, I shall willingly serve you. The King embraced and thanked him, and said, that great part of his fear was removed by having him on his part; they parted then, and Beltenebros and his Lady, Enil following, entered the forest, he having round his neck that green sword, and she that garland of flowers upon her head.

When they reached the fountain of the Three Channels, they saw a Squire on horseback coming down the mountain, who said, Knight, Arcalaus the Enchanter bids you send him that Damsel, if you make him fetch her, he will cut off both your heads. Where is Arcalaus the Enchanter? cried Beltenebros;

the Squire showed him where he and another Knight were under a tuft of trees, both being armed, and their horses ready by them. At hearing this Oriana could scarce keep her seat upon the palfrey. Lady Damsel, fear not! quoth he, if this sword fail me not I will protect you. He then took his arms—tell Arcalaus I am a stranger Knight, who know him not, and have no reason to obey him. When Arcalaus heard this he grew greatly enraged, and said to the Knight with him, Nephew Lindoraque, take that garland which the Damsel wears for your Mistress Madasima; if the Knight attempts to hinder you cut off his head, and hang the woman by the hair to a tree. Lindoraque mounted and moved on to do it: he was a huge man, and well might be so, being son of Cartadaque the giant of the defended mountain, by a sister of Arcalaus. But Beltenebros held him at nought, and placing himself right in his way, for he had heard his errand, cried, Knight, you pass no farther! You shall not hinder me, quoth he, from performing the pleasure of Arcalaus. Beltenebros answered, we shall see what your pride and his villainy can do. They couched their lances and ran, the lances broke, Lindoraque fell with the truncheon in his body, he rose, being of stout heart, and seeing Beltenebros about to strike him, bent from the blow, and reeled and fell upon the truncheon, and drove it clean through his back, so that he died instantly. Arcalaus was riding up to help him. Beltenebros galloped up to him and made him lose the joust, and struck at him with his sword a blow that cut off the lance, and with it half the hand, so that only his thumb was left. He turned to fly, and threw away his shield, and by the fleetness of his horse escaped. Beltenebros then bade Enil take the shield and hand of Arcalaus, and the head of Lindoraque to the King, and tell him what had happened. He and his Lady went on their way, and rested beside a fountain till it was near night, then rode to Miraflores. The Squires were ready, and Mabilia and the Damsel joyfully received them, for if there had been delay they only expected death. Fair prizes have you won, quoth Mabilia, but they have cost us a great alarm and many tears.

As Lisuarte and Galaor were returning to the town, a Damsel came up and gave them each a letter, and rode away. The King read his thus: To thee Lisuarte, King of Great Britain, I Urganda, the Unknown, send salutation, and I tell thee that in the perilous and cruel battle between thee and King Cildadan, Beltenebros, in whom you confide, shall lose his name and his renown, and for one blow that he shall give all his great deeds shall be quite forgotten. In that hour thou shalt be in the greatest extremity, and in all danger of death, when the sharp sword of Beltenebros shall shed thy blood. Cruel and dolorous will the battle be; there will be great rage and cruelty, and no compassion. But at last by three blows from the hand of Beltenebros his party shall remain conquerors. Look to it King, for she who sends thee this warning knows what is to come!

Brave as the King's heart was, this letter dismayed him; he believed that Beltenebros was to lose his life, and that his own would be in the utmost danger; howbeit he put on a good countenance, and gave the letter to Galaor, and asked his counsel. Sir, quoth Galaor, I stand in need of your counsel myself; but if this battle can honourably be avoided, I should advise that it be done so; if that cannot be, you should not be in the field; by the sword of Beltenebros your blood is to be shed, and by three blows from his hand his party are to remain conquerors. This I do not understand, for he is to be on your side; and yet the letter says otherwise. Friend, quoth the King, your love for me makes you advise me ill. I must not, for the knowledge of any one, how wise soever, distrust the power of him who ordaineth all things. My good friend, I will be in the battle, and take what fortune it please God to give. The King's answer roused Galaor; rightly are you esteemed the best King in the world! quoth he, and he then shewed him his own letter.

You Don Galaor of Gaul, the strong and the brave, I Urganda, salute as him whom I esteem and love; know from me what must befall you in the dolorous battle, if you be there. After many cruelties and deaths that you will have witnessed in the last press, your strong body and stout limbs will fail your brave and ardent heart, and at the end your head will be in his power, who, with the three blows that he shall give, is to decide the day.

Friend, quoth Lisuarte, if this say true, you will be slain if you enter the battle; I will so order that you may honourably decline it. Sir, said Galaor, it seems the advice I gave displeased you, that you would command me to my shame. God forbid that I should herein obey you. Don Galaor! you are right, the King answered, we will trust in God. Meantime say nothing of these letters lest our friends should be discouraged. Before they entered the town two Knights came up to be present in the battle, they were Don Bruneo of Bonamar, and Branfil his brother; and Bruneo grieved much that he had not arrived in time to prove the sword, for he had passed under the arch of Loyal Lovers, and by his love to Melicia doubted not that he should have won it. Him Galaor courteously saluted, and took to his lodging as a right worthy Knight. Presently Enil arrived with the head of Lindoraque hanging from the horse's breast-plate, and the hand and shield of Arcalaus. Then was the great prowess of Beltenebros more praised, and Galaor and Florestan more desirous, to prove in battle that he was not equal to their lost brother Amadis. At this time Filispinel returned who had been sent with the King's defiance to the giants; he brought word that they were gone to Ireland, and would in four days time land in the port of the plain where the battle was to be fought, and he brought with him this letter. To the great Lord Lisuarte, King of Great Britain, and to all our friends in his dominions. I Arban, a wretch, once King of North Wales, and I Angriote of Estravaus, inform you that our unhappy fortune hath thrown us into the power of the fierce Gromadaza, wife of Famongomadan, who, in vengeance for the death of her husband and her son, inflicts upon us such torments, that we wish for death to relieve us; but she will not kill us that she may lengthen our sufferings, the which are such, that we should have ridden ourselves of life, if it were not for losing our souls thereby; but being now near death, we write this letter with our blood, praying God to grant you the victory over these traitors, who, in such inhuman sort torment us. Great sorrow had the King hereat, and all his Knights; however he comforted them, assuring them that there was no other remedy, or way of helping their friends, than by conquering in this great battle: so they all prepared, and set forth for the place appointed.

CHAPTER 16.

Three days Beltenebros remained at Miraflores, on the fourth he departed alone at midnight. He had told Enil to meet him at the Castle of an old Knight, called Abradan, which was by the place of battle, and there on the next day he found him. The old Knight received him well, for he always, hospitably welcomed all Errant Knights. Presently two Squires arrived, the nephews of the host, and said, that King Cildadan was landed, and had pitched his tents upon the sea-shore, and his Knights with him, and they were landing their horses and arms. Grumedan and Giontes had been to them on the part of King Lisuarte, and made truce till the day of battle, and also concluded that neither party should bring out more than the hundred Knights appointed. Nephews, said the host, what think you of those enemies whom God confound! Good Uncle, said they, we must not speak of them; they are so strong and terrible, that unless God miraculously assist our King, he and his power will be nothing against them. Herewithal, the tears fell from the old man's eyes, who cried, O Lord, do not forsake the best and justest King in the world! Good mine host, quoth Beltenebros, be not dismayed for their fierceness, for worth and modesty often overcome proud valour. I pray you go to the King for me, and tell him that there is in your house a Knight called Beltenebros, who requests to know the day of battle that he may be there. How, Sir, cried old Abradan, are you he who sent Don Quadragante to the King my Master, and who slew Famongomadan and his son! Now am I overpaid for all the services that ever I have rendered to Errant Knights. So taking his Nephews to guide him, he went to King Lisuarte, who was arrived within half a league of his enemies. Greatly was the King rejoiced with what he said, and he told him the battle should be on the next day, and said, there lacked him but one Knight of the hundred. Don Grumedan replied, you are rather above the number, for Beltenebros should be counted for five. When the old man returned with these tidings, Enil took his Master aside, and kneeling down, said, Albeit Sir my services have not merited it, yet your great goodness emboldens me to ask a boon, and I beseech you for God's sake to grant it me. Beltenebros raised him and said, ask any thing that I can do. Enil would have kissed his hand; Sir, I ask you to make me a Knight, and to entreat the King that I may be one of the hundred since one is wanting. Friend Enil, replied Beltenebros, let it not enter your heart to begin so perilously. I do not say this because I will not make thee a Knight, but to advise thee to undertake lighter adventures first. My good Master, quoth Enil, where can I adventure so well? if I come from the field alive it will always be to my praise and honour, and if I die it will be dying well, and my memory will be joined with all those good Knights who must perish there. But then an affectionate pity was felt at the heart of Beltenebros, and he said within himself, thou dost well show thyself to be of the lineage of Gandales, my excellent and true fosterer! Be it so! said he, and he asked the host to give the Squire arms; and Enil watched them that night, and after dawn they heard mass, and Beltenebros knighted him, and they departed, their host and his Nephews carrying their arms. They found Lisuarte putting his battle in order to go against the enemies, who were ready in the plain. The King and his Knights rejoiced to see Beltenebros. Sir, quoth he, I come to perform my promise, and I bring with me this Knight to supply the one lacking. The King joyfully welcomed him, and placed his Knight to make up the complement. Then they moved on in one battalion: the King was in the middle of the rank, before him Beltenebros and his companion were placed, and Galaor, Florestan, and Agrayes; Gandalac, the Giant who had fostered Galaor, and his two sons Bramandil, and Gavus whom Galaor had knighted; Nicoran, of the Perilous Bridge, Dragonis and Palomir, and Pinorante, Giontes, nephew to the King, the renowned Don Bruneo of Bonamar, and his brother Branfil, and Don Guilan the Pensive. All these were together, and before them went that honourable and good old Knight Don Grumedan, Brisena's fosterer, with the banner of the King.

King Cildadan on his side placed the Giants in the front of the battle, and twenty Knights of his lineage of great valour. He stationed Madanfabul, the Giant of the Isle of the Vermillion Tower, upon a little rising ground, and with him ten of the best Knights, and directed them not to move till they saw that all were weary, and that then they should make way fiercely towards King Lisuarte, to kill him or carry him prisoner to the ships. In this array the two parties approached with deliberate pace till they came near, and then they met with such a shock that many a man fell, and many a horse ran over the field without a rider. That was a hard and dolorous day for all who were there present! for striking and struggling they continued thus without rest or intermission a third part of the day, with such toil and effort, being in the mid heat of summer, that they and their horses were so wearied, and the wounded bled so fast, that in many life could endure no longer, and there they fell dead, especially those whom the Giants had wounded with their great force. In that hour Beltenebros did wonders in arms with that good sword, striking and slaying all before him, though the care with which he kept watch over the King most employed him; for Lisuarte knowing that the great shame, or great glory of the day would be his, thrust himself into the hottest press of the battle. Galaor and Florestan, and Agrayes kept by him, being emulous to equal Beltenebros that day, and Don Bruneo watched to assist Galaor, who, like a lion made among the Giants, to equal him whom he thought the rival of Amadis, regardless of their great strength, and those whom he saw fall under their blows. In this heat he came before Cartadaque, the Giant of the Defended Mountain, who with a heavy battle axe, notwithstanding Florestan had given him a deep wound in the shoulder, had already killed six Knights at his feet. Galaor made at him, and with his sword struck him upon the helmet; it cut away all it touched, and lopt off his ear, and passing downward cut the battle-axe helve from his hand. When the Giant saw his enemy so near, and that he had no weapon to wound him, he laid hold on him with his hands, and plucked him so forcibly that the saddle girth broke, and he fell, but still the Giant held him; and Galaor thought he never could escape from that mighty grasp, and that all his bones were broken. Yet before his senses were gone he recovered his sword that hung from his wrist by the chain, and thrust it through the vizor of Cartadaque's helmet; the Giant's gripe relaxed, and he fell dead. Galaor arose then, but so weak and exhausted, that he could not pluck his sword from the Giant's head. The Knights on both sides pressed towards him, some to kill him at this disadvantage, his own friends to his help. The battle became fiercer there than it had yet been; King Cildadan came up, and on the other part Beltenebros. Beltenebros twice smote Cildadan on the head such stunning blows that the King fell from his horse at the feet of Galaor. Galaor caught up the sword of Cildadan, and laid about him till his strength and senses were gone, and he fell upon the body of King Cildadan.

At this time the Giants Gandalac and Albadanzor were engaged; they smote each other so furiously with their clubs, that they and their horses both fell. Albadanzor's arm was broken, and Gandalac's leg; howbeit he and his sons slew their enemy. The day was now half over, and on the two sides an hundred and twenty Knights had been slain. Madanfabul, the Giant of the Vermillion Tower, was looking on from the hill; he saw how the field was thinned, that they who remained were weary with their toil, their armour broken, and their horses stiff and exhausted. He thought that he and his companions could now have discomfited all that were left on both sides, and descended into the field, crying out, Leave not a man of them alive; I will kill or take King Lisuarte. Beltenebros had just mounted a fresh horse, which one of old Abradan's nephews gave him; he saw the Giant and his troop come on, and placed himself before the King, and called on Florestan and Agrayes, who were near; with these Don Bruneo of Bonamar joined, and Branfil, and Guilan the Pensive, and Enil, who had done much in that battle, and was therefore always held in high esteem, all these albeit they were grievously wounded, and their horses also, placed themselves before the King. Before Madanfabul came a Knight called Sarmadan the Lion, the Uncle of King Cildadan, and for strength and prowess the best of his lineage. Beltenebros stood foremost to meet him. Sarmadan drove his lance at him, it broke, yet pierced the shield and wounded him, though with no deep wound. Then Beltenebros hit him a thwart blow with his sword across the bever, straight over both eyes, and through both, that he fell dead. But Madanfabul and his other comrades came on so fiercely, that the most of those who were of King Lisuarte's part were beaten down before them, and he made right for the King, with such fresh strength, that the Knights about the King, bravely as they adventured, could not protect him; he seized Lisuarte round the neck, and grasped him so strongly that he lost all power of resistance, plucked him from the saddle, and carried him towards the ships. When Beltenebros beheld that he exclaimed, O Lord God, let not Oriana have this affliction! He struck the spurs into his horse and galloped after him sword in hand, and reaching him smote at him with his whole force. The sword fell on the right arm with which he held the King, and cut it clean through by the elbow; the weapon stayed not there, but passing on cut through the King's breast-plate, and wounded him so that the blood streamed down. Lisuarte was left upon the ground, and the Giant fled like a lost man, bleeding to death. When Beltenebros saw that with that one blow he had slain that mighty Giant, and rescued King Lisuarte from so great a danger, he shouted out, Gaul! Gaul! for I am Amadis. This he cried as he laid on among his enemies, felling them or slaying them, and in good season did he exert this prowess, for great havock had been made among the Knights of his party, so many slain, others wounded, and fighting on foot, and the enemies had come fresh against them with great strength, and an eager desire to kill all they could. For this cause Amadis put forth his strength, so that it might well be said his great prowess was the safety and support of his party that day; but what most kindled him was, that he had seen his brother Galaor afoot and sore wearied, and looking again saw him no longer, so that surely he thought him dead, and with this grief and anger he encountered no Knight whom he did not slay. When they of King Cildadan's party saw the great feats that he atchieved, they took for their leader a Knight of the race of the Giants, whose name was Gadancuriel, and who had made such slaughter that day that he was noted by all. They expected, being led by him to win the day, and at this time Amadis had thrust in so far among the enemy that he was beset by them and in great peril. King Lisuarte had mounted again, and with him were Don Bruneo of Bonamar, and Florestan, and Guilan the Pensive, and Ladasin, and Galvanes Lackland, and Olivas, and old Grumedan, from whose hand the banner had been cut. The King seeing Amadis in such danger made up to succour him like a worthy King, although he had many wounds, and all rejoicing that Beltenebros was Amadis, forced their way up to him, and released him from the press. He then turned whither he would, and chance guided him to where his cousin Agrayes, and Palomir and Dragonis were on foot, and many Knights upon them striving to slay them, but they standing together, and still defending themselves manfully. He seeing them thus, called upon his brother Florestan, and Guilan the Pensive, to their succour. There came against him a Knight of great renown, called Vadamigar, whose helmet had been struck off; he wounded the horse of Amadis in the neck, but Amadis reached him, and cleft him down to the ears, and as he fell cried out. Cousin Agrayes, take this horse! And Florestan struck down a good Knight, called Daniel, and gave his horse to Palomir, and Palomir then won one for Dragonis; and Guilan wounded Landin sorely, and unhorsed him, and gave his horse to Branfil: thus they were all helped, and then they followed in the path of Amadis, who went on cutting his way manfully, and shouting Gaul! Gaul! Amadis! that the enemy might know he was in the field. Such courage did he then display, and so well did Florestan and Agrayes, and those other Knights second him, and King Lisuarte also played his part so well, that they won the battle; the enemies who survived flying to their ships, and Amadis still among them raging for the death of Galaor. But Gadancuriel still made head with those whom he could turn from flight, and he turned upon the King. Florestan, who had seen his feats that day, thrust himself before Lisuarte to save him, though he had only a broken sword. Gadancuriel cut through the helmet and wounded him in the head, he with his broken sword smote him on the helmet so that it fell off, and then Lisuarte cleft his head; there was none other left to maintain the field: they who fled perished before they could reach the water, or in the water before they could reach their ships.

Then Amadis cried to Florestan and Agrayes, weeping as he spake, Good kinsmen, I fear we have lost Don Galaor, let us seek for him. They went to the spot where Amadis had smitten down King Cildadan, and seen his brother last on foot; but so many were the dead who lay there that they saw him not, till as they moved away the bodies, Florestan knew him by the sleeve of his surcoat, which was of azure worked with silver flowers, and then they made great moan over him. But when Amadis saw him thus with exceeding grief he threw himself from his horse, and his wounds over which the blood had clotted burst open with the fall, and bled abundantly, and he laying aside his shield and helm that were all hacked and bruised, went to Galaor and took off his helmet, and took his head upon his knees. Galaor at the fresh air began to move a little, and they all gathered round him weeping to see him thus. While they were thus standing twelve Damsels richly apparelled came up, and some Squires with them, who brought a bed covered with rich drapery. The Damsels knelt before Amadis and said, Sir, we are come hither for Don Galaor, if you would have him live give him to us: if not, all the Masters in Great Britain cannot help him. Amadis knew not the Damsels, and he saw the great danger of Galaor, and could not tell what to do; but those Knights advised him to trust his brother to this fortune, rather than see him die without any possibility of saving him. Good Damsels, said Amadis, may I know whither you would carry him? They answered, not as yet; but if you desire his life give him to us; else we must go our way. Then Amadis besought that they would take him also; this they refused, but at his request they suffered Ardian the Dwarf, and his Squire to follow them. Then they laid him in the bed, armed as he was, all except his helmet and gauntlets, and half dead; and Amadis and the Knights followed them, weeping, to the shore.

A ship was ready there in which the Damsels placed him, and then returned and went to King Lisuarte, and besought him that he would be pleased to give them King Cildadan also, who lay among the dead, bidding him remember that he was a good King, and had suffered this evil in doing what he was bound to do: and they prayed the King to have pity upon him, that he might look for pity himself in his need. Lisuarte readily assented. They took up Cildadan more dead than alive, and carried him in the same bed on board, then made sail, and were speedily out of sight.

Meantime Lisuarte had secured the enemies fleet that nothing might escape, taking prisoners all who were not slain in battle. He now came up to Amadis, and the Knights that were weeping with him, and when he heard their lamentation was for the loss of Galaor, he was grieved at heart, for Galaor had faithfully and affectionately served him from the hour wherein he became his Knight; then he dismounted, his armour being all stained with blood, and embraced Amadis, and bade him take comfort, for God would not suffer such a man as his brother to perish. They all then went to the tent of King Cildadan, and there took food, and he ordered that all the Knights who had fallen on his side should be buried in a monastery that was at the foot of a near mountain, and he ordered the due service for their souls, and assigned rents for masses for them. Moreover he ordered a stately chapel to be built there, and rich monuments therein for them, and that their names should all be engraved upon their tombs. Messengers were sent to inform Queen Brisena of his good fortune, and he and his Knights then went to Ganota, a town four leagues off, and there they remained till their wounds were healed.

While this battle was expected Queen Briolania went to visit Oriana at Miraflores. Oriana had her apartments hung with rich hangings to receive a guest whom she so greatly desired to see. When they met both were somewhat abashed, for neither the proof of the Enchanted Arch, nor of the Green Sword, could keep Oriana's heart so calm, but that it beat fast with fear, thinking that no affection, how true soever, could resist such beauty as she saw before her. And Briolania, who had seen the tears and thoughtfulness of Amadis, and knew what proof of love he had given at the Firm Island, presently concluded it could be only for this Princess, before whom she felt her own beauty even as nothing. So as they were freely communing together, Briolania related at length all that Amadis had done for her, and said how in her heart she loved him. Oriana then willing to learn farther, asked her why, as they were of equal rank, and she at her own disposal, she did not make him master of herself and her own dominions? Friend and Lady, replied Briolania, much as you have seen him, I think you know him not. Do you not believe I should think myself the happiest woman in the world if this could be? But you shall know all—and keep it I pray you secret, as one like you should do. I ventured upon this proposal, and it shames me whenever I remember it, but he replied, that he could neither bear affection to me nor to any other; the which I then believed, for unlike all other Knights, I never heard him speak of woman. You tell me wonders, quoth Oriana, glad at heart of what she heard; but unless Amadis loved some one he could not have passed under the Arch of True Lovers, which yet showed him more honour than ever any other had received. He may love, replied Briolania, but in his love he is the most secret that ever yet Knight was.

Briolania remained ten days with Oriana, and then they both went to join Queen Brisena at Fenusa, a town, where she was waiting for Lisuarte. Greatly rejoiced was she to see her daughter so recovered. There the tidings came of the victory, for joy whereat Brisena gave great alms to the churches and convents, and to those who were in want. But who can tell what joy there was to hear that Beltenebros was Amadis! What think you now of Amadis, quoth Briolania to Oriana, who affected the same surprise as the rest; I was in doubt whether he or Beltenebros most deserved my love. Queen and Lady, replied Oriana, we will ask him when he comes, wherefore he changed his name, and who the Damsel is that won the garland of flowers.

CHAPTER 17.

Now you shall know what became of King Cildadan and Galaor. The Damsels who removed them dressed their wounds, and on the third day they recovered their senses. Galaor found himself in a rich room, which stood upon four marble pillars, and had an iron grating on all sides, through which he saw that he was in a garden, surrounded with a high wall, in which was only one little door covered with plates of iron. Astonished to find himself in such a place, he thought he was in prison, and felt such pain from his wounds that he expected nothing but death; and he remembered the battle, but knew not who had carried him from it, nor how he had been removed there. King Cildadan also, when he came to himself, saw that he was lying in a rich bed in the vaulted chamber of a large tower. He looked round and saw no one, neither door nor any entrance into the chamber, but over the arch he heard voices. There was a window near his bed from whence he looked out and saw the sea, and it seemed that the tower he was in was a high tower upon a rock, and that the sea washed it on three sides. He too remembered the battle but nothing more: but he well knew that if he was thus a prisoner, his friends could not be in better plight, and seeing no remedy, lay down again in bed, groaning and in great pain with his wounds.

Don Galaor, as he was lying in the open chamber, saw the little door of the garden wall open, and raised his head with great difficulty; there came in a Damsel very fair and richly apparalled, and with her a man so feeble and old that it was a wonder how he could walk, they came up to the iron grating, and said to him, Don Galaor, look to your soul, for we cannot warrant you. The Damsel then produced two little boxes, one of iron the other of silver, and showing them to Galaor, said, She who brought you here wills not that you should die till she knows whether you will perform her will; if so, your wounds shall be healed, and you shall have food. Good Damsel, replied he, if what she desire be any thing that I ought not to do, it will be worse than death. Do as you please, quoth she, we care little for your answer: it is at your own choice to live or die. The old man then opened the door of the grating, and they both went in, and she took the box of iron, and told the old man to withdraw, and then she said to Galaor, Sir, I have such compassion on you, that I will venture my own life to save yours. I have been ordered to fill this box with poison, and the other with an ointment to make you sleep; the poison being then rubbed into your wounds will act more instantly and you would presently die; but instead of this I have put here a remedy, the which, if you take it daily for seven days, will so heal you, that by that time you shall be wholly recovered, and able to ride on horseback as before. She then applied the ointment to his wounds, and the pain was instantly assuaged. Good Damsel, quoth he, you do so greatly bind me to your service, that if by your help I may escape from hence, never was Damsel so well guerdoned by Knight as you shall be: but if you have not means for this and yet wish to serve me, contrive that Urganda the Unknown may know in what perilous prison I am laid, for in her I have great hope. The Damsel then began to laugh—what hope can you have in Urganda, who cares little for your weal or woe? So much, replied Galaor, that as she knows the wishes of all, she knows how greatly it is my wish to serve her. The Damsel then answered, Look for no other Urganda than me, Don Galaor; and take you good hope, for it is the part of courage, not only to encounter danger, but to endure its after-chances for the danger in which I place myself to heal you, and deliver you from hence, I ask one boon, which shall be neither to your dishonour nor hurt. I grant, quoth he, all that may rightly be performed. Now then, said she, it is time to depart, lie you down, and feign to sleep soundly. He did accordingly; she called the old man and said, Look how he sleeps! Now the poison will work. So it ought, quoth the old man, that he who brought him here may be avenged. Since you have obeyed so well you may come alone for the future, and see that you keep him fifteen days, that he die not, but live in great agony, and by that time they will be here who shall make him atone for the wrongs he hath done them. When Galaor heard this he found that the old man was his mortal enemy, howbeit he took hope for what she had said to him. The old man and the Damsel then went out of the garden; presently she returned, and brought with her two little girls, fair girls and well apparelled, who took food for Galaor; and she let them into the chamber to keep him company, and gave them books of history to read to him, that he might not sleep by day, and then she fastened the door and left them.

King Cildadan in the tower saw also a door open in the wall, a stone door so neatly fitted that it looked like the wall itself, and a Dame of middle age entered with two armed Knights, and approached the bed without saluting him; he on his part spake to them with courteous salutation, but they answered not. The Dame took off the bed cloaths, and applied salves to his wounds, then gave him food, and they went out again and fastened the stone door, not having spoken a word. The King thought that verily he was in prison, and where his life was not secure; howbeit having no remedy, he took as good comfort as he could.

When it was time the Damsel returned to Galaor, and asked him how he fared? So well, quoth he, that if it proceed so I shall be in good plight by the time you promised. Doubt not, said she, that what I have said shall be accomplished. But you must promise me the boon as a loyal Knight, for only by my help can you escape; the attempt would be to your mortal danger and hurt, and you could not effect it at last. That Galaor promised, and he besought her to tell him her name. What, quoth she, Don Galaor, know you not my name? I am deceived in you! Time was that I did you a service, which it seems you little remember. They call me the Wise[261:A] among the wisest. With that she departed, and he remained thinking who she might be; and remembering the good sword which Urganda had given him when he was knighted by Amadis, he thought it should be her, but Urganda was old, and this was a Damsel. He looked for the two little girls and they were gone, but in their stead he saw his Squire Gasavel, and Ardian the Dwarf of Amadis, both sleeping. He joyfully called them, they awoke; and when they saw who was there ran weeping for joy to kiss his hand, and exclaimed, O good Sir! blessed be God who has brought us here to serve you! He asked them how they came there: they replied, they knew not; only that Amadis and Agrayes, and Florestan, had sent them with him. Amadis, quoth he, was he found at such a time? Sir, said they, know that Beltenebros is your own brother Amadis, and that by his prowess the battle was won. Thou tellest me great things, cried Galaor, and great pleasure have I therein, though he has not given me cause for pleasure in keeping himself so long concealed from me. Thus abode King Cildadan and Don Galaor: the one in that great Tower, the other in the Garden-chamber, where they were both healed of their hurts. Then Urganda made herself known to them, for they were in her power in her Undiscovered Island; and she told them that the fear wherein she had put them was to effect their cure more speedily, for in their perilous state it so behoved. And she sent two Damsels to attend them and compleat their recovery; they were her nieces and fair Damsels, being the daughters of King Falangris, who was brother to Lisuarte by Grimota, Urganda's sister; by him begotten when he was a young batchelor. The one was called Julianda, the other Solisa: and it so chanced that the one bore a son named Talanque, to Don Galaor, and the other a son to King Cildadan, who was called Maneli the discreet, who were both valiant and strong Knights, and in this state of great pleasure these two Knights remained till it pleased Urganda to set them at liberty, as you shall hear hereafter.

When Lisuarte and Amadis, and the other Knights were all whole of their wounds, he went to Fenusa, where the Queen then sojourned, and there was he received with such joy by her, and by Briolania and Oriana, and the other Dames and Damsels, as never welcomed man before. But the joyful greeting which Queen Briolania gave to Amadis, that can in no way be written; she taking him by the hand made him sit between her and Oriana, and she said to him, my Lord, the grief and sorrow which I felt when they told me you were lost I cannot relate to you. I came hither with an hundred Knights immediately that your brothers might order them whither they would in your search, and because this battle delayed their departure, I resolved to remain here till it was decided. Now then direct me what I shall do, and it shall be done. Good Lady mine, quoth Amadis, if you felt sorrow for my mishap, great reason had you: for there is no man in the world who hath a better will to obey you; but since you desire me to direct you, I would have you abide here ten days, and dispatch your business with the King; in that time we may know something of my brother Don Galaor, and there will be a battle which has been appointed between Don Florestan and Landin, after that I will conduct you to your kingdom, and from thence I must go to the Firm Island, where I have much to do. So let it be, replied Briolania, and I beseech you tell us the wonders which you found in that Island. He would have excused himself, but Oriana took his hand and said, You shall not leave us till you have told us something of them. Good Ladies, quoth Amadis, trust me, labour however I should, I could never relate all; but this I say, that that Forbidden Chamber is the most rich and beautifullest thing in the world, and if by one of you it is not atchieved, I believe none else will ever win it. Briolania, after a while of silence, answered, I do not esteem myself such a one as can accomplish that adventure, yet such as I am, if you will not impute it to folly, I will prove it. Lady, quoth Amadis, I hold it no folly to attempt that wherein all have failed for want of beauty, especially in you whom God hath gifted so bountifully therewith, rather I hold it honourable to desire to win a fame which may endure through long ages. At this was Oriana greatly displeased, and her countenance fell, so that Amadis, whose eyes never left her, understood her feelings, and repented him of what he had said, albeit that all his design had been to her greater praise, for having seen the likeness of Grimanesa he knew that Briolania, fair as she was, did not equal her beauty, and of his own Lady's success he nothing doubted. But Oriana feared that whatever was to be won by beauty Briolania could win, and having requested her if she succeeded to let her know all the wonders of the Chamber, she withdrew, and went to Mabilia and told her what had passed. This always is the case with your Cousin, said she, my poor heart thinks only of pleasing him, neither regarding God nor the anger of my parents, and he knowing his full power holds me at little price, and then the tears came and coursed down her fair cheeks. Mabilia answered, I marvel Lady what manner of heart is yours! you are no sooner out of one trouble than you seek another. What great wrong is this that my Cousin hath committed? If Apolidon left this Chamber to be proved by all, shall he forbid the proof to Briolania? Certes I believe that neither her beauty nor yours will avail to accomplish that which none in a hundred years for lack of beauty could effect. But this is his over-ruling destiny that hath made him forsake all his lineage for your service, and thus it is you reward him; you do not desire his life, and will therefore drive him to death. This will be his reward! and mine, for all the friendship I have borne you, will be to see the flower of all my family, him who so dearly loves me, perish before my eyes. This will I never remain to see: for my brother Agrayes, and Galvanes my Uncle, shall take me home to my own country! and with that she wept and exclaimed, God grant that this cruelty toward Amadis may be well requited to you, and this wrong you do his friends! but their loss, great though it be, will be less than yours, destroying him who for your sake has deserted them, to give himself wholly to you. When Mabilia spake thus Oriana's heart was so overcharged that she could not speak, till at last the tears came, and she cried, wretch that I am above all others! I came to you for relief and you increase my sorrow, suspecting that which was never in my heart! Let God never help me if ever I had such thought! but what distresses me is, lest another woman should accomplish that proof which would be to me worse than death, and this fear has made me think wrongly of him who perhaps had but good in his intention: but come—forgive me—and for the love you bear your Cousin advise me! And then with a sweet smile she embraced Mabilia, True friend and dearest, I promise you I will never speak of this to your Cousin, nor let him know that I have had such a thought, but say you to him what you think best. Mabilia answered, I will forgive you on one condition, that whatever anger you conceive against him you never discover it to him till you have first consulted me, that no evil like the past may happen again. With this were they well reconciled, between whom there could never be a want of love.

But Mabilia sharply reprehended Amadis, and warned him to be wary in his conduct to Briolania, remembering what he had suffered on her account, and how difficult it is to root out jealousy from a woman's heart. Amadis replied, Lady and good Cousin, my thoughts were very different. Briolania is held by all for one of the most beautiful women in the world, so they make no doubt she can enter the Forbidden Chamber, but I who have seen the likeness of Grimanesa know that it will not be so. That honour which any one hitherto has won, that certainly will Briolania win: but Oriana has only to try and to succeed. But if Oriana atchieves the adventure before Briolania has essayed it, all will say that the other would have won had she been first; on the contrary, when she will have failed, as sure I am she must fail, my Lady will have her full glory. Well was Oriana satisfied at hearing this, and greatly repented her of her fault, to atone for which they appointed that Amadis should come to her apartment, through an old water way that issued into a garden. Presently Oriana and Briolania called Amadis, and requested him to answer them truly what they should ask, the which he promised. Tell us then, said Oriana, who the Damsel was who won the garland when you gained the sword? Then was Amadis grieved at the question because he was bound to answer it truly. As God shall help me Lady, said he, I know no more of her name than you do, though I was seven days in her company; but this I can say, that she had beautiful locks, and as far as I could see was right fair. Thus was Oriana sporting with him, when there came a Damsel to summon him on the King's part, saying, that Don Quadragante and his nephew Landin were come to acquit themselves of their promises. Being all assembled Quadragante rose and said, I come to discharge a promise made to Amadis of Gaul; and he then related how they had done battle together, and added, that both by the event of that battle, and by reason he was bound to forgive him the death of King Abies, who had been slain in fair combat, and to receive him for a friend even in what degree it pleased him. Then Amadis embraced him and thanked him; and notwithstanding this friendship appeared a thing constrained, yet did it long and faithfully continue. And because Florestan and Landin were to fight upon the same quarrel, it was judged, that since Quadragante, who was principal in the cause had forgiven it, their dispute should cease; the which pleased Landin not a little, for he had witnessed the prowess of Florestan in the great battle.

King Lisuarte now called to mind the cruel prison of King Arban of North Wales, and Angriote of Estravaus, and determined to pass over to the Island of Mongaza to deliver them; this resolution he imparted to his Knights. Then Amadis answered, Sir, you know what loss to your service is the absence of Don Galaor; if it please you I and my brother and my cousins will go in search of him, and if it please God return with him by the time that you make this voyage. The King replied, God knows with what good will I myself would seek him, if so many things did not prevent me, since I cannot, do what you say. Then more than an hundred Knights arose, all good men in arms, and said that they would enter upon that quest, for in no worthier adventure could they be employed. Thereat was King Lisuarte well pleased, and he besought Amadis not to depart, for he would speak with him.

FOOTNOTES:

[261:A] Sabencia sobre sabencia.

CHAPTER 18.

After supper, it being almost the hour of sleep, as the King was in the gallery looking toward the sea, he saw two fires coming on through the water, whereat all were greatly astonished, marvelling how the fire and water could exist together. As they drew nearer, a galley was seen between the two fires, and on its mast there were great torches burning, so that the whole vessel seemed ablaze. The uproar was great, for all the people ran to the walls to see this wonder, expecting that if the water could not quench this fire nothing else could, and the city would surely be consumed; so they were greatly terrified. The Queen with all her Ladies went in their fear to the chapel, and the King mounted, and with his guard of fifty Knights rode down to the shore, and found there the most part of his Knights, and in the front of all Amadis, and Guilan the Pensive, and Enil, so near the fires that he wondered how they could endure them; then spurring his horse, whom the tumult had frightened, he rode up to them. Presently he saw come from under a cloth that covered the deck a Dame clad in white holding a golden casket in her hands, the which she opened and took out a lighted candle and threw it into the sea, where it was extinguished. At once the two great fires were quenched so that no trace of them remained, only the torches upon the mast remained burning, and cast a light along the shore. Then was the cloth which covered the galley withdrawn, and they saw how it was all hung with green boughs, and strewed with roses and flowers, and they heard instruments within sounding very sweetly; and when the instruments ceased, ten Damsels came forth, all richly garmented, with garlands on their heads and wands of gold in their hands, and before them was the Lady who had quenched the candle in the sea: and they coming to the galley's edge opposite to the King made obeisance to him, and he on his part returned the greeting. Then said Lisuarte, Dame, you have put us in great fear with your fires, if it please you tell me who you are, though I believe with little difficulty we can divine. Sir, quoth she, in vain should he labour who strove to strike fear into your great heart, and into these Knights in whom no fear is; these fires I bring to protect me and my Damsels: and if you think I am Urganda the Unknown, you think aright; I come to you as the best King in the world, and to behold the Queen, who for virtue and goodness hath no peer. Then said she to Amadis, Sir, draw nearer, and I will tell you of your brother Galaor to save you and your friends the labour of searching him; for though all in the world were to seek him it would be but labour lost: he is healed of his wounds, and leads a life of such pleasure as he never till now enjoyed. Lady, quoth Amadis, I always thought that next to God the safety of Don Galaor was in your hands, else would I rather have died than suffer him to be carried from me as he was. You shall soon see him, quoth she. The King then said, it is time that you should leave the galley and come to my palace. Many thanks, she answered, but this night I will remain here, to-morrow I will be at your command; then let Amadis and Agrayes, and Don Bruneo of Bonamar, and Don Guilan the Pensive come for me, for they are all lovers and of high heart, even as I am myself. Use your own pleasure, replied Lisuarte, in this and every thing; then ordering all the people to return into the town he took his leave, and appointed twenty cross-bowmen to keep guard that none should go down to the shore.

In the morning the Queen sent twelve palfreys richly accoutred for Urganda and her Damsels. Amadis and the other Knights whom she had named, being clothed in costly garments, went with them; they found Urganda and her company in a tent which she had pitched upon the sand, and they placed them on their palfreys, and went towards the town, the four Knights surrounding Urganda. Now, said she, is my heart glad, because I see those around me who are like myself, and this she said because of the love she bore to that fair Knight who was her friend. When they arrived at the palace the King welcomed her right courteously, and she kissed his hand; and looking round and beholding the Knights on every side how many they were, she said, Sir, you are well accompanied, and this I say, not so much for the valour of these Knights as for the love they bear you, for when princes are loved by their people then are their kingdoms safe. Therefore preserve their love, and beware of evil counsellors! Now if it please you I will see the Queen. So she and the four Knights went to Brisena, by whom and by Oriana, and Briolania, and all the Dames and Damsels, she was lovingly received. Much did she admire the beauty of Briolania, and saw that it fell far short of Oriana's perfection. Lady, quoth she, I came to this court to see the greatness of the King and you, the height of prowess and the flower of beauty, and the perfection of true love; for as valour was proved in the conquest of the Firm Island, and in the death of the giants, and in that dolorous battle with King Cildadan, so was true love in the proofs of the burning sword and of the garland. When Oriana heard her say this her colour changed, and she greatly feared, as did Mabilia and the Damsel of Denmark, fearing that Urganda should tell all; and Oriana looked at Amadis, but he seeing her apprehension drew near to her and said, fear nothing, she will not say what you imagine; and then he went to the Queen and said, Lady, ask Urganda who she was who won the garland, and the Queen replied, if it please you friend, tell us what Amadis desires to know! She smiled and answered, he better ought to know than I for he was in her company, and with great toil delivered her from Arcalaus and

Lindoraque. I? quoth Amadis; it cannot be that I should know either her or myself better than you know us, for from you nothing is concealed. Then, said she, I will tell you what you know of her, and raising her voice that all might hear her she pursued: Though Amadis brought her here as a Damsel she is certainly no Damsel: and because she loves so truly she won the garland. She is a native of this kingdom, and in this kingdom she dwells and hath here her heirship; but her mother is not of this land; and if she lacks any thing it is only because she cannot have him whom she loveth. He who would discover her must seek her in this kingdom, and he will lose his labour. She said no more, and Oriana's heart was then at rest. Then went they to their meal.

Urganda besought the Queen that she might be lodged with Oriana and Queen Briolania. That shall you, replied Brisena, but I believe their follies will disquiet you. Their beauty, quoth Urganda, will more disquiet the Knights, whose valour cannot protect them against that danger. They may easily, replied the Queen, be pardoned the deaths of all they have yet slain! So taking her leave Urganda went to Oriana's apartment, where there were four beds, one for Briolania, and one for Mabilia, and for Urganda and herself. When Urganda saw that they were all asleep except Oriana, she said to her, Lady and friend, if you do not sleep reason it is that he should keep you waking who has no rest but in your sight. Oriana was abashed at her words: but she added, fear nothing, I will not divulge your secrets. Speak low, cried Oriana, that they may not hear you. I will relieve you of that fear, quoth Urganda; therewithall she took forth a book which was so little that a hand might have shut over it, and began to read. Now, said she, do what you will they shall not awake, and if any one should enter the room she would fall down asleep. Oriana rose and went to awaken Briolania but she could not, and she laughed and took her by the head and hands and pulled her out of bed, and did the same to Mabilia, but they neither of them awakened; and then she called the Damsel of Denmark, who was just without the door, and she, so soon as she entered, fell upon the floor in a deep sleep. Then Oriana joyfully went into Urganda's bed and said, I beseech you, since you know what is to come, tell me what will happen to me! Urganda looked at her and smiled. Dear daughter, said she, do you think to escape it, if it be evil, by knowing it aforehand? Believe not so! for that which is permitted and ordained by the Most High none can alter, whether it be good or ill, unless he remedies it; but since you so greatly wish me to say something I will speak: look now, if when you have the knowledge you can profit by it! At that time, when great sorrow shall be present with you, and many shall because of you be greatly afflicted, the strong Lion with his beasts shall come forth, and with his loud roaring shall in such sort astonish those who have you in their keeping, that you shall be left in his strong talons. And the famous Lion shall throw from your head the lofty crown which shall no longer be yours, and the hungry Lion having your body in his power shall bear it into his den that his extreme famine may be slacked. Now daughter dear look how you act, for this must come to pass! Lady, quoth Oriana, I should have been better content if I had not enquired, for you have made me in great terror of this strange and cruel end. Lady and daughter fair, replied Urganda, seek not to know that which neither your prudence nor strength can avert. Of these dark things men often dread that for which they ought to be joyful. Meantime be you happy, for God has made you daughter of the best King and Queen in the world, and has gifted you with such beauty that it is ever spoken of as a wonder, and has made that Knight love you, who shines above all other in prowess, even as day above darkness. Now it is time to awaken these ladies; she then opened her book again, and read, and they recovered.

After some days Urganda besought the King to summon all his Knights, and the Queen to assemble her Dames and Damsels, that she might speak to them before her departure; accordingly they met together in a spacious hall that was richly furnished, and Urganda placed herself where all might hear her. Then she said to the King, Sir, since you have kept the letters which I sent to you and Don Galaor just after Beltenebros had won the sword, I beseech you let them be produced, that all here may know that I knew what was to come to pass. The letters were then read, and it was seen how all had been accomplished, whereat the Knights marvelled, and still more admired the courage of the King who, notwithstanding that fearful forewarning, had dared enter the battle. In like sort was it certainly known that by three strokes from Beltenebros the battle was won; the first when he felled King Cildadan at Galaor's feet, the second when he slew Sarmadan the Lion, the third when succouring the King he lopt off the arm of Madanfabul the fierce giant of the Vermilion Tower. That also was fulfilled which had been written of Don Galaor, that his head should be in the power of him who should strike the three strokes, for so it was when Amadis held it in his lap as dead. Now, said Urganda, I will tell what shall come to pass in process of time. Contention shall arise between the great Serpent and the strong Lion, in which many fierce beasts shall take part; anger and fury shall come upon them, so that many shall suffer cruel death. The great Roman Fox shall be wounded by the claw of the strong Lion, and his skin cruelly torn, whereby a part of the great Serpent shall be in great affliction. In that time the gentle Sheep covered with black wool shall come between them, who by his humble and loving blandishments shall assuage the fury of their hearts. But presently the Wolves shall come down from the mountains against the great Serpent, who being with all his animals by them conquered, shall be blocked up in one of his dens; and the tender Unicorn putting his mouth to the ear of the strong Lion shall rouse him from his sleep, and make him hasten to the succour of the great Serpent, whom he shall find so wounded and bitten that the blood shall flow over his scales, and he shall deliver him from the mouths of the Wolves, and they shall all be destroyed. Then the great Serpent having his life restored, and casting all his poison from his entrails shall consent that the white Doe shall be placed in the cruel talons of the Lion. Now good

King, let all this be written, for so it must be. The King said it should be done, albeit he understood it not. Time will come, she answered, when it shall be manifest to all. Then looking at Amadis, who was musing, she said, Amadis, you muse upon that which cannot avail you: let that be, and think of a bargain you have to make. At that time you shall be brought near to death for another's life, and for another's blood shall expend your own, and of that bargain the martyrdom will be yours, and another will have the gain; and the guerdon which you shall have will be wrath and the long delay of your will; then shall that keen and beautiful sword so pierce thy flesh and bones that you shall be poor of blood, and in such plight that if half the world were yours you would give it so that that sword were broken or thrown into some lake from whence it could never be recovered. Look to it! for so it must be. Amadis saw that all eyes were upon him, and he answered chearfully as he felt. Lady, by what you have said of the past we may believe this also, but I knowing that I am mortal, and that my life cannot be prolonged one minute longer than it pleaseth God, am desirous to end it justly in some great and honourable enterprize. It were as easy, quoth Urganda, to rob your heart of its courage as to drain the sea dry. Then said she to the King, Sir, I must depart; remember what I have said as one who desire your honour and would serve you,—shut your ears to those whose works you know to be evil! With that she departed, suffering none but the four Knights whom she had chosen to conduct her to the shore; then she embarked, and the ship put forth to sea, and was presently covered with a great darkness.

CHAPTER 19.

Some few days after, as King Lisuarte was consulting with his Knights about the passage which he would make to the Isle of Mongaza, to deliver King Arban of North Wales, and Angriote of Estravaus, they saw a ship making toward the port, and went thither to see whom it brought. When they came near a Damsel and two Squires were in the boat, and when they landed the Damsel asked if King Lisuarte were there? They answered yes, but they were all astonished at her greatness, for there was not a Knight in the court who equalled her by a full palm in stature, and her features and limbs were in proportion; she was fair enough, and richly attired. Sir, said she to Lisuarte, I bring you a message which, if it please you, I would deliver before the Queen. Be it so, said the King, and he returned to the palace, and the Damsel with him. Then being in presence of the Queen and of all the Knights and Ladies of the Court, she asked if Amadis of Gaul were there, he who had called himself Beltenebros. He answered, good Damsel I am he. She looked at him with an evil eye and said, you may well be he! but now it will be seen if you are as good as you are famous! Then she produced two letters with seals of gold; the one she gave the King, the other to the Queen; they were letters of credence, and the King bade her say her bidding.

Sir, quoth the Damsel, Gromadaza, the Giantess of the Boiling Lake, and the fair Madasima, and Ardan Canileo the Dreadful, who is with them for their defender, know that you design to come against their country, and as that cannot be attempted without great loss, they are willing to put it upon trial of a battle in this guise, that Ardan Canileo shall combat Amadis of Gaul. If he conquer or slay him the land shall be free, and he shall be allowed to carry his head to the Boiling Lake; if he be conquered or slain himself, the land shall be yours, and King Arban of North Wales, and Angriote of Estravaus shall be delivered. They shall be brought hither, and if Amadis loves them as they believe, and will fulfill the hope they have in him, he will accept the battle to deliver two such friends; if he be conquered, Ardan Canileo will still hold them prisoners, and if he will not accept the defiance he shall presently see their heads cut off before him. Good Damsel, quoth Amadis, if I accept the battle, how shall the King be certain that the terms will be accomplished? She answered, the fair Madasima, with twelve Damsels of great birth, will put themselves as prisoners in the Queen's power, in security that the terms shall be observed, otherwise they are content to lose their heads, and they demand no other assurance than that she may carry away your head if you be overcome; and moreover the old giant Andanguel and his two sons will enter the King's prisons, and nine Knights beside, who have the towns and castles of the Island in their keeping. Said Amadis, if this be done the security is sufficient; but from me you shall have no answer unless you and your Squires come and eat with me. Why do you invite us? quoth she; this is no wisdom, your trouble will all be lost, for I hate you to death. Good Damsel, said Amadis, I am sorry therefore, for I love you, and will show you all the honour that I can; if you desire to be answered you must grant this. I grant it, quoth she, more to get my answer than for any good will. Then said Amadis, good Damsel to venture myself for two such friends, and to increase the dominions of the King is a just thing, and therefore I undertake the battle in the name of God, let therefore those whom you have named come as hostages. Truly you have answered to my will, replied the Damsel; but let the King promise, that if you fail to perform your word he will never protect you against the kindred of Famongomadan. That promise, quoth Amadis, may be excused, the King would have no one in his company who lacked truth: now let us go eat, for it is time.—I will go, more joyfully than I expected; to-morrow Madasima and her Damsels will be here, and the Knights will put themselves in the King's hands, for Ardan Canileo would have the battle without delay; but you must give him a safe conduct from all but Amadis, whose head he will take from hence. Don Bruneo of Bonamar answered, Lady Damsel, sometimes it happens that he who thinks to take away anothers head loses his own, and so it may fall out to Ardan Canileo. Amadis besought him to be silent, but the Damsel replied to Bruneo, who are you who speak for Amadis? A Knight, quoth he, who would willingly bear a part in the battle if Ardan Canileo will bring a companion. She answered, you may be excused from that battle, but if you are desirous of combat, after that is finished I will produce a brother of mine to answer you, as much the mortal enemy of Amadis as you are his friend, and one who will prevent you from taking up the quarrel again. Good Damsel, quoth Don Bruneo, your brother had need be as you boast to perform all that you have promised! See, here is my gage that I defy him, and he stretched out the end of his cloak towards the King. The Damsel took a silver net from her head—here Sir, you see mine that I will make good my words. The King took the pledges, though against his will, for he thought the combat of Amadis against Ardan Canileo enough to trouble him, for that enemy was so dreadful that for four years he had found no Knight hardy enough to do battle against him.

This being settled Amadis took the Damsel to his lodgings, which he ought not to have done for the best castle in his father's lands; and to do her more honour he lodged her in the Chamber where Gandalin kept his arms and accoutrements. She looking round saw the sword of Amadis, and seeing how strange a one it was, she told her two Squires, and the others who were present, to leave her alone[288:A] for a little while; when they were gone she drew the sword, and leaving the sheath and belt so that the theft might not be discovered, she wrapt it under her mantle; then opening the door she gave it secretly to one of her Squires under his cloak, and bade him carry it to the vessel—this she spake softly; then spake aloud, go bring me my cup! and all present thought that the Squire was sent for that. Then Amadis and Branfil entered, and they made the Damsel be seated on the Estrado, and Amadis asked at what hour of the morrow Madasima would arrive.—Before breakfast: but why ask you?—Because we would go out to receive her and show her every honour, that if she have received any displeasure from me I may make her such amends as she shall demand. If you keep your promise, quoth she, and Ardan Canileo be what he always hath been in arms, you will give her your head for amends; any other amends will be good for little. That, said Amadis, I shall keep if I can; but if it could be I should gladly obtain her pardon. With that he went out, leaving Enil and others to attend her, but she was so desirous to be gone, that the number of dishes provoked her, and as soon as the cloths were removed she rose and said to Enil, Knight, tell Amadis that I am gone, and that all the pains he has taken to please me are lost. God save me, quoth Enil, as I believe it! and whoever should strive to please such a one as you would lose his pains. She answered, you please me little, and he still less! Enil replied, neither he nor I nor any one else can like so insolent a Damsel. With these words they parted.

The Damsel entered the ship glad for the sword which she had stolen, and she told Ardan Canileo and Madasima how she had sped. Ardan thanked her for what she had done, and he said to Madasima, my Lady, account me not for a Knight if I do not bring you back with honour; and if I give you not the head of Amadis in less time than a man can go half a league, how swift soever he be, never grant me your love. She answered him not, for albeit she greatly desired vengeance for the death of her father and her brother, yet for nothing in the world would she have seen herself married to Ardan Canileo, for she was fair and noble, and he foul and deformed and hideous, that there was none like him, and this agreement was made at her mother's will, not at her own, who had promised, if he would defend and revenge her, to give him Madasima and leave him all her lands. Now whereas this Ardan Canileo was a Knight famous in the world, and of great prowess, the history shall tell you of what land he was native, and the fashion of his body and face, and what else to him appertaineth. Know then that he was born in the province called Canileo, of the blood of the Giants, who abound there more than in other parts; he was not unreasonably great of body, albeit exceeding in stature any man who was not a giant; his limbs were large, and his breast broad, and his shoulders square, and his hands and legs proportioned; his face was large and flat and like a dog, wherefore he was called Canileo, and his nose was flat and spreading, and his colour purple freckled with black spots, which were all over his face and neck and hands; his look was fierce like a lion, and his lips were thick and curling out, and his hair so woolly that it could scarcely be combed, and the beard like it. He was now five and thirty years old, and for ten years past neither Knight nor Giant had been able to withstand him, and so bony was he that there was scarcely a horse could carry his weight. When the Insolent Damsel heard him promise the head of Amadis to Madasima, she said to him, we may well hope so Sir, since Fortune already shows herself adverse to your enemy. Here is his good sword which I bring you, which could not have been gained for you without great mystery of his ill fate, and your good fortune; then she gave it him and related how she had stolen it. He took it and replied, I thank thee for the gift, more for the good manner in which you took it than for any fear I have of a battle against a single Knight. Then he ordered tents to be taken from the ship, and pitched in a plain near the town, and there they all went with their horses and palfreys, and the arms of Ardan Canileo, expecting the next day to appear before King Lisuarte. Right joyful was Ardan that the combat was thus appointed, and for two reasons: the one because he made no doubt that he should carry off the head of Amadis, who being so famous all his glory would remain upon him, and the other because he should win the fair Madasima whom he loved so well.

Meantime Amadis was with his friends who greatly feared this combat, so dangerous did they esteem it. Presently Agrayes, and Don Florestan, and Galvanes Lackland, and Don Guilan the Pensive, came in, knowing nothing of what had past, for they had been hunting in the forest; but when they heard how the combat had been appointed, they complained that it had not been fixed for a greater number of Knights, that they might have entered it, and he who most passionately lamented this was Don Guilan who had heard how Ardan Canileo was the strongest of any Knight in arms, and the most powerful, and it grieved him to death, for he thought that Amadis would never escape with life from him, fighting him man to man in lists, and he greatly wished to share his fortune if Ardan had brought a companion. Don Florestan too exclaimed in great anger, as God shall save me, brother, you think me of no account as a Knight, or you do not love me, since you did not remember me on such an occasion! you make me perceive that it is bootless to accompany you longer, for you always withhold me from such perils. Agrayes also and Don Galvanes complained in the like manner. Sirs, quoth Amadis, you blame me with little cause; the combat was demanded of me alone, so that without showing cowardice I could not otherwise have answered; else, if I might have had assistance whom else should I have looked to but you, whose great valour might have aided mine in danger. Thus having excused himself he said, it will be well that we ride forward to-morrow before the King goes forth, to meet Madasima, who is greatly esteemed by all who know her.

In the morning they apparalled themselves richly, and having heard mass mounted on palfreys and rode to receive Madasima. Don Bruneo of Bonamar went with them and his brother Branfil, and Enil, who was a goodly Knight and of great worth, and of chearful heart, so that he was beloved and esteemed by all, so they were eight companions. And as they drew nigh the tents they saw Madasima coming, and Ardan Canileo and their company. Madasima was arrayed in black, mourning for her father and brother, but her beauty was so lively and excellent that it was a marvel, and her Damsels went near her all drest in the same cloth. Ardan Canileo led her bridle, and there came the old Giant and his sons, and the nine Knights who were to be hostages. As they drew near to each other the Knights made their obeisance, and she in like manner bowed to them with good semblance; then Amadis approached her and said, Lady, if you are praised it is with great reason I see, and happy ought he to be esteemed who is allowed to honour and serve you; that would I willingly do in what it might please you to command me. Ardan Canileo, who looked at him and saw how handsome he was, so that he had seen none like him, was nothing pleased at this. Knight, quoth he, give back, and dare not speak to one whom you know not. It is that we may know her and serve her, replied Amadis, that we are come. And who are you? cried Ardan scornfully; let me know if you are worthy to serve her? Such as I am, quoth Amadis, I have the will to serve her, and shall not cease to have that will, however unworthy I may be, and since you ask who I am, tell me who are you?—I am Ardan Canileo, who can better serve her in a day than you can in your whole life, though you were of twice your worth.—That may well be: but your great service would not proceed from so good a heart as my trifling one, this is plain from your pride and evil mind. Know that I am Amadis of Gaul of whom you have demanded battle. If I have offended and grieved that Lady by doing that which without great shame I could not have left undone, right willingly would I atone for it by some good service. Ardan Canileo answered, if you dare perform your promise, certainly she shall receive atonement with your head which I will give her. That amends, quoth Amadis, she shall not have with my good pleasure, but she shall receive a greater; for I will break off your marriage. No man can so lack judgment as to hold it good that your beauty and hers should be united! At this Madasima being nothing displeased, laughed a little, and her Damsels likewise, but Ardan became so wroth that his whole body shook, and his face became so exceeding terrible, that many thought Amadis was nothing in comparison with him, and that this would without doubt be his last battle, and the last day of his life.

Thus they proceeded till they came before the King, to whom Ardan Canileo said, you see here the Knights ready to become your hostages, if Amadis dare keep his word. Then Amadis came forth and answered, you see me here: let the battle be without delay, and I tell you that though I had not promised it, I would undertake it now solely to save Madasima from so monstrous a marriage; but let King Arban of North Wales, and Angriote of Estravaus be brought here, that they may be delivered if I conquer. They shall come, replied Ardan, but let Madasima be where she may see the combat and the vengeance which I shall take for her. So the old Giant and his sons, and the nine Knights put themselves in the King's power, and Madasima and the Damsels went to the Queen, and so meekly and decorously did Madasima demean herself, that albeit by her means Amadis was brought into this great danger, yet were they greatly pleased with her, and did her all honour. But Oriana and Mabilia seeing the fierceness of Ardan Canileo were greatly affrighted and retired in great fear and weeping to their chamber, for they thought the strength of Amadis was not enough to resist that Devil: yet did they remember his good fortune, how often it had brought him off with honour, and Mabilia comforted her friend the best she could. The following day was appointed for the battle; King Lisuarte ordered his huntsmen and bowyers to surround the lists with chains and stakes, that neither Knight might lose honour by the fault of his horse. The lists were before the palace, and when Oriana saw them preparing them from her window, the thought of how great a danger was there designed for her Amadis so overpowered her, that she fell almost senseless in Mabilia's arms.

Lisuarte went to the lodging of Amadis where many Knights were with him, and said to him, that as the Queen and his daughter, and Queen Briolania and the other Dames and Damsels would pass that night in the chapel, beseeching God to preserve their Knight, he would have him return in his company to the palace, and with him Florestan and Agrayes, and Don Galvanes, and Guilan and Enil, and that there they should regale themselves, and he desired Amadis to send his armour to the chapel, that he might arm himself to-morrow before the Virgin Mary, that so she and her glorious son might be his protectors. They went therefore with the King, and Amadis ordered Gandalin to carry his arms thither as Lisuarte had advised. But he taking them in obedience missed the sword from the scabbard, whereat so amazed was he and exceeding sorrowful that he wished himself dead, not only because the loss fell out at a time of such danger, but because he held it as a sign that his Master's death was nigh at hand. He sought for it every where, and enquired of all who might know any thing; but when he could learn no tidings he was on the point of throwing himself from a window, if the thought had not come upon him that in that case he should destroy his soul; forthwith in trouble of heart he went to the palace, and calling Amadis apart said to him, Cut off my head Sir, for I am a traitor to you; and if you do not kill me I must slay myself. How now? quoth Amadis: are you mad? or what mishap is this? Better Sir, he said, that I were mad or dead than that such a mishap should have befallen. I have lost your sword, it has been stolen from the scabbard. Is it for this you are so distressed? replied Amadis, I thought something worse had chanced; trouble yourself no more, there will be no want of another wherewith God will assist me, if it be his good pleasure. But though he spake thus to comfort Gandalin, yet was he grieved at heart for the loss of that sword, as well for the lack of it now in such need, being one of the best in the world, as because he had won it by the force of his true love, and it was a comfort to him to look at it, and remember that when he was absent from his Lady. Howbeit he bade Gandalin say nothing thereof to any person, but bring him the scabbard, and he bade him learn of the Queen if he could have the sword which Don Guilan had brought there together with his own arms; and if he could see Oriana he made him request her in his name that she would be somewhere where he might see her when he was in the lists, for the sight of her would make him become conqueror in that or in a worse danger. Gandalin went to perform his bidding, and the Queen commanded the sword should be given him; but Briolania and Olinda said to him, Ah Gandalin, what think you can your Master do against that Devil? he answered smiling, and with a chearful countenance, Ladies, this is not the first perilous enterprise which he hath undertaken, and as God as hitherto preserved him so he will now. God grant it, cried they. Then went he to Mabilia and told her what his Master requested of Oriana, and then returned to Amadis, and said that all things were done as he desired, whereat he had great pleasure and took more courage, knowing that his Lady would be where he might see her from the lists. Amadis then took the King aside, and said to him, Sir, I have lost my sword, and knew it not till now; they have stolen it and left the sheath. The King was grieved thereat and answered him, although I had determined and promised never to give my sword to any Knight who was to fight man to man before me, yet will I now give it you, remembering how many dangers you have encountered for my sake. God forbid, quoth Amadis, that I who ought to maintain your royal word should make you break it, and that too when you have pledged it before so many good men. The tears came into Lisuarte's eyes, and he said, such a man are you for maintaining justice and right! but what will you do?—I have here the sword which was laid in the Ark with me, which Don Guilan brought hither, herewith and with your prayers to the Lord which will avail before him, I may be assisted. Then he placed the sword in the sheath, which became it well, although the sword was somewhat short, and the King was glad he took the sheath because of its virtue, which would protect him from exceeding heat or cold, for the bones of the serpents whereof it was made were of such a constellation; but of very different goodness was this sword from the other.

Thus they passed that day till it was the hour of sleep, and then all those Knights had their arms around the King's bed. But all that night Ardan Canileo had merry-making in his tents, with music and dancing, and ever at the end of his songs his people all cried out, come Morning, come! and let the day be clear, that Ardan Canileo may perform what he has promised to the fair Madasima! but it fell out otherwise than they expected. That night Amadis slept in the King's chamber, but the sleep which he slept was of no avail, for presently at midnight he rose without speaking, and went to the chapel, and having awakened the chaplain confessed all his sins to him, and there they both were before the altar of the Virgin Mary making prayers, and beseeching her to be his patroness in this battle. When it was dawn the King and those other Knights arose, and heard mass, and Amadis was armed by such Knights as well knew how to do it; but before his breast-plate was put on Mabilia came up and hung round his neck certain reliques shrined with gold, saying, that the Queen her mother had sent them to her by the Damsel of Denmark; but it was not so, for Elisena had given them to Amadis when she knew him for her son, and he gave them to Oriana when he delivered her from Arcalaus. When he was armed they brought him a goodly horse, which Corisanda had sent with other presents to her friend Florestan. Florestan carried his lance, and Don Guilan his shield, and Don Bruneo his helmet, and the King went before on a great horse, holding a wand in his hand. All the people of the court and town were assembled about the lists to see the battle, and the Dames and Damsels were at the windows, and the fair Oriana and Mabilia were at their chamber window, and with the Queen were Briolania and Madasima, and other princesses. As Amadis came up to the lists they loosened one of the chains and he entered and took his arms, and as he put on his helmet he looked at his Lady, and felt therewith such strength as though no one in the world could withstand him. Then the Judges entered the field, who were to assign to each his right; they were three in number, that good old man Don Grumedan, who was well skilled in such things, and Don Quadragante, who was now the King's vassal, and Brandoyuas; then came Ardan Canileo well armed, and upon a great horse: his harness was of thick mail, and his shield and helmet were of steel, so polished that it was bright like looking-glass; and he had girded at his side the good sword of Amadis, which the Damsel had stolen, and he bent his huge lance as if he would have broken it, and thus he entered the lists. When Oriana saw him, she said in great agony, ah my friend, how fierce and terribly my death approaches, unless God in his mercy prevent it. Leave this, quoth Mabilia, and make good chear, for so shall you encourage your friend.

Then Don Grumedan led Amadis to one end of the lists, and Brandoyuas placed Ardan Canileo at the other, with their horses heads fronting each other; and Quadragante at an equal distance between them held a trumpet in his hand to sound the signal. Amadis, who was looking at his Lady, exclaimed, What is Quadragante about that he does not blow the trumpet? Quadragante then blew the blast, and the two Knights ran full speed, and encountered lance against shield so fiercely that the lances shivered, and they hurtled with such force that the horse of Ardan Canileo fell and broke his neck and died, and the horse of Amadis broke his shoulder and could not rise. Amadis presently arose, though with some difficulty, for a truncheon of the lance was sticking in his shield, and through the lappets of his armour, though it had not reached the flesh; he plucked it out, and laid hand to sword and made at Ardan, who had risen hardly and was adjusting his helmet. But Ardan seeing his approach drew his sword, and they joined battle so furiously that there was not a man who saw them but was greatly amazed, for their strokes fell so fierce and so fast that flames of fire seemed to proceed from their helmets and swords as if they burnt, and chiefly from the shield of Ardan Canileo, for that being of steel, and the blows of Amadis so rapid and heavy, it appeared as if the whole shield and arm were in a blaze of fire, but the great hardness of the shield protected him and saved his body, which was to the mortal evil of Amadis; for as his arms were not so good, and as Ardan had one of the best swords in the world, never blow reached him that did not pierce through and reach his flesh, so that in many parts the blood ran down, and his shield was all hacked. The sword of Amadis could make no impression upon the shield and helmet of his enemy, and though his own harness was of thick and strong mail, it was pierced in more than ten places, and the blood streamed from them all. What then most profited Amadis was his activity, for by that he made Ardan miss all his heaviest blows, though Ardan was well practised and expert with the sword. Thus they continued till the hour of tierce, striking and foyning, and grappling and struggling so manfully that Ardan Canileo was in great amazement, for he had never before found Knight nor Giant so strong as to resist him thus much; and what made him doubt the issue was, that he always found his antagonist more active and stronger than at the beginning, whereas he himself waxed weary and faint, being full of blood. Then Madasima knew that he had boasted vainly when he promised to conquer Amadis before the swiftest footman could run half a league, whereat she was little grieved, nor would she though Ardan were to lose his own head there, for such was her mind, that she would rather lose all her lands than be joined in marriage with such as he. The Knights still continued in battle, striking at each other in every part where they could work most harm, each striving for the other's death; and if Amadis had then had arms good as his own activity and breath, Ardan could not have held the field against him, but all his efforts were now needed, for his arms were broken, and his shield broken, and the blood flowing from many wounds, and he had to deal with a Knight fierce and strong in battle. When Oriana saw him in such plight her heart failed her for sore anguish, and she threw herself upon the ground, and beat her face, thinking that Amadis was come to his death. Mabilia seeing this, notwithstanding her own exceeding trouble, put on an appearance of much anger, and told her that at such a time and in such danger she ought not to forsake her lover, and because she could not endure to see his danger, Mabilia made her stand with her back to the window that Amadis might see her long hair. At this time Brandoyuas, who was one of the Judges, said, I am grieved to see the arms and shield of Amadis so battered! and I, quoth Grumedan, I am much troubled. Sirs, said Quadragante, I have proved Amadis in combat, and his strength seems to double while he fights, and of all Knights whom I have seen he endures the best, and is the best breathed; he is now in his full strength, which is not the case with Ardan, if any fault be in Amadis it is that he is too eager: he should suffer his enemy to press on him, and then his own weight would weary Ardan. But his great courage will not let him thus spare himself. When Oriana and Mabilia heard these words they were greatly comforted; but Amadis, who had seen his Lady retire from the window, knew that it was for sorrow at beholding him, and he made a blow at Ardan with exceeding fury, and smote him so rudely upon the helmet that he brought him down upon one knee, but that blow was so mighty, and the helmet so hard, that the sword broke in three pieces, and a piece only remained in his hand. Then was Amadis in all fear of death, and they who beheld him expected his death also. When Ardan saw this he rose and drew back, and took his shield by the straps, and brandishing his sword cried aloud to Amadis, Look! here is the good sword which thou hast won to thy own destruction. Look at it! this is it, and thou shalt die by it. Come, Lady Madasima! come to the window, and you shall behold the full vengeance which I will give you! When Madasima heard this she fell at the Queen's feet, and besought her to protect her from Ardan, which, said she, you may lawfully do, for Ardan promised to win the battle before a man could run half a league, and it has now lasted four hours. I hear you, replied Brisena, and will do what is just. But when Amadis saw in what plight he stood, his arms in pieces and without a sword, he remembered the words of Urganda when she told him that he would give half the world if it were his, so that that sword were sunk in a lake; and he looked toward Oriana's window, and seeing her back towards him, knew why she had turned away, and his courage revived so that he resolved to die rather than fail to do his utmost. He made at Ardan Canileo as if he were about to strike him; Ardan raised his sword and awaited him, and struck at him as he came up, but Amadis bent aside and closed with him so close that Ardan could not interpose his sword, and he seized the shield by the rim, and plucked it with such force that he tore it from his arm and well nigh brought him to the ground, then he drew back, and put that shield upon his own arm, and took up the truncheon of a lance which had its point, and again turned to Ardan, being now defended by Ardan's shield. Ardan in great fury for this loss ran at him thinking to smite him on the helmet; Amadis caught the blow upon his shield, and though it was of fine steel, such was the temper of that good sword that it pierced through the rim and entered three fingers' depth, and with the broken lance Amadis wounded him in the right arm by the wrist, thrusting the iron half through between the two bones, therewith Ardan lost all power to pluck the sword out, and Amadis forced it from his hand; if he was then right glad and satisfied need neither be asked nor said; he cast away the broken lance, and drew the sword from the shield, thanking God for his mercy. Mabilia, who beheld, caught hold of Oriana and made her turn and see her lover obtain this victory over so imminent a danger. Ardan Canileo grew faint as he beheld his death at hand, howbeit he attempted to recover the shield in the like manner as he had lost it, but Amadis smote him upon the left shoulder, and cut through armour, and flesh and bone. Ardan felt the use of his arm was gone, and he fled round the lists, fearing that good sword. Amadis followed close and caught him by the helmet, and plucked it off, and brought him to the ground at his feet, then knelt upon him and cut off his head, to the great joy of all, especially of King Arban of North Wales, and Angriote, who had endured great agony while they witnessed the danger of Amadis. Then Amadis cast the head out of the lists, and he dragged the body to a rock and threw it into the sea, then he wiped the blood from his sword and placed it in its sheath.

The King sent him a horse, on which he rode well accompanied to his lodging, but he was sore wounded and had lost much blood. With him he took King Arban and Angriote, whom he had delivered from their cruel chains. Brisena sent for her nephew Arban, and Angriote remained in the chamber of his true friend Amadis, and there were they both healed; and they were lovingly visited there by many Knights and Dames and Damsels of the court, and his cousin Mabilia came to Amadis, and brought with her that true medicine wherewith his heart could heal all lesser evils.

FOOTNOTES:

[288:A] Y pensando que alguna cosa de las naturales que no se pueden escusar hazer queria, dexaron la sola.

CHAPTER 20.

On the day after the battle Don Bruneo of Bonamar appeared before the King, and there he found the Insolent Damsel, who said that her brother was ready to do combat with him, and take that poor vengeance for Ardan Canileo. Forthwith they armed and went to the field, Don Bruneo accompanied by many good Knights, and Madaman the Envious, for so he was called, by them who bore his arms. At the first encounter Madaman was thrown and Bruneo slightly hurt in the breast; he kept his seat, but when he turned the reins Madaman cried out to him, sword in hand, Don Bruneo, if you would not lose your horse, alight or let me mount. Take your own choice, quoth Bruneo. Alight then, said Madaman, for being of huge stature he thought to have the advantage afoot; then began a brave battle, and while they were thus engaged there happened a strange thing, whereby it was manifested that beasts know their masters, for the horses being loose in the field attacked each other, fighting with their feet and teeth so furiously that all were amazed thereat, and this lasted till Madaman's horse being no longer able to hold out ran away, and in his fear leaped over the barriers, the which, all they who wished for the victory of Bruneo, held as a good sign; and turning their eyes now to the two combatants they saw how Don Bruneo prest upon the enemy hard, so that Madaman drew back and said, Why do you fatigue yourself? is not the day long enough? Hold awhile and let us rest; look at your arms and the blood which you have lost, and you will find it needful. Madaman, quoth he, if our combat were of another nature you should find in me all courtesy, but for this pride and hatred I will not suffer thee to rest, and show thy own faint-heartedness, lest my own fame should be lessened; with that he prest upon him and foyned so fast at him, that Madaman had enough to do to defend himself from the blows; and he thinking he might protect himself better among the rocks drew back towards the cliff, and there he stood upon the edge, being affrighted at the depth, till Bruneo came up, and with his shield and hand thrust him over, so that he was all shattered before he reached the water; then Bruneo knelt and returned thanks to God.

But when Matalesa the Insolent Damsel beheld the fall of her brother, she ran furiously to the cliff and looked over, and seeing the bloody fragments floating on the waves, she caught up his sword which he had dropt and cried,

Here, where the blood of my Uncle Ardan Canileo and my brother has been shed, shall mine be shed also, that my soul may be with theirs; and she ran herself through, and fell backward into the sea. Don Bruneo then rode to the lodging of Amadis, and his bed was placed by the beds of Amadis and Angriote, and there were they all healed, and during their confinement the Knights and Ladies of the court often went there to amuse them.

Now Briolania perceiving that the malady of her love increased, with the advice of Amadis departed for her own kingdom; but she determined first to see the wonders of the Firm Island, and prove the Forbidden Chamber. So she took Enil with her, and promised to tell Oriana all that she should see there, as shall be related hereafter.

As this history now proceeds you will see the little power of human wisdom when it pleases God to leave man to himself. You have heard how King Lisuarte being a prince, and possessing nothing but his arms and his horse, and going about with only a few servants seeking adventures, came to Denmark, where Brisena, the King's daughter, preferred him to all her many suitors, and chose him for her husband; this was his first good fortune. But ere long his brother died, and he became King of Great Britain, and subdued other Kingdoms, and the sons of Kings, and Princes, and Dukes, abode in his court, so that his name was famous above all Emperors and Kings in the world. Now there were two Knights in his court who had served his brother King Falangris, and for this, and because of their age more than for their goodness, they were of Lisuarte's counsel: the one was named Brocadan, the other Gandandel. This Gandandel had two sons who were thought passing good Knights in arms, before Amadis and those of his lineage arrived there, whose exceeding worth and courage had now made them be forgotten. On this account Gandandel neither fearing God nor regarding his duty to the King, nor the good deeds done by Amadis to himself, devised in his evil heart a foul treason. He led the King apart and said to him, Sir, I have long forborne to speak to you upon this matter, hoping some other remedy might be devised, and therein have I greatly sinned against you; but I should sin both against you and God if I were longer to keep silence, and I have been always careful to preserve my soul and honour, and do evil to no one, so that my judgment is free from all passion. You know Sir what great quarrels have subsisted between the kingdoms of Gaul and Great Britain, because that country ought to be subject to this as all the other neighbouring countries are, and this is an evil which will never be thoroughly healed till it be so. But now Amadis, who is not only a native of Gaul, but the chief person of his lineage, is come hither with his kinsmen, and has acquired such power that the kingdom is in his hand, as if he were right heir thereto. True it is that from him and his friends I have never received any wrong, but great honour and pleasure; but you are my natural Lord, and I must discharge my duty lest I fall into a wretched plight in this world, and my soul be cast into hell in the other. The King without any seeming alteration answered him, These

Knights have already served me well to my honour and profit, so that I cannot think of them otherwise than well. Sir, quoth Gandandel, that is the worst sign, for if they did any thing against your service you would be upon your guard against them, but the treachery is concealed under their good services. Thus have you heard all the talk, for the King answered nothing farther. But Gandandel took counsel with his cousin Brocadan, whose evil mind was like his own, and they two both working upon the King to the same effect wrought in him a great change against those who had done him such services, so that he seemed to have forgotten how Galaor rescued him from the ten Knights of Arcalaus, and Amadis from the arms of Madanfabul, although in both cases they saved his life and his [315:A]kingdoms.

So much was Lisuarte moved thereby that he now began to hate Amadis and his friends, and he left off visiting Amadis where he lay wounded, and would pass by his lodging without asking how he fared. All who saw this novelty marvelled much thereat, and they sometimes talked concerning it before Amadis, but he knowing his own true meaning would not believe but that the King also was like himself, and that business occupied him, and this he said to his friends, and particularly to Angriote of Estravaus, who was the most troubled. While things were in this state King Lisuarte sent for Madasima and her Damsels, and the old Giant and his sons, and the nine Knights whom he held as hostages, and he told them that if they did not forthwith cause the Island of Mongaza to be given up to him, according to terms, he would have their heads cut off; which, when Madasima heard, the tears came abundantly, and not knowing what to reply her flesh all shook with exceeding fear. But Andaguel the old Giant replied, that if he would send him with a certain force he would cause the Island to be surrendered to him, or else return again. The King therefore dismissed him with this force, and Madasima returned to prison, accompanied by many Knights, among whom was Don Galvanes Lackland; he beholding the tears on that fair face was moved to exceeding pity, and yielded up that liberty which he had before preserved, and without delay speaking apart to her, he opened his heart and said, that if it pleased her to marry him he would so deal that both her life and lands should be safe. Madasima, who well knew his great worth, and of what lineage he was, was nothing averse; then Galvanes knelt down and kissed her hand, and it was not long before he acquainted Amadis and Agrayes of his love, and besought them to enable him to perform what he had promised as they regarded his life. They marvelling at this sudden change told him that, considering his good services to King Lisuarte, what he required was a little thing, especially as the Lordship of the Island would remain to the King, and Amadis promised, as soon as he could ride, to request the boon for him.

Meantime Gandandel often went to visit Amadis with semblance of great regard, and always spoke to him of the King as being changed, and warned him to beware of him lest some evil should happen, which, said the old traitor, would be a great grief to me, because of the many favours I and my sons have received at your hands; but never could he kindle any wrath or suspicion in the mind of Amadis, though he persisted so that Amadis grew angry at him, and told him to say no more, for if all in the world were to tell him so he never would believe that so wise and good a King could be moved against one, who sleeping and waking had no thought of any thing but his service. After some days, when the three Knights were healed of their wounds, they rode out one morning being richly apparelled, and after hearing mass went to the palace, where they were right welcomed by all except by the King, who neither looked at them nor received them as he was wont. Amadis did not conceive that this proceeded from any ill will, but that traitor Gandandel came up to him, and embracing him, said with a smile, people are sometimes not believed when they tell the truth. Amadis made him no answer, and he seeing how Angriote and Don Bruneo were offended that Lisuarte did not notice them, went up to the King and said, so that no one could hear him, Do you not see Sir how those Knights look towards you? Lisuarte did not reply, and Amadis then, who suspected no evil, came up with Galvanes and Agrayes and said courteously, Sir, if it please you we would speak with you, and let whom you will be present; the King said, Gandandel and Brocadan; thereat was Amadis well pleased, for he believed them to be his true friends. Then they went together into a garden, where the King seated himself under a tree, and they round about him, and Amadis said, Sir, it has not been my fortune to serve you according to my good will, yet though I may not have deserved it, relying upon your virtue and great nobleness, I venture to ask a boon, which shall be to your service, and wherein you shall show great courtesy and do what is right. Certes, said Gandandel, if it be as you say you ask a fair boon, but let the King know what you would have. Sir, replied Amadis, what I and Agrayes and Galvanes, who have served you also, now request, is the Island of Mongaza, that reserving to yourself the Lordship you would give it with Madasima in marriage to Don Galvanes, wherein you will show favour to him who is of such lineage and hath no lands, and will gain a good vassal for yourself, and also deal courteously with Madasima, who by us hath been disherited. Gandandel and Brocadan hearing this looked at the King, and made signs to him that he should not grant it; but he remained silent for awhile, calling to mind the great worth of Galvanes, and the services which he had received from him, and how Amadis had won that Island with the extreme peril of his life, and knowing also that what they asked was a reasonable and becoming thing, and just. But because his will was perverted he answered as one who had no inclination to consent, He is not wise who asks for what he cannot have. I say this with respect to you, for you ask that which five days ago I promised the Queen for her daughter Leonoreta; this answer he made to excuse himself, not because it was true. At this Gandandel and Brocadan were well pleased, and made signs to him that he had said well, but Agrayes, whose heart was warm, when he heard with how little courtesy the King had refused them would not keep silence. You make us feel Sir, quoth he, that our services will profit us little here; if my advice be taken, our lives shall be differently employed. Nephew, exclaimed Galvanes, services are worth little when they are done to those who know not how to reward them: men should look where they bestow them. Sirs, quoth Amadis, do not complain that the King cannot give you what he hath already promised to another. I will ask the King to give you Madasima and let him keep the land, and I will give you the Firm Island till the King shall have something else to bestow upon you. The King answered, Madasima is in my prison in hostage for her lands, and if they be not surrendered I will have her head cut off. Then Amadis replied, of a truth Sir you should have answered us more courteously, and you would not have committed this wrong if you had known us better. If I do not know you, said Lisuarte, the world is wide enough; go through it, and look for those who may know you better. Certes Sir, quoth Amadis, till now I thought there was no King in the world who had wisdom such as yours; but seeing how strangely different you are from what I believed, since you are in this new mood we must seek a new way of life. Lisuarte answered, Do your own will as I shall mine, and he rose angrily and went to the Queen.

Gandandel and Brocadan commended him much for what he had done in thus dismissing such dangerous enemies, and he told Brisena all that had passed, and how he rejoiced thereat. But she told him that what he rejoiced at was to her cause for sorrow, for Amadis and his friends had ever served him faithfully and well; and that other Knights seeing how they were recompensed would have great reason to seek one who would know and reward them better. Say no more, cried he, I know what I am doing, and remember to say what I tell you, that you asked that Island for Leonoreta, and that I have given it her. I will do as you command me, replied Brisena, but God grant that it come to good!

Amadis returned to his lodging in a more melancholy mood than he was wont, he would say nothing to the Knights of his company till he had spoken with Oriana, so calling Durin aside he bade him tell Mabilia that he must see Oriana that night, and that they should expect him by the water course in the garden. Then he ate and regaled with the Knights as he used to do, and he desired them to assemble there on the morrow for he had something to impart to them. When day was gone and night was come, after they had retired and all were at rest, he went with Gandalin to the water course, and having entered it went forthwith to the chamber of Oriana, where she with as true love expected him; and being in her arms she asked him why he had sent that message by Durin, and he told her all that had past. Now Lady mine, said he, since it is so that for my honour I must depart I beseech you do not command me otherwise, for I am more yours than my own, and if I am shamed the shame will be yours also. But Oriana, though she felt as though her heart were breaking, took courage as she could and answered, True friend, with little reason can you complain of my father, for it is not him but me whom you have served, for my sake you abode here, and for my sake have done so many great actions, and from me you have had your guerdon, and shall have while I live; yet should not my father have done thus, seeing what you have been to him. Howbeit, though your absence will be like as if my heart were breaking, I will regard reason more than my unbounded love. Do as you think best! my father will find when you are gone that all that is left will be to him cause of sorrow and evil! Amadis kissed her hands; my own true Lady many and great kindnesses have I received from you which have saved me from death, but for this I thank you above all, inasmuch as honour is above all delights. Thus past they that night mingling tears with their love, thinking of the long solitude that was to come, and towards day-break Amadis rose; that dear cousin Mabilia and the Damsel of Denmark went out with him, and he embraced them, and commended Oriana to their consolations, and so they parted weeping.

Amadis went to his lodging and slept the remainder of the night and some part of the morning, but when it was time he arose, and the Knights assembled, they heard mass and rode forth, and being assembled in the field he addressed them after this guise:—It is notorious to you good Sirs and honourable Knights, whether the affairs of King Lisuarte have prospered or declined since I and my brethren and friends for my sake came to Great Britain. I may therefore be excused from recalling what is past to your memory, this only I ought to say, that ye as well as myself might reasonably have expected great recompence; but either that Fortune hath been using her accustomed inconstancy, or by the influence of evil counsellors, or perhaps because age hath altered the conditions of the King, we have found him different from what we expected; for when I myself and Agrayes, and Don Galvanes besought him that he would give Madasima to Don Galvanes in marriage, and with her her lands in vassallage, he nothing regarding the worth of this Knight nor his high lineage, not only would not grant us the boon, but denied it in terms so discourteous and dishonourable, that because they proceeded from a tongue so true, and from a judgment so sound, I would not willingly repeat them were not things at this extremity that it cannot be excused. Know then Sirs that towards the end of our talk, when we said to him that he did not know our services, he replied, the world was wide enough and we might seek those who would know them better. So therefore as we have hitherto obeyed him in concord and friendship, now must we in discord and enmity, fulfilling that which he thinks fitting; it seemed right to me that you should know this, because it not only concerns us in particular but all in general.

When these Knights heard what Amadis had said they were greatly astonished, and they talked one with another and said, that ill would their poor services be recompensed when what Amadis and his brethren had done was so forgotten, so that their hearts were moved against the King. And Angriote of Estravaus, as one who had resolved to take his share in the good or evil which might befall Amadis, said to them, Sirs, I have long known the King, and have always seen him temperate in all his actions, and never moved without great and just cause, therefore I cannot believe that this should proceed from his own nature or inclination but from some meddling traitors who have bereft him of his wisdom. Not for this do I excuse the King! for many days I have seen him speak more with Gandandel and Brocadan than he was accustomed to do, they being false and treacherous men, and I believe that they have done this thing hoping to obtain thereby for themselves and their sons that which they have never merited, and that you may see how the justice of God comes to pass I will arm myself, and challenge them for their villainy which they have done to the King and to Amadis, and will do combat against them both, or against their sons in their stead, if they dare sustain their father's treason. Forthwith he would have departed but Amadis withheld him saying, God forbid my true and loyal friend that your life should be put in danger for an uncertain cause. I am certain, quoth Angriote, that it is as I say by what I have long known of them, and if it pleases the King to speak truth he will confirm it. If you love me, replied Amadis, let this rest at present, that the King may not be offended; if these men who seemed so friendly are indeed my enemies, that will be known hereafter, and then may you better proceed against them. Then Angriote albeit unwillingly consented to delay vengeance. Amadis then turned to the assembled Knights and said, Sirs, I will take leave of the King and Queen if they chuse to see me, and will go to the Firm Island, where they who shall please to live with me shall be partakers with me in all the honour and pleasures that I can command. The land is rich and aboundeth with all things, there is store of forests and of fair women. I have treasure enough for our wants; they who know us will come thither to see us, and strangers to demand our help, and there we may return from our adventures to recover strength. While my father King Perion lives the kingdom of Gaul will not fail us, nor after his days. I have letters from the lesser Britain telling me that they give me that land, that then you may esteem our own; I must remind you also of Scotland, the country of my Cousin Agrayes, and of Queen Briolania's kingdom, which will not fail us for weal or for woe. That you may say truly Sir Amadis, quoth a Knight present, whose name was Tantiles, and who was governor of that kingdom. Sobradisa and its fair Queen, whom you have established there, will be always at your service. Now then Sir, cried Don Quadragante, take leave of the King and then will it be seen who they are who love you, and will continue in your company. Amadis answered, greatly shall I esteem those who at this time will so honour me, yet do I not say, that if they can profitably remain with the King they should not do so, for of a truth so good a Lord cannot soon be found. As they were thus talking the King and Gandandel past by with many other Knights, hawking with merlins, and sported near them awhile without speaking to them or noticing them, and then returned to the palace.

FOOTNOTES:

[315:A] Here follows a column of caution against evil Counsellors.

CHAPTER 21.

Then Amadis taking with him all those Knights went to take leave of the King; they who were in the palace, when they saw with how altered a countenance he entered, and at that hour when the tables were placed, all drew nigh to hear what he should say. He being before the King spake thus: Sir, whether or not you have dealt ill with me God and yourself can witness: of this I say no more, for though my services may have been great, much greater was the will I had to requite those honours which I from you received. Yesterday you told me that I might go about the world and seek for one who would know me better, giving me to understand that what you wished was my departure from your court; since this would please you it becomes me so to do. I do not come to discharge myself of vassallage, for I never was subject to you, nor to any but God alone; but I take leave of that good will which you once manifested to honour and favour me, and of that great love wherewith I ever strove to requite and serve you. Then Don Galvanes also took leave, and Agrayes and Florestan, and Dragonis and Palomir, who were cousins to Amadis, and Don Bruneo of Bonamar and his brother Branfil, and Angriote of Estravaus, and Grindonan his brother, and Pinores his nephew. Don Quadragante then came before the King and said, Sir, I abode with you only at the request of Amadis, and because I have been yours for his sake, for the same reason I will continue so no longer; small hope of recompence can there be for my poor services when he is so rewarded! for ill have you remembered how he saved you from the hands of Madanfabul, from whence none other could have saved you, and how he won for you that battle against King Cildadan, and how his brethren and kinsmen there shed their blood for you; how he delivered you from my enmity, and from Famongomadan and his son Basagante, who were the strongest giants in the world, and from Lindoraque, who was so mighty a Knight, and from Arcalaus the Enchanter—all this you have forgotten; but I tell you that had all we been in the field and Amadis away, how think you would it then have fallen out? The King answered, Don Quadragante I well perceive by your words that you have no love towards me, neither are you so beholden to Amadis that you should desire his welfare; perchance what you say of that is not so true as it sounds. Quadragante replied, you are of that rank that you may say what pleases you, but sure am I that you will not move Amadis with mischief-making words as others have been moved, who will discover their error when too late. Then Landin came up and said, Sir, of all your household I could find no help or healing for my wounds save only from Amadis, therefore shall I go with him and with my uncle Don Quadragante. Certes, quoth Lisuarte, if you staid I should not have a friend the more. Landin replied, such as they are towards you will I be. At this time were assembled together in another part of the palace, Don Brian of Monjaste, a right good Knight, who was son of King Ladasan of Spain and of a sister of King Perion, and Gandal, and Orlandin, son to the Count of Orlanda, and Grandores, and Madancil, he of the Silver Bridge, and Listoran of the White Tower, and Ladadin of Fajarque, and Branfiles the haughty, and Don Gavarte of the Perilous Vale; and when they saw how all those other Knights were about to depart for the love of Amadis, they also went before the King and said, Sir, we came to your court to see Amadis and his brethren, and to obtain his friendship, and as he was the cause of our coming so will he be of our departure. These Knights having departed, and there remaining no other, Amadis would have taken leave of the Queen but Lisuarte would not permit him, because she had always opposed this quarrel, so he sent his excuses by Don Grumedan. Then went he to his lodging, and after they had made their meal they all mounted being fully armed, five hundred Knights were they in all who followed Amadis, among whom were the sons of Kings and of Counts, and others, who for their prowess as well as birth, were renowned throughout all the world.

Mabilia beheld them from a window of the Queen's palace, in what order they went, their arms how rich they were, and how glittering in the sun, so that none who saw them depart but marvelled and thought the King unhappy, that he would so lose such a Knight and so goodly a company. Then Mabilia went to Oriana and said, Cease thy sorrow and come look at your vassals! and let your heart rejoice that you have such a lover; for if till now he has led the life of an Errant Knight serving your father, now that he has left his service, he appears like a powerful Prince, and that Lady will redound to your honour. Oriana being comforted by her words looked at the company, subduing by her fortitude that grief and passion which tormented her heart. There went out with Amadis to honour him, King Arban of North Wales, and Grumedan the Queen's fosterer, and Brandoyuas and Quinorante, and Giontes the King's nephew, and Listoran the good jouster. All these rode with him apart from his company and very sorrowful for his departure, and Amadis besought them that they would still be his friends so far as they could without breach of honour, for he should still esteem and love them as he had done; nor though the King had ceased to love him, having no cause for this change, should they do so likewise, nor for that cease to serve the King and honour him as for his worth he deserved. They answered, that they should never cease to love him however they were bound by loyalty to serve the King. Then said Amadis, I beseech you tell the King that what Urganda said before me is now made manifest, how I should gain for another, and my guerdon should be wrath, and the long delay of my will! So has it come to pass! but the just Judge of all will allot to every one his right. Don Grumedan cursed Urganda for prophesying so truly, and then they returned to the town. Presently Don Guilan came up and he was in tears; and he said, Sir, You know how it is with us, that I have neither will nor heart of my own, but must obey her for whom I suffer so much, and she has forbidden me to follow you, and thus am I put to great shame: now would I repay those honours which I have ever received from you and your brethren, but I may not! But Amadis, who knew the great and excessive love of this Knight, and remembered how he himself loved and obeyed Oriana, embraced him and said, Don Guilan my dear friend, God forbid that a Knight like you should disobey your Lady, not so would I advise you, nor so advising should I be your friend; obey her and serve the King, and sure am I that you will keep your loyalty and yet that I shall have in you the same friend. So Guilan answered, he trusted in God to serve him yet; and he took his leave. They rode on about three leagues to the shore where Amadis had ordered tents to be pitched; there they regaled that night, congratulating each other that they had not remained longer in the service of one so thankless, but Amadis felt his heart fail him, for he knew not when he should again see Oriana. In the morning they set forth again and took the straight road to the Firm Island.

On the day after Amadis had departed, the King when mass was over sate in his palace according to custom, and looked on one side and on the other, and beholding how desolate the place appeared without those Knights who were gone, he began to muse upon his own conduct, and was lost in thought. Gandandel and Brocadan, who knew what Angriote had said of them, when they saw him thus thoughtful began to fear that he was ill satisfied with what had been done. Howbeit as they could not now retreat they resolved to push farther on, for this is the ill fate of all great errors. So Gandandel went up to Lisuarte and said to him, henceforth Sir you may rest secure since those who could have injured you are dismissed from your service; the trouble of your state and household you may lay on us and we will attend to it more carefully than to our own concerns, and when you think of the treasures which you must have bestowed upon those Knights but which are now your own, you should greatly rejoice. Lisuarte looked sternly at them and answered, I marvel much at what you say, that I should commit the management of my state and household to you! that I and those about me are not equal to the task—but you, in whom I did not perceive such great ability are capable thereof! Even if you were, my vassals and household would be ill contented with the authority of such as you! You tell me too that I shall save the wealth which would else have been bestowed among those Knights. I would know how it could be better employed than to my own honour and service, my honour was defended by it, my dominion increased, and so it at last returned to me again, for the wealth that is bestowed where it ought, lies in a good treasury whence it never can be lost. No more of this! I shall not take your counsel! He then arose and called his huntsmen and went forth to the field, leaving them in amazement and great dismay.

At this season arrived a Damsel from Queen Briolania with tidings to Oriana, whereat all greatly rejoiced for that Queen was much beloved by all. Lady, quoth she, I come from Briolania to tell you the wonders of the Firm Island, that you may know all, for I was witness. God grant long life to her! said Oriana, and good fortune to you for the trouble which you have taken. So all drew round to hear her. Then said the Damsel, when Briolania and her company had arrived at the Firm Island she was asked if she would attempt the Forbidden Chamber or the Arch of True Lovers, but she answered, that she would leave those two proofs till the last. They then led us to a fair dwelling about a league from the Castle, which, because of its goodly situation, was one of the chief habitations of Apolidon, and when it was dinner time they led us to a large hall, at the one end whereof was a deep cave so dark and fearful that none durst go nigh to it, and at the other end of the palace was a fair tower where they led us, and we found the tables and benches placed by the windows, and from thence we could see all that past below in the large hall. So there were we well served by Dames and Damsels, and the Knights and our people feasted below in the hall. But when the second service was brought in loud hissings were heard from the cave, and a hot wind came forth therefrom, and there issued out a great serpent into the middle of the hall, so fierce and terrible that none dared look on him, and he breathed smoke from his mouth and nostrils, and lashed the ground with his tail so that the whole palace shook; presently two Lions came out of the cave and attacked him, and began such a battle that there is not heart of man which would not have felt fear at beholding it. The Knights and people fled with all speed from the table, and though the windows whereat we were were very high, yet were we greatly terrified. Half an hour that battle lasted till the Lions were so wearied that they lay as though they were dead, and the serpent so exhausted that he could scarce draw breath; but after he had rested a little he took one Lion in his mouth and carried him into the cave, then returned for the other, and they were seen no more that day. The men of the Island laughed at our fear, and assured us that they would appear no more that day, so we then returned to the tables and finished our meal.

The next day they led us to a place still fairer, where we were well feasted, and at night they showed us a rich chamber, marvellously fair where there was a rich and costly bed for Briolania, and other good ones for us. But about midnight the doors flew open with so great noise that we all awoke in terror, and a hart came in, having lighted candles upon his horns, so that the whole chamber was as light as day. One side of that hart was white as snow, and the neck and the head were black as pitch, and the one horn seemed gilt and the other was red; four dogs pursued him in full cry, and behind them an ivory horn moved and sounded in the air as if a man were sounding it, and gave the proper sound of the chase, and cheared the dogs so that they pursued the hart and allowed him no respite, and drove him from one part of the chamber to another, and sometimes they leaped over our beds, and sometimes they fell on them, so that we rose up in our shifts and our hair hanging about and fled from them, and some hid themselves under the beds, till the Hart finding no safety there leaped through a window and the dogs after him; then were we right glad, and taking up the cloaths which were thrown about covered ourselves, and gave a robe to Briolania wherein she drest herself, and then as the fear was past we laughed at the confusion into which we had been thrown. While we were making our beds again, a Dame and two Damsels entered and a little girl with candles, and she spake to Briolania and said, How is it Lady that you have risen at such an hour? but when she heard they laughed and answered, Now then Ladies go to sleep again, for you have nothing more to apprehend to-night.

Early in the morning we went to a wood where there were fine groves and fair gardens, and there we had tents pitched by a brook side. We found there a round building with twelve marble pillars, the walls were of crystal so curiously made that they who might be within could see all without; the doors were made of plate of gold and of silver, and by every pillar there was placed the image of a Giant made in copper, and these images had bows in their hands, and the arrow heads were of fire. We were told that nothing could enter that chamber but would be presently reduced to ashes by those arrows which never failed of their mark; and they put in two fallow deer and a stag, immediately the images shot at them and they were reduced to ashes, and the arrows returned to the bows from whence they fled. On the doors of the chamber there were letters written which said, Let no man or woman dare enter here except they twain who love each other truly, as truly as did Grimanesa and Apolidon, and they must enter here together, else will they die the cruellest death that ever was seen. This enchantment will endure till they twain shall have entered the Forbidden Chamber, and then shall all the enchantments of the Firm Island be done away. Then Briolania called Ysanjo and Enil, and told them she wished to see nothing more except the Arch of True Lovers and the Forbidden Chamber, and she asked Ysanjo the meaning of the Lion and Serpent, and of the Hart and the Dogs. Lady, he replied, we know nothing more than that always at that hour they appear; and the Hart and the Dogs run from the window into a lake which we believe proceeds from the sea, but were you to remain here a whole year you could not see half the wonders that are in this Island.

On the morrow we mounted our palfreys and returned to the Castle; without delay Briolania went to the Arch of True Lovers and past through the Forbidden Perrons like one who had never failed in her love, and the image with the trumpet made so sweet a sound that we were all astonished, and when she entered where the images were of Apolidon and Grimanesa, it ceased with so sweet a finish as was marvellous to hear. There beheld she those images as fair and fresh as life, and being alone with them she thought herself in good company; and while there she saw letters newly written in the Jasper, saying, this is the name of Briolania, daughter to King Tagadan of Sobradisa, the third Damsel that hath entered here. Then she felt a fear of being alone and returned. The fifth morning she went to attempt the Forbidden Chamber; she was in rich attire, and she wore nothing upon her beautiful head except a gold clasp with jewels, and all who saw her said, that if she did not enter the Chamber there was none in the world who could, and that they should now see the end of all those enchantments. She commended herself to God, and passed through the copper Perron, and came up to the marble Perron and read the writing there, and proceeded so far beyond that all surely thought the adventure was atchieved; but when she was within three paces from the door three hands seized her by those beautiful locks, and pitilessly cast her out of the Forbidden ground as they had done all others, and she lay in such plight that we could not soon recover her. Till now Oriana's heart had been misgiving her, but now she looked at Mabilia and the Damsel of Denmark, and they at her, being all well pleased; the next day pursued the Damsel, Briolania departed for her own kingdom. So the Damsel then received her bidding from Brisena and Oriana, and the other Ladies, and set out on her return to her Mistress.

Now Amadis and his company arrived at the Firm Island, where they were joyfully received by all the dwellers therein, who, as they had felt great sorrow for the loss of their new Lord, so now had they double pleasure in welcoming him. But when those Knights who were with him beheld the Castle how strong it was, and how there was no other entrance to the Island large as it was, and that the land was so fertile, and peopled with so many and such inhabitants, they thought it might maintain war against all the world; so they were lodged in the largest town which stood under the Castle. You are to know that this Island was nine leagues long and seven wide, all full of villages and rich dwelling-houses of the Knights of the land. And in the pleasantest parts thereof Apolidon had built four palaces for himself, the strangest and most delightful that ever man could behold. One was that of the Serpent and the Lions. Another that of the Hart and the Dogs. The third was called the Whirling Palace, for three times in the day and as often in the night it whirled round, so that they who were in it thought it would dash to pieces; and the fourth was that of the Bull, because every day a wild Bull issued out of an old covered way, and ran among the people therein as though he would kill them, and when they fled from him he ran against the iron door of a tower and burst it open and went in, and presently he came out again being quite tame, and ridden by an old Ape, so wrinkled that his skin hung all in folds, which Ape flogged him into the place from whence he came. Great pleasure had all these Knights in beholding these enchantments, and enough pastime had they there, and they were all firm in their love to Amadis, and ready to follow him wherever he would.

At this time came Andalod the Hermit of the Poor Rock to establish the monastery as had been appointed, and he seeing Amadis gave thanks to God for giving life to so good a man, and looked at him and embraced him as if he had never seen him before. But Amadis kist his hands, and with all humility thanked him for his preservation and for his life, which he owed to God and to him. So a monastery was founded at the foot of the rock, where that Chapel of the Virgin stood, wherein Amadis had prayed in his despair before he departed into the mountain. A good man called Sisian, whom Andalod brought, remained there, and thirty Friars with him, and Amadis assigned to them rents enough, and Andalod then returned to the Poor Rock as before. Then Balays of Carsante arrived, he whom Amadis had released from the dungeon of Arcalaus, who had gone to take leave of King Lisuarte, so soon as he knew that Amadis had left him in discontent; with him also came Olivas whom Agrayes and Don Galvanes had helped in battle against the Duke of Bristol. They asked of Balays, what news in the court? he answered, enough to tell. King Lisuarte Sir has summoned all his people; for Count Latine and they whom he sent to take possession of the Island of Mongaza, have informed him that the old Giant had given up to them all the Castles which he and his sons had in their keeping. But Gromadaza refused to yield the Castles by the Boiling Lake, which is the strongest place in the Island, and also three other strong Castles, for she says she will never yield the place where she was Mistress in the life of her husband Famongomadan, and Basagante her son, but always annoy Lisuarte to the utmost of her power, and for Madasima and the Damsels she cares not what may become of them so she can do any harm to the King. The King therefore has summoned his forces, and hath sworn, if Gromadaza does not yield up her Castles within a month, that he will behead Madasima and the Damsels, and that he will go against the Castle of the Boiling Lake, and not depart from before it till he shall have won it, and if he can take the old Giantess he will throw her to the Lions. At this news they were all greatly troubled, and Galvanes said to them, Sirs, you all know the promise which I have made to Madasima, to defend her with reason, or if that failed by force of arms; and for this cause was it that Amadis and all of us forsook Lisuarte; now I beseech you, if he will not hear reason, assist me in arms to fulfil my word. At that uprose Don Florestan, and said, Don Galvanes, there are better advisers here than I, but if reason fail I will undertake the battle in the name of God. Good friend, replied Galvanes, I thank you with all my heart; but if it must be by battle I have promised and I will perform it. Then Don Brian of Monjaste and Quadragante said that the quarrel appertained to all, and all ought to bear a part, for all Knights were bound to succour Damsels who were opprest, and as Madasima and her Damsels had gone as hostages in obedience to her mother, they were innocent before God. Sirs, said Amadis, you rejoice me in what you say; for whatsoever is undertaken with such concord will have good issue. But I will tell you what seems to me good: these Damsels are twelve in number, and therefore ought to be succoured by twelve Knights. Sure I am that such as ye will think such danger but pastime, if it please ye I will name twelve champions, and let the other Knights remain here for greater perils if they should befal us. You, Sir Don Galvanes shall be the first, as it is your quarrel, and Agrayes your nephew, and my brother Florestan, and my cousins Palomir and Dragonis, and Don Brian of Monjaste, and Nicoran of the White Tower, and Urlandin and Gavarte of the Perilous Vale, and Ymosil brother to the Duke of Burgandy, and Madansil of the Silver Bridge, and Ladadin of Fajarque; let those twelve go, there are among them the sons of Kings and Dukes and Counts, so that their peers will not be found. Hereat were all well pleased, and the Knights appointed made ready forthwith, and shortly after midnight armed themselves and rode towards Tafilana, the town where Lisuarte then was.

CHAPTER 22.

Now Oriana felt herself great with child, and she asked counsel of Mabilia and the Damsel of Denmark in that danger; they albeit they were sore dismayed dissembled that, and Mabilia bade her take heart for all should be remedied. I always expected, said she, that to such[347:A] a saint such an offering would be brought. Oriana could not forbear a smile. I will feign myself worse, she said, and withdraw as much as I can from all company; and if the Damsel of Denmark will hazard her honour for me, my honour and life may both be saved. Lady, quoth the Damsel, I am at your command even were it to my death. Good friend, quoth Oriana, this I hoped, and if I live you shall recover your honour and with great praise. Then the Damsel knelt and kissed her hands, and Oriana proceeded: continue to visit Adalasta the Abbess of my Nunnery as you have hitherto done, and when it is time tell her that you are pregnant, and beseech her to help you, so that you may lay the child at the church door, and that she will order it to be taken in and brought up for Charity's sake; thus will my secret be safe, nor will you be shamed, for none but this honourable Lady will know what you shall tell her, and she loves you much. Thus they determined that it should be.

When Lisuarte knew how Gromadaza persisted in her warfare, by advice of Gandandel and Brocadan he sent for Madasima and her Damsels, and told them that they must all be put to death for an example. When she heard this so rigorous doom the fair and fresh colour of her cheeks suddenly changed to a pale and deadly hue, and falling at the King's feet she said, Sir, the fear of death doth make my heart weaker than it naturally is, weak Damsel as I am, so that I have neither thought nor words to answer you; but if in this court there be any Knight willing to uphold the right let him speak for me as a Knight is bound to do, for I did not enter your prison willingly but in obedience to my mother. If there be none such here, do you O King, whom hitherto never distressed Dame or Damsel hath implored in vain, do you deal justly by me, and let not anger have the mastery over you. Gandandel, who was present, was greatly desirous that Madasima should be slain, knowing that then Amadis could never be reconciled with the King; and he said, Sir, do not hear her, these Damsels were given you as hostages to die if the conditions were not performed, and therefore justice ought to be executed without delay.

But Don Grumedan, who was a good Knight, and well versed in all the laws of Knighthood, as one who had not only practised but read much, replied, that shall not the King do if it please God! nor ever shall such cruelty and wrong be by him committed. This Damsel came hither in obedience to her mother, and as that obedience will in secret be by God rewarded, so should it be in public by the King as his servant, and one who obeys his will. Moreover I have learnt that within three days here will arrive certain Knights from the Firm Island to take up their quarrel; and if you Gandandel, or your sons are willing to maintain the justice of your advice; you will there find those who will answer you. Gandandel answered, Don Grumedan, tho' you wish me ill I have never deserved it at your hands; if you had offended my sons you know they are such Knights that they can maintain what I have said. We shall soon see that, quoth old Grumedan; as for you I only wish you well or ill as it shall be found that you have counselled the King. Albeit that Lisuarte had acted much amiss toward Amadis, and had it in his heart to do him all displeasure, yet could not that new passion subdue his old virtue, so that he was glad at what Grumedan said, and asked who the Knights were that were coming to defend the Damsels, and when Grumedan had told their names, he observed that they were enough good and prudent Knights. But then was Gandandel sore dismayed, and he repented him of what he had said concerning his sons, knowing that they were nothing equal in arms to Florestan and Agrayes, and Don Brian of Monjaste, and Gavarte of the Perilous Vale. So when Madasima was remanded to prison he went to his brother-in-law Brocadan in trouble of heart, receiving now the guerdon which the merits of his misdeed deserved.

Here came to pass what the Gospel saith, That no hidden thing but shall be made known; for Gandandel retiring with Brocadan to a private chamber to consult with him how they might prevail upon the King to execute Madasima and her Damsels before the Knights of the Firm Island arrived, Brocadan began to reproach him for the wrong he had done to Amadis, greatly repenting his own wickedness now that he saw his own honour and his sons in danger. Now it happened that a niece of Brocadan was enamoured of a young Knight called Sarquiles, who was nephew to Angriote of Estravaus, and she had hidden him near this chamber, so that he heard the whole secret of this treachery; and when it was night he went out and armed himself, and mounting his horse he rode on the morrow into the town as if he came from another place, and he went before the King and said to him, Sir, I am your natural subject and was brought up in your household, and therefore would save you from all treachery, that you may not commit wrong in compliance with another's will. It is not three days since I was in a place where I heard persons counselling how to instigate you to do an evil thing against your own honour and good reason. I say to you, give no heed to Gandandel and Brocadan in what they say to you, touching Madasima, for there are others in your court who more honestly advise you; you and all here shall know wherefore I say this, within twelve days, if you will delay following their will for so long. Now Sir, God be with you, for I go to my Uncle Angriote. God be with you, replied Lisuarte, and remained musing on what he had heard.

Sarquiles rode on by the shortest way he knew to the Firm Island, and when he arrived there his horse was so overspent with the speed he had made that he could scarcely carry him. He found Amadis, and Angriote, and Don Bruneo, riding on the shore to hasten the equipment of some vessels which they had ordered to pass over to Gaul, for Amadis was desirous to see his parents. Right well was Sarquiles received, and Angriote said to him, Nephew, what business have you that your horse is in such plight? Very great, replied he, and he told him how his Mistress Gandaza had hidden him in Brocadan's house, and what he had there heard. Now Sir, quoth Angriote to Amadis, was my suspicion right? You would not suffer me to bring the matter to an end, but now if it please God neither you nor ought else shall let, but that this great treason against the King and against you shall be made manifest. Good friend, replied Amadis, you may now do it with reason and certainty, and God therewith will speed you. I will depart to-morrow, said Angriote, and Sarquiles upon another horse with me. Accordingly on the following morning they twain set out for the dwelling of King Lisuarte.

Meantime the King mused much upon that Sarquiles had told him. One day Gandandel and Brocadan came before him and said, Sir, we are grieved to see how little you regard your own welfare; that, quoth Lisuarte, may well be, but why say you this?—Because these Knights who are your enemies are coming to your Court without any fear to defend these Damsels for whom you ought to have the land given up. If you will take our advice you ought to behead them before these champions arrive, and send to forbid the Knights to enter your kingdom; thus would you make them fear you, and Amadis would not venture to offer you any wrong, for if they do not forbear for fear, for nothing else will they; the sooner this is done the better will it be, and the more terror will it strike. The King then called to mind the words of Sarquiles, and saw how he had spoken truth. You tell me two things, he replied, against all reason: the one that without any form of judgment I should have these Damsels slain, what account could I give to the Lord whose minister I am if I should do this? He has appointed me here in his stead to administer right in his name, and if I did this wrong which you counsel to strike fear into others, it would fall upon my own head at last. Those Kings who follow their own will instead of what is reasonable rely on themselves and not on God, which is the worst error into which they can fall. Their best security is to chuse out good counsellors, and honest ones, and to remember that however evil actions appear at first, the just Judge directs, and the end thereof cannot be good. You tell me also to forbid these Knights from coming to my court; a dishonourable thing would it be to prevent any one from claiming justice before me, much more they being my enemies, for it is to my honour that I have the power and inclination to do what they request. I do not like your counsel! you have done ill to those who deserved no ill at your hands! I have sinned and I have my punishment; and if you have been false so I trust will you have yours at the end. And with that he went away and left them.

The following day Lisuarte rode forth after mass with a great company, and seeing that the twelve Knights were approaching he rode forward to receive them, for he was a courteous man to all, and they well deserved such honour being what they were. They made obeisance to him, and while their people pitched tents in the field Don Galvanes spake to the King. Sir, confiding in your virtue and in your wonted goodness, we are come hither to request that you will hear Madasima and her Damsels, that they may have their right; we are come to plead their cause, and if by that means we cannot succeed, let it not offend you Sir if we support it by arms, for there is no cause wherefore they ought to die. The King answered, go now and rest yourselves, I will do all that can justly be done. Don Brian of Monjaste then replied, So Sir we hoped, that you would do what behoved your royal dignity and your conscience, and whenever you have failed so to act it has been the work of evil advisers, and that, if it did not offend you, I would prove upon any one who dared gainsay. Don Brian, quoth the King, if you would listen to your father I know that you would neither forsake me for another, nor come hither to plead against me. Sir, replied Don Brian, my pleading is for you, it is that you should do justice, and not listen to those who would serve you less faithfully than I, and stain your worth. You say Sir, that if I had listened to my father I should not forsake you: I have not forsaken you Sir, for I never was yours, albeit I am of your lineage. I came to your court to seek my kinsman Amadis, and when you were pleased that he should be no longer yours, then I departed with him; in all this I have not erred a single point of duty. The King then returned to the town, and they remained in their tents where they were visited by their friends. But for Oriana I tell you she never left the window, looking at those who so loved her lover, and beseeching God to give them the victory in this appeal.

That night did Gandandel and Brocadan pass in great perplexity, wishing that they could recall what was past, but now perforce must they go on. On the morrow the twelve Knights heard mass with the King, and that done accompanied him to his palace. He then called for Gandandel and Brocadan, and said to them, You must now support the advice which you have always given me in the affair of Madasima, and make these good men understand why she ought not to be heard, and he bade them stand where all might hear them. Ymosil of Burgandy, and Ladadin of Fajarque then came forward and said, We Sir, and these Knights beseech you of your goodness that Madasima and her Damsels may be heard, for so we conceive it is right. Then answered Gandandel, many talk about the right and few know what it is; you say that of right these Damsels ought to be heard, which of right they ought not, for without any such condition they bound themselves to death, and entered the prison of the King thereupon, that if Ardan Canileo were slain or vanquished, and the whole Island of Mongaza were not then freely surrendered, they and the Knights with them should suffer death. The Knights delivered up the Castles in their keeping, which Gromadaza will not do, therefore there neither is nor can be reason for which they should be excused from death. Ymosil replied, Certes Gandandel, you might have been excused from uttering such reasons before so good a King and such Knights as are here! It is manifest to all who have any knowledge, that man or woman are to be heard, of right in their own defence, in all cases except in treason and conspiracy; this is the custom in all lands wherein justice is observed, and this is what we require. Gandandel replied, that nothing more was to be said: the King was to decide, so the matter was at issue, and the King remained with certain Knights, all the others leaving the hall.

The King wished his Uncle Argamonte, an honourable Count and of great prudence, to deliver his opinion, but he referred it to the King, saying that none so fully understood what was right as he himself; the other counsellors did the same. Lisuarte seeing this then said, Since you leave the decision to me, I think Ymosil of Burgundy hath spoken to the purpose, and the Damsels should be heard. Certes Sir, quoth the Count, and all they who were present said the same, you have determined justly, for thus it ought to be. They then called in the Knights and said what had been resolved; for this Ymosil and Ladadin of Fajarque kissed his hands and said, be pleased therefore Sir to let Madasima and her Damsels be summoned, and we will save them by fair reason, or by arms if need shall be. Let them come, replied the King, and see if they will commit their cause to you. Presently they came before the King so modestly and in such fear that not a man could behold them without great pity. The twelve Knights of the Firm Island took them by the hand, and Agrayes, Florestan, Ymosil and Ladadin said to Madasima, Lady Madasima, these Knights come to save you and your Damsels from death, will you commit your cause to us? Sirs, she replied, if the cause of Damsels so forlorn and wretched may be undertaken, we commit it to you, and trust in God and you. Since it is so, quoth Ymosil, let who will come forward against you! if he be one I will defend you by reason or by arms; if more, twelve shall be answered. The King looked at Gandandel and Brocadan, and saw that they looked down, and were dismayed, and did not answer. Return to your lodgings till the morrow, said Lisuarte, and meanwhile those who are to answer you will take counsel. The Knights then conducted Madasima to her prison and went to their tents.

Lisuarte led Gandandel and Brocadan aside, and said to them, you have often urged me to put those Damsels to death, and said you would maintain the justice of the deed by reason, or your sons should in arms, if need should be, now then do as you said, for what Ymosil advances seems just to me, and I will not appoint any of my Court to combat against these Knights. Look ye to it! Else will the Damsels be delivered, and I shall have been ill advised by ye, and wrongfully. They replied, that to-morrow they would be ready with their reply, and returned very sorrowfully to their homes. And they agreed to persist in their advice and maintain it by reason, but not put their sons in danger, because the cause was not just, and they were not such in arms as those Knights. But that same evening tidings came to the King how Gromadaza the Giantess was dead, and had ordered her Castles to be delivered up to save her daughter and the Damsels, and that they had accordingly been yielded to Count Latine. Greatly pleased thereat was Lisuarte, and when the Knights came before him on the morrow he said, proceed no farther in this cause, for you are quit of your defence, and the Damsels are free; the Castles for which I held them in pledge having been surrendered. Gandandel and Brocadan then rejoiced, for they surely expected to be dishonoured. Then Lisuarte sent for Madasima and the Damsels, and said to them, ye are free; do what it pleases you, the Castles have been given up; but he would not tell her that her mother was dead. Madasima would have kissed his hand but the King permitted not that, for he never suffered Dame or Damsel to kiss his hand save when he bestowed upon them some boon. Then said she, since you leave me at my own disposal; I give myself to my Lord Galvanes, who hath been so willing to help me. Agrayes took her by the hand and said, good Lady, you do that which is right; and though you are now disherited of your own land, you shall be honoured in another till it please God to remedy your loss. But Ymosil then said to the King, Sir, if right be done to Madasima she will not be disherited, for children who are in the power of their parents must obey them, however unwillingly, but not for that should they be disherited, when obedience and not free will hath made them bind themselves to what their parents commanded. And because you Sir are appointed here to make every one render to another his right, so ought you yourself to do as an example. Ymosil, replied the King, you have the Damsels at liberty, say no more upon this other matter; I have had sufficient trouble about that land, and will defend it now it is mine, nor can I take it from my daughter Leonoreta, to whom I have granted it. Don Galvanes then said, Sir, that right which Madasima has to the land of her fathers is now mine. I beseech you remember some services which I have done you, and do not disinherit me, for I would willingly be your vassal and stand in your favour, and serve you as loyally as it is possible. Say no more Don Galvanes, quoth Lisuarte, that is done which cannot be undone. Since it is so, quoth he, that I find neither right nor courtesy here, I shall strive to win it how I can. Do your utmost, replied the King, it was in the power of those who were stronger than you, and easier will it be to defend it from you, than it was to win it from them. You won it, answered Galvanes, by means of one who was badly guerdoned, he will help to recover it. If he helps you, cried Lisuarte, many others will serve me who would not serve me before for his sake, when I had him in my household and protected him from them. Agrayes then grew angry and exclaimed, Certes all here, and others beside can tell whether Amadis was protected by you or you by him, though you are a King and he was always as an Errant Knight. Don Florestan seeing how Agrayes was moved laid hand upon his shoulder and drew him back, and then said himself, it seems, Sir, you prize the services of these you speak of above those of Amadis, whether they be so indeed, we shall soon see. Don Brian of Monjaste then stept forward, however little you esteem the services of Amadis and his friends, they must be of great worth indeed who can reasonably make them to be forgotten. It is plain Don Brian, replied the King, that you are one of those friends!——Sure Sir I am; he is my kinsman and I shall do what he pleases. We have enough, quoth Lisuarte, to dispense with you. All you have, replied Don Brian, will be wanted to resist what Amadis can do. The Knights on both sides drew nigh to answer, but Lisuarte stretched out a wand which he held and commanded them to say no more, and they returned to their places.

Just then Angriote of Estravaus, and his nephew Sarquiles entered, compleatly armed, and approached to kiss the King's hand. The twelve Knights marvelled at their coming being ignorant of the cause thereof, but Gandandel and Brocadan were put in fear, and they looked at each other, for they knew what Angriote had said of them before, and albeit they held him for the best Knight in the King's dominions, yet they took courage to answer what he might say; and they called their sons and bade them say nothing more than they should tell them. Angriote stood up before the King and said, Sir, let Gandandel and Brocadan come hither, and I will say that to them which shall make you and all present know them better than ye have hitherto done. The King accordingly called on them to come forward, and all the Knights drew nigh to hear. Then said Angriote, know Sir that Gandandel and Brocadan are disloyal and false toward you, they counselled you wickedly and lyingly, neither regarding God, nor you, nor Amadis, who had so honoured them, and had never done them wrong. They, villains as they are, told you that Amadis designed to seize your kingdom, a thing which never was in his thoughts, for what he desired hath ever been your service, and thus have they made you lose the best Knight that ever King had to serve him, and many other good Knights with him, for no fault of their own. Therefore I say that these wicked and false men, in whom you trusted, have committed a great treason against you, which if they deny, I will do battle with them both; but if their age excuses them, let their sons come forward, and by God's help I will make them confess the disloyalty of their fathers before you, that you shall understand it. Sir, replied Gandandel, you see how Angriote comes to dishonour your court! and this is because you permit those to enter your land who do not seek your service, if you had prevented that at first this would not have happened; and now Sir do not marvel if Amadis should come hither to-morrow and defy you yourself! If Angriote had met me in those days when I did good service in arms for this kingdom, and for your brother King Falangris, he would not then have dared to say what now he says, but now he sees me old and weak, and dares insult me as one already overcome; this shame Sir falls more upon you than me. No Sir Knave, quoth Angriote, I am not come hither to dishonour the Court, but for its honour to destroy treason, and root out the tares which you have scattered among the good seed! Then said Sarquiles, Sir, you know the words which I spake to you upon this matter; with my own ears I heard the villainy which these old traitors were devising; they are old, but their sons are young and strong; let them answer for them, they are three and we are two, then will God discover the truth, and it will be seen if they are such as to make amends for the loss of Amadis and his lineage as their fathers have boasted! When the two sons of Gandandel heard this, and saw that the whole Court were smiling to see their fathers so prest, they thrust angrily through the throng, and came before the King and said, Sir, Angriote lies in all that he hath said and we will combat with him; here are our gages, and they threw their gloves into his lap. Angriote then held out the lappet of his armour—here Sir is mine! let them go arm themselves, and do you Sir behold the battle. The King answered, the day is far spent and there will not be time, let it be after mass to-morrow. With that Adamas came up, the son of Brocadan by a sister of Gandandel; he was great of stature and strong, but of so villainous a nature that none esteemed him. He said to the King, Sir, Sarquiles lies in all he hath said, and if he dare enter the field with his Uncle I will combat him! at this Sarquiles right joyfully gave his gage; the Court then broke up. Angriote and Sarquiles went with the twelve Knights and Madasima, who had taken leave of the Queen and of Oriana, and Brisena sent her a rich tent to lodge in.

The King remained with Don Grumedan and Giontes his nephew; he sent for Gandandel and Brocadan, and said to them, I marvel at you! you have so often told me that Amadis designed treason and meant to seize my kingdom, and now when the proof was necessary you shrunk from it! and have suffered your sons to risque themselves who know not what is the justice of their cause. You have sinned against God and me; great evil have you done me in making me lose such a man and such Knights, but you will not escape without your punishment, for that just Judge will give to every one his due. Sir, said Gandandel, my sons came forward hastily thinking that the proof was delayed. Of a truth, quoth Grumedan, they thought right; for there neither is nor can be proof that Amadis in this or in aught else hath done wrong toward the King, and if you suspect it, it is against all reason; even the devils in hell cannot think so! If you had a thousand heads, and the King were to cut them all off, he would not be enough revenged for the wrong you have done him, and now you will be left for more mischief, which God forbid! and your wretched sons must suffer for your fault! Don Grumedan, said they, whatever you believe and wish we trust that our sons will save their honour and our own. God never save me, replied he, if I wish more than that you be rewarded as your counsel deserves. The King then bade them cease, and he went to table, and they departed to their homes.

That night the arms and horses of the champions were made ready. Angriote and Sarquiles past the remainder of the night from midnight in a chapel of Saint Mary, which was near their tents. At day-break the twelve

Knights armed themselves, for they doubted the King seeing how wroth he was against them, and with Madasima and her Damsels, each upon her palfrey, they rode through the town to the field of battle, Angriote and Sarquiles going before them. The King and his Knights were already assembled, and three Judges were appointed: King Arban of North Wales, and Giontes the King's Nephew, and Quinorante the good Jouster; they placed Angriote and Sarquiles at one end of the lists. Presently the two brothers Tarin and Corian came with their cousin Adamas, well armed and mounted, and disposed to do their part well, if the wickedness of their fathers had not been against them. They being opposed each to the other, Giontes blew his trumpet and they ran the career, Corian and Tarin at Angriote, and Adamas against Sarquiles. Tarin broke his lance upon Angriote, who encountered Corian, and bore him from his saddle, then turned and saw Tarin sword in hand. Tarin struck at him but the blow fell upon the horses' head and wounded him, and cut away the headstall, so that the reins fell on his neck, and the horse being thus at liberty, Angriote was carried against his enemy, and they dashed against each other and Tarin fell; then Angriote leaped lightly from his horse as one accustomed to such perils, and took his shield, and laid hand upon that sword with which he had heretofore dealt so many and mighty blows. He saw his nephew maintaining a brave sword-combat on horseback, and then made at the two brethren who stood by each other, and laid on him a heavy load like brave and strong Knights. But Angriote well defended himself, holding out his shield against one and laying on the other with the sword, so that he made them give back, for never stroke came from him that did not shear away the armour, for as I have told you this Knight was the best foyner with the sword of any in the King's dominions. So that their shields were soon chipt away, and their harness broken that the blood started through, nor was he so whole but that the blood ran from many wounds. When Sarquiles saw how his Uncle sped, and that he was still coping in equal battle with Adamas, he spurred his horse and grappled with his enemy, and there they struggled each to overthrow the other. Angriote seeing them drew nigh to succour Sarquiles if he should fall undermost, and the two brethren followed him to help their cousin. At length the two Knights fell from their horses, still grappling; then might you have seen a great conflict, Angriote pressing to help his nephew and the brethren to assist Adamas. But in that hour Angriote did such wonders in arms, and laid on such terrible and heavy blows that the brethren, albeit they did their utmost, could not save Adamas from the hands of Sarquiles. When Gandandel and Brocadan saw this, who till now had hoped that the valour of their sons might have defended their wickedness they withdrew from the window in great sorrow and pain of heart, and the King withdrew also, for all the good fortune which befell the friends of Amadis displeased him, and he would not witness the victory of Angriote. But all else who were present rejoiced to see that Gandandel and Brocadan would suffer some part of the punishment on earth which they deserved. The four Knights meantime continued their fierce conflict, but it did not long endure, for now Tarin and Corian gave ground and fled, seeking some place of safety, but finding none they turned, and struck again at their pursuers and then again fled, till they were smitten down and slain to the great joy of Madasima and her Damsels, and the Knights of the Firm Island, but above all of Oriana, who had never ceased praying to God to grant her friends that victory. Angriote then asked the Judges if there was aught more to be done? they replied, he had done enough for his honour, and led the two champions from the lists; their comrades then received and took them with Madasima to their tents where they were healed of their wounds.

Here endeth the Second Book of Amadis of Gaul.

FOOTNOTES:

[347:A] This is D'Herberay's phrase, it is better than the original: Siempre me tuve por dicho que de tales juegos auriades tal ganancia.

END OF THE SECOND VOLUME.